"*The St. Zita Society*, a brilliantly crafted novel of psychological suspense, further enforces [Rendell's] rightful place as the queen of British mystery writing."

—*Shelf Awareness*

"Over her last several outings, Rendell has been returning to the stripped-down dyspepsia of her earliest work, adding freak-show sociology to her velvet nightmares. Instead of exhausting the possibilities of her collection of plausible misfits, this group portrait leaves you longing for more."

—*Kirkus Reviews*

"This novel radiates tension . . . like vintage Evelyn Waugh or Muriel Spark, informed with a psychological subtlety worthy of Iris Murdoch."

—*Publishers Weekly* (signature review)

The Copper Peacock & other Stories
The Secret House of Death

The Inspector Wexford Novels

From Doon with Death
The Sins of the Fathers
Wolf to the Slaughter
The Best Man to Die
A Guilty Thing Surprised
No More Dying Then
Murder Being Once Done
Some Lie and Some Die
Shake Hands Forever
A Sleeping Life
Death Notes
The Speaker of Mandarin
An Unkindness of Ravens
The Veiled One
Kissing the Gunner's Daughter
Simisola
Road Rage
Harm Done
The Babes in the Wood
End in Tears
Not in the Flesh
The Monster in the Box
The Vault
No Man's Nightingale

BARBARA VINE NOVELS

A Dark-Adapted Eye

A Fatal Inversion

The House of Stairs

Gallowglass

King Solomon's Carpet

Asta's Book

No Night Is Too Long

The Brimstone Wedding

The Chimney Sweeper's Boy

Grasshopper

The Blood Doctor

The Minotaur

The Birthday Present

The Child's Child

The Brimstone Wedding

King Solomon's Carpet

THE ST. ZITA SOCIETY

A Novel

Ruth Rendell

Scribner

New York   London   Toronto   Sydney   New Delhi

SCRIBNER

A Division of Simon & Schuster, Inc.
1230 Avenue of the Americas
New York, NY 10020

First Scribner trade paperback edition August 2013

SCRIBNER and design are registered trademarks of The Gale Group, Inc., used under license by Simon & Schuster, Inc., the publisher of this work.

For information about special discounts for bulk purchases, please contact Simon & Schuster Special Sales at 1-866-506-1949 or business@simonandschuster.com.

The Simon & Schuster Speakers Bureau can bring authors to your live event. For more information or to book an event, contact the Simon & Schuster Speakers Bureau at 1-866-248-3049 or visit our website at www.simonspeakers.com.

Map by Roger Walker

Manufactured in the United States of America

3 5 7 9 10 8 6 4 2

Library of Congress Control Number: 2012014259

ISBN 978-1-4516-6668-7
ISBN 978-1-4516-6669-4 (pbk)
ISBN 978-1-4516-6670-0 (ebook)

For my cousin Sonia, with love

Number 7
Preston and Lucy Still *Ex Vactor Rad Sothern*
Their children, Hero, Matilda,
and baby Thomas
Rabia, the nanny
Montserrat, the au pair

daughter of Studley
Beacon-driver

Number 5
Mr. and Mrs. Neville-Smith

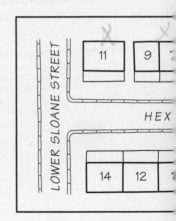

Number 3
Dr. Simon Jefferson
Jimmy, the driver
Dex, the gardener

Number 11
Lord and Lady Studley
Richard, the butler and cook
Sondra, Richard's wife
Henry Copley, the driver

2 daughter Ingette

The Dugong

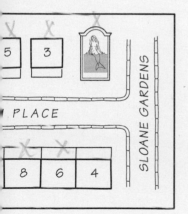

Number 6
Princess Susan Hapsburg
June Caldwell
Zinnia, the cleaner
Gussie, the dog

Number 8
Roland Albert and Damian
Thea
Miss Grieves

THE ST. ZITA
SOCIETY

1

S OMEONE HAD TOLD Dex that the queen lived in Victoria. So did he, but she had a palace and he had one room in a street off Warwick Way. Still he liked the idea that she was his neighbour. He liked quite a lot about the new life he had been living for the past few months. He had this job with Dr. Jefferson that meant he could work in a garden three mornings a week, and Dr. Jefferson had said he would speak to the lady next door about doing a morning for her. While he was drawing his incapacity benefit, he had been told he shouldn't get any wages, but Dr. Jefferson never asked, and maybe the lady called Mrs. Neville-Smith wouldn't either.

Jimmy, who drove Dr. Jefferson to work at the hospital every day, had asked Dex round to the pub that evening. The pub, on the corner of Hexam Place and Sloane Gardens, was called the Dugong, a funny name that Dex had never before heard. There was going to be a meeting there for all the people who worked in Hexam Place. Dex had never been to a meeting of any sort and didn't know if he would like it, but Jimmy had promised to buy him a Guinness, which was his favourite drink. He would have drunk a Guinness every evening with his tea if he could have afforded it. He was halfway along the Pimlico Road when he got out his mobile and looked to see if there was a message or a text from Peach. There sometimes was and it always made him feel happy. Usually the message called him by his name and said he had been so good that Peach was giving him ten free calls or something like that. There was nothing this time, but he knew there would be again or that Peach might even speak to him. Peach was his God. He knew that because when the lady upstairs saw him smiling at his mobile and making a message come back over and over, she said, "Peach is your God, Dex."

He needed a God to protect him from the evil spirits. It was quite a while since he had seen any of them, and he knew this was because Peach was protecting him, just as he knew that if one was near him he should look out for, Peach would warn him. He trusted Peach as he had never trusted any human being.

He stopped outside the Dugong, which he knew well because it was next door to Dr. Jefferson's house. Not joined on to but next door, for Dr. Jefferson's was big and standing alone and with a large garden for him to look after. The pub sign was some kind of big fish with half its body sticking out of blue, wavy water. He knew it was a fish because it was in the sea. He pushed the door open and there was Jimmy, waving to him in a friendly way. The other people round the big table all looked at him, but he could tell at once that none of them were evil spirits.

"I AM NOT a servant." Thea helped herself to a handful of mixed nuts. "You may be but I'm not."

"What are you then?" said Beacon.

"I don't know. I just do little jobs for Damian and Roland. You want to remember I've got a degree."

"Blessed is she who sitteth not in the seat of the scornful." Beacon moved the bowl out of Thea's reach. "If you're going to eat from the common nuts, you ought not to put your hand in among them when it's been in your mouth."

"Don't quarrel, children," said June. "Let's be nice. If you're not a servant, Thea, you won't be eligible to join the St. Zita Society."

It was August and the day had been sunny and warm. The full complement of those who would compose the society couldn't be there. Rabia, being a Moslem and a nanny, never went out in the evening, let alone to a pub; Zinnia, cleaner for the Princess and the Stills and Dr. Jefferson, didn't live in; and Richard was cooking dinner for Lady Studley's guests while Sondra, his wife, waited at table. Montserrat, the Stills' au pair, said she might come, but she had a mysterious task to perform later; and the newly arrived Dex, gardener to Dr. Jefferson, never opened his mouth except to say "Cheers." But Henry was still expected, and as June was complaining about the Dugong's nuts being unsalted and therefore tasteless, he walked in.

With his extreme height and marked resemblance to Michelangelo's David, he would in days gone by have been footman material. Indeed, in 1882 his great-great-great-grandfather had been footman to a duke. Henry was the youngest of the group after Montserrat, and although he looked like a Hollywood star of the thirties, he was in reality driver and sometime gardener and handyman to Lord Studley, performing the tasks that Richard couldn't or wouldn't do. His employer referred to him with a jovial laugh as his "general factotum." He was never called Harry or Hal.

Beacon said it was his round and what was Henry going to have. "The house white, please."

"That's not for men. That's lady juice."

"I'm not a man, I'm a boy. And I'm not drinking beer or spirits till next week when I'm twenty-five. Did you see there's been another boy stabbed? Down on the Embankment. That makes three this week."

"We don't have to talk about it, Henry," said June.

One who plainly didn't want to talk about it was Dex, who drank the last of his Guinness, got up, and left, saying nothing. June watched him go and said, "No manners, but what can you expect? Now we have to talk about the society. How do you set up a society, anyway?"

Jimmy said in a ponderous tone, "You pick a chairman, only you mustn't call him a chairman because he may be a lady. You call him a chair."

"I'm not calling any bloke a piece of furniture." Thea reached for the nuts bowl. "Why can't we make Jimmy the chairperson and June the secretary and the rest of us just members. Then we're away. This can be the inception meeting of the St. Zita Society."

Henry was sending a text on his iPhone. "Who's St. Zita?"

June had found the title for the society. "She's the patron saint of domestic servants, and she gave her food and clothes to the poor. If you see a picture of her, she'll be holding a bag and a bunch of keys."

"This boy that was stabbed," said Henry, "his mum was on the TV and she said he was down to get three A-levels and he'd do anything for anyone. Everybody loved him."

Jimmy shook his head. "Funny, isn't it? All these kids that get murdered and whatever, you never hear anyone say they were slimeballs and a menace to the neighbourhood."

"Well, they wouldn't when they'd died, would they?" Henry's iPhone tinkled to tell him a text had come. It was the one he wanted, and he grinned a little at Huguette's message. "What's the society for, anyway?"

"Solidarity," said Jimmy, "supporting each other. And we can have outings and go to shows."

"We can do that anyway. We don't have to have a servants' society to go and see *Les Miz*."

"I'm not a servant," said Thea.

"Then you can be an honorary member," said June. "Well, that's my lot. It's got quite dark and the Princess will start fretting."

Montserrat didn't come and no one knew what the "mysterious task" was. Jimmy and Thea talked about the society for an hour or so, what was it *for* and could it restrain employers from keeping their drivers up till all hours and forced to drink Coke while they awaited their employer's call. Not that he included Dr. Jefferson, who was an example to the rest of them. Henry wanted to know who that funny little guy with the bushy hair was, Dex or something, he'd never seen him before.

"He does our garden." Jimmy had got into the habit of referring to Simon Jefferson's property as if it belonged equally to the paediatrician and himself. "Dr. Jefferson took him on out of the kindness of his heart." Jimmy finished his lager, said dramatically, "He sees evil spirits."

"He what?" Henry gaped as Jimmy had intended him to.

"Well, he used to. He tried to kill his mother and they put him inside—well, a place for the criminally insane. There was a psychiatrist saw to him and he was a pal of Dr. Jefferson, and when the psychiatrist had cured him, they let him out because they said he'd never do it again and Dr. Jefferson gave him that job with us."

Thea looked uneasy. "D'you think that's why he left when he did without saying good-bye? Talking about stabbing was too near home? D'you think that's what it was?"

"Dr. Jefferson," said Jimmy, "says he's cured. He'll never do it again. His friend swore blind he wouldn't."

Henry left last because he fancied another glass of lady juice. The others had all gone in the same direction. Their employers' homes were all in Hexam Place, a street of white-painted stucco or golden brickwork houses known to estate agents as Georgian, though none had been built before 1860. Number six, on the opposite side to the Dugong, was the property of Her Serene Highness, the Princess Susan Hapsburg, a title incorrect in every respect except her Christian name. The Princess, as she was known to the members of the St. Zita Society among others, was eighty-two years old and had lived in this house for nearly sixty years, and June, four years younger, had been there with her for the same length of time.

Steps ran down into the area and June's door, but when she came home after having been out in the evenings, she entered by the front door even though this meant climbing up eight stairs instead of walking down twelve. Some evenings June's polymyalgia rheumatica made climbing up a trial, but she did it so that passing pedestrians and other residents of Hexam Place might know she was more of a friend to the Princess than a paid employee. Zinnia had bathed Gussie that day and brought in a new kind of air freshener so that the doggy smell was less pronounced. It was warm. Mean in most respects, the Princess was lavish with the central heating and kept it on all summer, opening windows when it got too hot.

June could hear the Princess had *Holby City* on but marched in just the same. "Now, what can I get you, madam? A nice vodka and tonic or a freshly squeezed orange juice?"

"I don't want anything, dear. I've had my vodka." The Princess didn't turn round. "Are you drunk?" She always asked that question when she knew June had been to the pub.

"Of course not, madam," June answered as always.

"Well, don't talk any more, dear. I want to know if this chap has got psoriasis or a malignant melanoma. You'd better go to bed."

It was a command, and friend or no friend, after sixty years June knew it was wiser to obey. The young ones in St. Zita's might be pals with their employers, Montserrat even called Mrs. Still "Lucy," but when you were eighty-two and seventy-eight, things were different, the rules had not relaxed much since the days when Susan Borrington was running away with that awful Italian boy and June was going with her to his home in Florence. June went off to bed and was falling asleep when the internal phone rang.

"Did you put Gussie to bed, dear?"

"I forgot," June murmured, barely conscious.

"Well, do it now, will you?"

THE AREAS OF these houses were all different, some with cupboards under the stairs, others with cupboards in the wall dividing this area from next door's, all with plants in pots, tree ferns, choisyas, avocados grown from stones, even a mimosa, the occasional piece of statuary. All had some kind of lighting, usually a wall light, globular or cuboid. Number seven, home of the Stills and next door but three to the Dugong, was one of those with a cupboard in the wall and no pot plants. The hanging bulb over the basement door had not been switched on, but enough pale light from a streetlamp showed Henry a figure standing just inside the wall cupboard. Henry stopped and peered over the railings. The figure, a man's, retreated as far as it could go into the shallow recesses of the cupboard.

Possibly a burglar. There had been a lot of crime round here recently. Only last week, Montserrat had told him, someone had just walked through the window of number five, home of the Neville-Smiths, taken the television, a briefcase full of money, and the keys to a BMW and walked out the front door to drive away in the car. What could you expect if you had no window locks and you had actually left a downstairs window open two inches? This man was obviously up to no good, a phrase Henry had heard his employer use and which he liked. Lord Studley would tell him to call the police on his mobile, but he didn't always do what Lord Studley recommended and was in fact off to do something of which he would have deeply disapproved.

Henry was turning away when the basement door opened and Montserrat appeared. She waved to Henry, said hi, and beckoned the man out of the cupboard. Must be her boyfriend. Henry expected them to kiss but they didn't. The man went inside and the door closed. Fifteen minutes later, having forgotten about the burglar or boyfriend, he was in Chelsea, in the Honourable Huguette Studley's flat. These days the pattern of Henry's visits followed the same plan: bed first, then arguing. Henry would have preferred to forgo the arguing and spend twice as long in bed, but this was seldom allowed.

Huguette (named for her French grandmother) was a pretty girl of nineteen with a large red mouth and large blue eyes and hair her grandmother would have called frizzy but others recognised as the big, curly bush made fashionable by Julia Roberts in *Charlie Wilson's War.* The argument was always begun by Huguette.

"Don't you see, Henry, that if you lived here with me, we could stay in bed all the time? There wouldn't be any arguing because we'd have nothing to argue about."

"And don't you see that your dad would sack me? On two counts," said Henry, who had picked up a certain amount of parliamentary language from his employer, "to be absolutely clear, like not living at number eleven and like shagging his daughter."

"You could get another job."

"How? It took me a year to get this one. Your dad'd give me a reference, would he? I should coco."

"We could get married."

If Henry ever thought of marriage, it would be when he was about fifty and to someone with money of her own and a big house in the suburbs. "No one gets married anymore, and anyway, I'm outta here. You want to remember I have to be outside number eleven at seven a.m. in the Beemer waiting for your dad when he chooses to come, which may not be till nine, right?"

"Text me," said Huguette.

Henry walked back. An urban fox emerged from the area of number five, gave him an unpleasant look, and crossed the road to plunder Miss Grieves's dustbin. Upstairs at number eleven a light was still on in Lord and Lady Studley's bedroom. Henry stood for a while, looking up, hoping their curtains might part and Lady Studley look down, preferably in her black lace nightgown, bestow on him a fond smile, and purse her lips in a kiss. But nothing happened. The light went out and Henry let himself in by the area door.

INSTEAD OF OPENING the door to her bedsit with en suite bathroom (called a studio flat by her employers), Montserrat had led the caller up the basement stairs to the ground floor and then the next flight, which swept round in a half circle to the gallery. The house was silent apart from the soft patter of Rabia's slippered feet on the nursery floor above. Montserrat tapped on the third door on the right, then opened it and said, "Rad's here, Lucy." She left them to it, as she put it to Rabia five minutes later. "If they're all asleep, why don't you come down for a bit. I've got a half bottle of vodka."

"You know I don't drink, Montsy."

"You can have the orange juice I got to go with the vodka."

"I wouldn't hear Thomas if he cries. He's teething."

"He's been teething for weeks, if not months," said Montserrat. "If he belonged to me, I'd drown him."

Rabia said she shouldn't talk like that, it was wicked, so Montserrat started telling the nanny about Lucy and Rad Sothern. Rabia put her fingers in her ears. She went back to the children, Hero and Matilda fast asleep in the bedroom they shared, baby Thomas restive but silent in his cot in the nursery. Rabia puzzled sometimes about calling a bedroom a nursery because as far as she knew—her father worked in one—a nursery was a place for growing plants. She never asked, she didn't want to look foolish.

Montserrat had called out good-bye and left. Time passed slowly. It was getting late now and Rabia thought seriously of going to bed in her bedroom at the back. But what if Mr. Still came up here when he got home? He sometimes did. Thomas began to cry, then to scream. Rabia picked him up and began walking him up and down, the sovereign remedy. The nursery overlooked the street, and from the window she saw Montserrat letting the man called Rad out by way of the area steps. Rabia shook her head, not at all excited or amused as Montserrat had expected her to be, but profoundly shocked.

Thomas was quiet now but began grizzling again when laid down in his cot. Rabia had great reserves of patience and loved him dearly. She was a widow, both of whose children had died young. This, according to one of the doctors, was due to her having married her first cousin. But Nazir himself hadn't lived long either, and now she was alone. Rabia sat in the chair beside the cot, talking to Thomas softly. When he began to cry again, she picked him up and carried him to the table where the kettle was and the little fridge in the corner and began making him a warm milky drink. She was too far from the window to see or hear the car, and the first she knew of Preston Still's arrival was the sound of his rather heavy feet on the stairs. Instead of stopping on the floor below where his wife lay sleeping, they carried on up. As she had expected. Like the duck in *Jemima Puddle-Duck*—a book Rabia sometimes read to the children and which, they said, sounded funny in her accent—Preston was an anxious parent. Quite a contrast to his wife, Rabia often thought. He came in, looking tired and harassed. He had been at a conference in Brighton, she knew, because Lucy had told her.

"Is he all right?" Preston picked up Thomas and squeezed him too hard for the child's comfort. His playing with Thomas or even talking to him was a rare occurrence. His care was concentrated in concern for Thomas's health. "There's nothing wrong, is there? If there's the slightest thing, we should call Dr. Jefferson. He's a good friend, I know he'd come like a shot."

"He's very all right, Mr. Still." The use of given names to Rabia's employer did not extend to the master of the house. "He doesn't want to sleep, that's all."

"How peculiar," Preston said dismally. The idea of anyone not wanting to sleep, especially someone of his own blood, was alien to him. "And the girls? I thought Matilda had a bit of a cough when I saw her yesterday."

Rabia said that Matilda and Hero were sound asleep in the adjoining room. Nothing was wrong with any of the children, and if Mr. Still would just lay Thomas down gently, he would certainly settle. Knowing what would please Preston, get rid of him, and let her go back to her own bed, she said, "He was just missing his daddy, and now you are here, he will be fine."

No paediatrician then, no more disturbance. She could go to bed. She could sleep for maybe five hours. What she had said to Mr. Still about Thomas's missing his daddy wasn't true. It was a lie told to please him. Secretly, Rabia believed that none of the children would miss either of their parents for a moment. They seldom saw them. She put her lips to Thomas's cheek and whispered, "My sweetheart."

2

O N THE TRAY was a small tub of the kind of yogurt that claims to regulate the consumer's bowel movements, a fig and a slice of buttered toast, marmalade and a pot of coffee. The Princess was halfway through her yogurt phase. June knew she was halfway through because her phases always lasted about four months and two had elapsed. June fished out the tray-on-legs— neither of them knew its name—and set it up on top of the duvet. The Princess always put her hair in rollers at bedtime and now proceeded to take them out, shedding dandruff onto the toast.

"Sleep well, dear?"

"Not so bad, madam. How about yourself?"

"I had a most peculiar dream." The Princess often had peculiar dreams and now began to recount this one.

June didn't listen. She pulled back the curtains and stood in the window, looking down at Hexam Place. Lord Studley's black BMW stood outside number eleven on the opposite side, poor Henry at the wheel. June knew for a fact he would have been there for two hours. He looked as if he had fallen asleep, and no wonder. It was a pity really that the St. Zita's Society wasn't a union, but perhaps it could take on some of the prerogatives of a union and put its spoke in at such heartless treatment of an employee. June wondered if Henry's human rights might be infringed.

The classy school bus, silver with a blue stripe along its side, came round the corner from Lower Sloane Street. Hero and Matilda Still were already waiting outside number seven, each holding one of Rabia's hands. She saw them onto the bus and it bore them off to their expensive school in Westminster. Now why couldn't their mother have done that? Still in bed, thought June. *Still* by name and still by nature. What a world! Damian and Roland had emerged from number eight, whose front door June couldn't see from where she stood. Those two always went everywhere together. If they had been of opposite sexes, they would have held hands, and June, an ardent progressive, thought it a crying shame that this development in the fight against prejudice and bigotry had not yet been attained. Mr. Still had just come out of number seven when the Princess wound up her dream story. June had an instinct born of years of experience as to when this point was reached.

". . . And it wasn't my mother at all but that girl with the red hair that cleans for those queers, and then I woke up."

"Fascinating, madam, but we don't say 'queers,' do we? We say 'gay couple.'"

"Oh, all right. If you insist. I'm sure Lady Studley doesn't allow Sondra to talk to her like that."

"Probably not, madam," said June. "Is there anything else you'd like me to bring you?"

There wasn't. The Princess would sulk for a while and then get up. June had heard Zinnia arrive. She went downstairs, happy to have won that round and prepared, once she had persuaded the cleaner to wash the paint in the dining room, to get on with the agenda of the next St. Zita meeting.

June Caldwell had been fifteen when her mother, a widow and housekeeper to Caspar Borrington, had got her the job of lady's maid (well, maid of everything really) to Susan Borrington, his daughter. Within two months of her eighteenth birthday Susan had got herself engaged to Prince Luciano Hapsburg, scion of a dubiously aristocratic Italian family she met while skiing in Switzerland. Perhaps not exactly the scion, as he had two older brothers and was a ski instructor. There was no money, and the title tended to make Italians laugh, for Luciano's father had changed his name from Angelotti to Hapsburg some years before. He had a couple of lingerie shops in Milan. This, oddly enough, gave them something in common. Caspar Borrington, who had plenty of money, who owned three houses and a flat in Mayfair, had made it out of something not dissimilar but even less dignified. His factories produced sanitary towels. The advent of Tampax ruined that, but when Susan met Luciano her family was enormously rich and Susan was an only child.

They got married and June went to live with them in the apartment Susan's father paid for in Florence. The city amazed June, the people and their funny talk, the weather, always glorious (Susan got married in May), the buildings, the Arno, the bridges, the churches. June was just getting used to it, learning to say *Buon giorno* and *Ciao*, when Susan and Luciano had a more than usually spectacular row, coming to blows, and Susan told June to pack, they were going home.

They were never divorced, Susan having an idea divorce was impossible in Italy. Caspar Borrington gave Luciano a large sum of money to shut him up and Susan never saw him again. Years later he got the marriage annulled. He was not a Serene Highness, there was some doubt if he was a prince at all, but Susan called herself Her Serene Highness the Princess Susan Hapsburg, had this name printed on her cards, and entered it on the register of voters in the City of Westminster. Her father bought her number six Hexam Place, not quite so smart an address as it later became, and she had lived there ever since, finding herself a circle of friends among the widows of generals, ex-wives of sportsmen, and superannuated single daughters of company directors. There had been lovers, but not many and not for long.

Zinnia was another who had a name she had adopted, disliking *Karen*, with which she had been baptised in Antigua. She genuinely had the surname St. Charles. Working for a princess in the heart of Knightsbridge brought her a lot of kudos and made it easy for her to get jobs cleaning at number three, number seven, and number nine. Having got her to agree to washing the dining-room paint, June asked her if she'd like to join the St. Zita Society.

"What does it cost?"

"Nothing. And the chances are you get a good many free drinks."

"OK," said Zinnia. "I don't mind. Is Henry Copley a member?"

"He is," said June. "But don't get your hopes up. He's got enough on his plate."

She went into the study, which the Princess never entered, sat down at the desk the Princess never used, and began composing the society's constitution and teaching herself to write minutes.

ALL THE HOUSES in Hexam Place had gardens, front and rear, and number three had a bit more round the side dividing it from the Dugong. The front gardens needed little attention, consisting of pebbled squares with a tree planted in the middle of each, a Japanese flowering cherry, for instance, in the squares in front of number four, two monkey puzzles at Simon Jefferson's. Dex was glad there was little to do in that front garden as the monkey puzzles rather alarmed him. They looked unlike any trees he had ever before seen, more like something you might expect to find growing under the sea near a coral reef. Dex knew about such things from his television viewing. The television went on the moment he entered his room and remained on, irrespective of what might be showing, until he went to bed. Sometimes, if he was frightened or simply wary and Peach wasn't speaking to him, he left it on all night.

He liked Dr. Jefferson's back garden because it was big and walled and had a lawn. He cut that lawn more often than he needed to because the lawn mower was so beautiful and smooth. Dr. Jefferson said he could buy plants if he wanted to and got Jimmy to give him the money, so Dex went along to the Belgrave Nursery and bought annuals in May and hebes and lavender in September on the advice of the big, tall Asian man called Mr. Siddiqui. Dr. Jefferson was pleased with Dex's work and recommended him to Mr. and Mrs. Neville-Smith at number five. So now Dex had two jobs, which he could easily handle.

He had seen no evil spirits since coming to work in Hexam Place, but the fact was that he was not always sure about identifying evil spirits. Sometimes it took him weeks of observing them, often following them, before he could be sure. But he had to remember that he had made a promise to Dr. Jefferson's friend Dr. Mettage, the psychiatrist in the hospital, that he would do nothing to them unless they threatened him. He said that depended on what you meant by "threaten." Women themselves were a threat to him, but he had never told Dr. Mettage or Dr. Jefferson that. He told his God, but Peach had not responded.

If he had no work to do in the front garden of number three, there was plenty in the front garden of number five. A hedge grew round the pebble patches on either side of the front steps, with narrow flower borders round the hedge. Dex knelt to weed these borders, first laying down an old doormat given him by Mrs. Neville-Smith to protect his knees from the little stones.

He liked to watch the people of Hexam Place without wanting to talk to them, the redheaded woman opposite who sat on the steps to smoke a cigarette, the old lady called June taking a little fat dog round the block, the young man who looked as if he ought to be on TV, sitting at the wheel of a big, shiny car, doing more sitting and waiting than driving. Two men lived in the same house with the redhead. The two always left together in the morning just after Dex had started work, always wore suits and ties and, on cold days, tight-fitted overcoats.

He had to go and work in the back, and then he saw nothing but clematis and dahlias and roses. Mr. Neville-Smith was fond of roses. Next door at number seven lived a lot of children, two and a baby, and a girl Jimmy said was an au pair. Dex saw her go up and down the area steps at number seven, and he saw a lady in a long black gown wearing a black headscarf and pushing the baby in a pushchair. But if he had chanced to see any of them away from the places where they lived, he wouldn't have recognised them. Faces meant nothing to him. He saw them as blank, featureless masks.

3

F EW OF ITS patrons knew what a dugong was. The hanging
sign above its doors showed a picture of an animal halfway
between a seal and a dolphin with a woman's pretty face. This led
some to say it was a mermaid and others a manatee. The licensee
said to google it, but if anyone did, the results weren't known. It
didn't seem important. The Dugong was one of those London pubs
which were surviving the recession and the drunk-driving laws and
the adjurations to everyone to drink less. This was because it had a
wealthy and mainly youthful clientele and was tastefully appointed
with a garden at the rear and a wide pavement at the front on which
to gather, drink sauvignon, and chat.

The St. Zita Society had its first meeting round the biggest table
in the garden, the evening being fine and warm for mid-September.
Jimmy should have been in the chair, but if he didn't exactly panic,
he protested that he had no idea what to do. He'd never actually
said he'd be chairman. Let June do it. So June read the rather sparse
minutes of the inception meeting, and they were agreed as a true
record by Jimmy, Beacon, Thea, Montserrat, who hadn't been
there, and Henry. The first item on the agenda was the question of
Henry's human rights.

June had scarcely begun on the speech she had written describing poor Henry waiting for hours at the wheel of the BMW for Lord Studley to arrive, had in fact not reached the point of uttering Lord Studley's name, when the subject of her complaint leapt to his feet with a cry of "Stop, stop, stop!"

"What on earth's the matter?" The Dugong's garden was infested with wasps. "Have you been stung?"

"You want me to lose my job?" Henry lowered his voice, in the belief that not only walls but bushes and plants in tubs have ears. "It took me a bloody year to get my job and what about my flat?" He continued in a sibilant whisper, "You want me to lose my flat?"

"Well, I'm sure I'm very sorry," said June. "I meant well. It went to my heart seeing you half-asleep at the wheel at that hour of the morning."

"We'll change the subject if you don't mind. Come to that," Henry said with a glare at her, "even if you do mind."

"Time for another drink," said Beacon. "What are we all having?" He was trying to think up a suitable biblical quotation, but no cars and not much in the way of human rights were in the Bible. "What'll it be, Henry?"

Henry and Montserrat wanted white wine, June a vodka and tonic, and Thea merlot. Jimmy had lager and Beacon settled for sparkling water "with a hint of black currant" because there was always a chance Mr. Still might call him on his mobile for a lift from Victoria Station.

With nothing more on the agenda but "expenditure and income," as yet a blank page, "Any Other Business" was quickly reached. Montserrat suggested a recruiting drive to find more members. Even if membership was confined to Hexam Place, they were still lacking Rabia, Richard, and Zinnia. Beacon said everyone had been given notice of the meeting and you couldn't make people come if they didn't want to.

"You can *persuade* them," said June. "You can appeal to their public-spiritedness." She suggested that an outing to "a show" should be discussed at the next meeting and a date fixed. The kind of fidgety apathy that often settles on meetings that continue for too long was causing eyes to close, shoulders to slump, and pins and needles to cramp legs. Everyone was relieved to agree to the outing, especially as it was not to be raised again until October, the meeting was over, and serious drinking began.

While sticking to his no-spirits rule, Henry had drunk his wine and was in need of something stronger. Eyebrows were raised when he ordered a Campari and soda and "go easy on the soda." Ahead of him was an ordeal which he both looked forward to and dreaded, but there was no escape from it. Huguette expected to see him and, knowing that her father was away on a two-day parliamentary visit to Brussels, also knew that Henry could not be on call to drive the Beemer. She would have to wait in vain, for he had another engagement in the Studley family at nine.

Beacon was the first to leave. His call had come through. Mr. Still was in a train heading for Euston, not Victoria, and was due to arrive in twelve minutes. This was a cue also for Montserrat, who watched him go, checked that the Audi had left, and ran upstairs at number seven to knock on Lucy's door and warn Rad to be out of there in three minutes at the most. When she had escorted him down to the drawing-room floor, down the steep and narrow staircase to the basement and the area, and seen him disappear in the direction of Sloane Square, she ran all the way to the top. Thomas, for once, was asleep, the girls were watching television while they got ready for bed, and Rabia was having a cup of tea.

Number eleven, home of the Studleys, was the largest house in Hexam Place, not only bigger but different from those in the terraces, being detached, and with more elaborate rails round its balconies. You entered it between fluted columns and through double doors. Above these doors French windows opened from the principal bedroom onto a large balcony on which stood palm trees and pampas in Grecian urns. This window, though fastened and locked, somehow made the bedroom seem more exposed and less secure than if a solid wall had been there, and this was why Oceane Studley preferred to visit Henry than have him visit her.

He was back from the Dugong at ten to nine, quickly changing the sheets on his bed, pulling down the blinds, and setting out the wineglasses. She would bring the wine, she always did. Not that it had happened more than twice—this would be the third time. He hadn't time for a shower but he'd had one that morning. That would have to do. Henry couldn't make up his mind if he wanted to see Oceane or if he'd prefer his mobile to ring and her to say she couldn't make it. All the time she was in his room he was terrified. Only because of his youth, he supposed, could he function at all and not be inhibited by fear. Things were quite different with Huguette because they did it in Huguette's flat, which was a mile away and not her dad's, though no doubt her dad paid the rent. The whole of this house was Lord Studley's, Henry's room as much as the master bedroom, and even when he knew his employer was in Brussels, he was still afraid of spies. Letting himself in here this evening, he had encountered Sondra on the stairs, and though she had been perfectly pleasant, he couldn't rid himself of the idea that she had been keeping an eye on him.

The trouble was that Oceane was an attractive woman and not yet forty. Henry thought her basically more attractive than her daughter, but Huguette was young and that was a great advantage. Anyway, while he hadn't even thought about refusing Huguette, he had been afraid to say no to Oceane. Henry was unacquainted with the story of Joseph and Potiphar's wife, but the plot was obvious to anyone who imagined the scenario. You say no, thanks, you'd rather not, and she tells her husband, who happens to be your boss, that you made a pass at her.

He was coming to the end of envisaging this outcome when the door opened and Oceane came in. She never knocked. Whatever else he might be to her, Henry was her husband's driver. "Oh, darling," she said, "are you in a seventh heaven to see me?" She pressed her pelvis against him and stuck her tongue in his mouth.

Henry responded. He hadn't really any option.

MONTSERRAT KNEW ALL about it. She made it her business to know who was having an affair with whom, who was skiving off, and who was borrowing a Beemer or a Jaguar when such a loan was strictly forbidden. She had never blackmailed anyone, but she liked to keep the possibility of a modified sort of blackmail in reserve. The only friend she had in Hexam Place was Thea, and the only member of the St. Zita Society who possessed a car of their own was herself, keeping her rather old VW in a garage in the mews that belonged to number seven.

Attempts at persuading Rabia to join the society had failed. "You wouldn't have to drink anything. I mean, you wouldn't have to drink anything alcoholic. You'd just sit at a table and talk. And then you could come with us to shows."

Rabia said she couldn't afford it, and if she asked her dad if she could go into a pub, he would say no.

"Why tell him?"

"Because he's my father," said Rabia in her simple, direct way. "I no longer have a husband to tell me what to do." Ignoring Montserrat's rolling eyes, she offered her another cup of tea.

Montserrat said she'd rather have a glass of wine and she didn't suppose Rabia would let her bring the bottle up here. "No, that's right," said Rabia. "I'm sorry but this is the children's place," and she went to see to Thomas, who had begun whimpering.

JUNE AND THE PRINCESS and Rad Sothern, who was June's great-nephew, were having coffee in the drawing room at number six. The Princess only tolerated this relative of June's because he was a professional man, an actor, and a celebrity. Besides this, he was good-looking and played Mr. Fortescue, the orthopaedic surgeon, in one of her favourite hospital sitcoms. Mr. Fortescue was an important character in *Avalon Clinic*, appeared every week, and was a famous face when seen crossing Sloane Square. June was fond of him in a halfhearted way but was well aware that he only came round when he had nothing better to do. She had seen him admitted to number seven by the basement door and disapproved of his having an affair with Montserrat, whom she thought of as sly. It puzzled her how he had ever managed to meet the Stills' au pair. As far as she knew, Rad's only contact with the occupants of number seven had been when the Princess introduced him to Lucy Still at a party the Princess gave in this house a few months before.

The Princess addressed him as "Mr. Fortescue" because she thought this was funny. Rad had told her not to but she took no notice. The conversation was always centred on gossip. Film and TV gossip, not Hexam Place scandalmongering, as this might be rather close to the bone for Rad. June knew he came to number six as often as he did not because of his fondness for the Princess, but so that when he was seen, the neighbours would think his visits were to his great-aunt rather than to Montserrat.

The Princess, as always, wanted him to tell her about the private lives of the cast of *Avalon Clinic*, and he obliged with a diluted version. It seemed to satisfy her.

"Can I offer you a brandy, Mr. Fortescue?"

"Why not?" said Rad.

None was offered to June but she helped herself just the same. She was tired and she still had to walk Gussie round the block. Rad wouldn't leave for hours if she didn't give him what she called a nudge, though it was rather more than that. "Time you went, Rad. HSH wants to go to bed."

Gussie was put on his lead, and Rad, in June's habitual phrase, was seen off the premises, out of the front door and down the steps.

It was a fine night but growing cold. Rad picked up a taxi in Ebury Bridge Road, and June and Gussie walked on round the block. It was late but some lights were on in bedrooms, while Damian and Roland were still up in their living room, though the blinds were down. There was no one about, no one to see June let herself in by the front door, so she and Gussie entered the house by the more comfortably negotiated stairs to the basement.

THEA LIVED IN the top flat at number eight, Damian and Roland occupying the ground and first floors. Roland did some of the cleaning in a grudging way, and Thea did what he didn't do, but no one cleaned for Miss Grieves in the basement. She couldn't afford it. Thea already shopped for her and sometimes took her the kind of food that was an improvement on Meals on Wheels, but now Thea also pushed the vacuum cleaner around and dusted the ancient furniture. It was one of the many tasks she performed unasked but because she felt she ought to. For the same reason she did what they called "little jobs" for Damian and Roland, staying in to open the door when a plumber was coming or the postman with a parcel, phoning Westminster City Council whenever a complaint was to be made, putting out their recycling, changing lightbulbs and mending fuses. She disliked doing these things but didn't see how she could stop now. Nor was she proud of her goodness in helping her neighbours. If only doing these things made her happy, if she could acquire a consciousness of virtue, a sense of satisfaction in performing useful and *unpaid* services, but all it amounted to was a weary fed-up-ness and sometimes resentment. She just did it in a weary, fed-up sort of way.

Montserrat always seemed to have someone, but Thea hadn't had a boyfriend in two or three years. The years were passing, as her married sister, Chloe, told her, or in Roland's words, quoted from something or other, "time's winged chariot" was "hurrying near."

She sometimes thought that if any man asked her out, so long as he wasn't positively ugly or gross, she would say yes. He was becoming a dream lover, this faceless man, as she envisaged him arriving in a nice car to take her for a drive and then for lunch, and she saw herself waving to him from the window, saying good-bye for now to Damian and Roland, and running down the stairs to the front door.

She knew no one, however vaguely, to fill this role. On her way to work in the Fulham Road she would look at the passengers on the bus or the men who passed her on foot and wonder. What did you have to do, how did you have to look, to gain the attention of this one or that? She had once known and put her knowledge into practice. They had married other people, those men. Probably she would end up like Miss Grieves, single and solitary, a crone.

4

ABRAM SIDDIQUI WAS walking along the aisle between shrubs and conifers, checking that everything was in its proper place and everything clearly labelled. He was tall and sturdy, handsome like the majority of those from that part of the world where he was born, with a strong aquiline face rather softened by his black beard. For work he dressed like an English country gentleman, even though the Belgrave Nursery was in the heart of Victoria, and today he wore fawn-coloured cavalry-twill trousers, a brushed-cotton check shirt with dark green knitted tie, and a lighter green tweed jacket with leather pads on the elbows.

If half his mind was intent on checking that the full complement of cypresses, Macrocarpas, and thujas were in stock, the other half was thinking about his daughter, Rabia. As he worried about her and the sad, disappointed life she led, and she so pretty and modest and quiet, he turned the corner into the next aisle, the one between the ericas and the lavenders, and saw her coming towards him from the Warwick Way entrance. She was pushing a new baby carriage, the grandest Abram had ever seen, a coach fit for a prince, but she looked rather small to be in charge of such a splendid equipage and such a big, lusty boy. Rabia wore a long black skirt and gray blouse, a spotted black scarf tied round her head in such a way as to hide all her hair and cover the neckline of the blouse.

"It is a whole week's time since I've seen you, Father. Are you too busy for Thomas and me this morning?"

"Come, my daughter," said Abram in Urdu, "we will take him into the hothouse and let him look at the tropical fish."

Thomas crowed with delight at the fish, red and green and yellow-striped fish and blue fish sparkling like jewels, as they wove their way between the fronds of green weed and the pillars of artificial coral. Abram picked a red flower from a branch and gave it to him to hold, assuring Rabia that it would do him no harm if he put it in his mouth.

"I was thinking of you before you came," he said to his daughter. "I worry that these people you work for will corrupt you. I worry that they are ungodly and immoral."

He seemed to have guessed, as he so often did, at the problem which these days was often in her mind. But she was sure she was not yet ready to consult him, if she would ever be. Strange then that a man so sensitive should believe that his attempts to get her to marry again, to let him find her a husband, were so wide of the mark. He took her to the nursery's café, bought her a cup of coffee and an ice cream for Thomas, choosing a tub rather than a cornet because he liked children to be kept clean and tidy. Rabia tied a huckaback napkin round Thomas's neck and fed him the ice cream by means of a silver sugar spoon.

Her father moved on to a different tack. "Rabia, you know you don't have to work. I am not a rich man but I am what they call in UK comfortably off. You come home and stay at home and I can keep you. It would be a pleasure to me."

She was looking at Thomas and he saw such love and yearning come into her eyes that he had his answer. "I know you have suffered. There is no worse suffering for a woman than to lose her children, but only marry and there will be more children. Yes, my daughter, more children will come. There is a good man who works for me here. No, he is not in today, he is driving one of the vans. He is your auntie Malia's sister-in-law's brother, he has seen you and admired you as any sensible man must. And he is not your cousin or even a relative, so your fears—mind you, I don't believe in them—of something to do with a gene mix-up, that you could forget. I will speak to him for you and a meeting can soon be arranged. Rabia, you are thirty years old but you look no more than twenty-one or -two . . ."

She let him finish. She removed the ice cream from Thomas's mouth with a cleansing wipe, took another to clean his hands, and kissed the top of his head before she answered. In a calm, quiet voice she said, "I cannot go through that again, Father. You are right about the suffering and I can't go through it again. As for living with you, you are so kind, you always are, but it won't do. I am best with children, I love these children, and you are best on your own with your nice friends and your good neighbours."

"Come, then," he said, and she knew he had given up—but only for now. It would begin again next time she saw him. "I have customers to attend to."

They were mostly women. The older ones wore Knightsbridge clothes and Bond Street jewellery, their hair dyed the colour of freshly squeezed orange juice or like the mahogany in Lucy's drawing room. The young women all looked like Lucy Still in tight jeans made for teenagers, white T-shirts, and shoes with four-inch heels. One had taken hers off, put them in the trolley she was pushing towards BULBS AND CORMS, and was hobbling along barefoot. Thomas had fallen asleep, thumb in mouth. Rabia pushed him home, walking slowly, enjoying the sunshine.

Montserrat was outside the house, standing beside her car, talking to Henry. On the ground between them was an object that looked to Rabia like a cross between a boat and a coffin. Henry told her it was his and neither a coffin nor a boat but a box to go on a car roof rack and contain extra baggage or camping equipment.

"Montsy's going to buy it."

"Wait a minute," said Montserrat, "that depends if the price is right. Why you want to get rid of it is another thing."

"Because I had to get rid of my car."

"You fasten it to the roof rack on your car and put stuff in it and drive off somewhere," said Rabia. "Where are you going, Montsy? You go to your mother in Spain?"

"Not this time. I'll be skiing in France and I'll put my skis in it and all the gear I've bought. You wait till you see my new ski pants."

Bought with the money Lucy gave her and Rad Sothern gave her, Rabia thought uncomfortably. A twenty-pound note here and a fifty-pound note there. Of course Rabia said nothing. It wasn't her business—unless it was her business and her moral duty to say something to someone. Back to that again. It always came back to that, however much she argued with herself.

"You want to come to a lunchtime meeting of the St. Zita Society?" said Montserrat. "It's an extraordinary general meeting and it's to be in the Dugong's garden so you can bring Thomas, and when Henry starts asking an inflated price like he's bound to, you can take my side and support me."

"Lucy would be angry."

"Lucy won't know."

Rabia smiled and began dragging the heavy pushchair up the steps of number seven. Henry ran up to give her a hand, calling back to Montserrat that he couldn't take less than seventy-five pounds.

"You're joking. It's about a hundred years old."

"*If* you don't mind, I paid two hundred for it in 2005."

"Fifty," said Montserrat.

"Seventy."

"Fifty-five."

"Now look who's joking."

June appeared at the front door of number six and, in spite of the rheumatism, tripped down the steps like someone half her age. "You two are making as much noise as a gang of yobs in Brixton. This is supposed to be one of the most select neighbourhoods not just in the UK but in the Western world. HSH has got a headache."

"I can give you a couple of paracetamol for her but it'll cost you," said Henry, laughing.

June ignored him. "We shall have to raise this question of street noise at the meeting. I'll put it on the agenda."

Henry put the roof box inside the basement door of number seven, then they all trooped off to the Dugong. Beacon and Jimmy, both once more on the wagon because Mr. Still would want fetching from the City at four and Dr. Jefferson from Great Ormond Street at five, and Thea were already there, drinks for all already bought. In October it wasn't warm enough to sit outside, so they crowded round the biggest table in the saloon bar and June read the minutes of the last meeting, adding that this was an extraordinary general meeting called because of the full agenda.

They had barely begun on the business when Thea broke in to say she had seen Rad Sothern in Hexam Place earlier in the week. Late at night, as it happened. "I wondered who he'd been calling on." Thea packed a great deal of suggestive innuendo into this speculation. Sometimes she was bitchy to counteract her goody-two-shoes behaviour.

"The Princess and me, as a matter of fact," said June.

"You?" It seemed almost too much for Thea to believe. "How on earth did you meet him?"

"Meeting him wasn't necessary." June could be icy when she chose. "He's my great-nephew."

"That's funny," said Montserrat. "If anyone had asked me, I'd have said he'd be a relation of the Princess."

June raised her eyebrows. "HSH hasn't got any relations, she's all alone in the world but for me. And no one did ask you that I heard."

"There's no need to be nasty."

"Sometimes there's every need. And may I remind you all that this is supposed to be an extraordinary general meeting of the St. Zita Society, and the main item on the agenda is increasing street noise made by members."

"And I've got some 'Any Other Business,'" said Henry.

Dex turned up at the meeting, or rather, he walked into the Dugong while the meeting was going on and sat down at the big table where the others were already sitting. He bought himself a Guinness and, having nothing to say as usual, listened to the discussion while observing everyone. One of the women had red hair. She was one of those people whose eyes he could see and see too that they were a bright blue. Otherwise her face was the usual blank, not very different from the rest of the faces. Another one was talking on a mobile. Maybe they had gods living in theirs too or just fruits, Dex had heard—orange and blackberry and apple. The others were talking about shouts in the street and shrieks of laughter and loud talking late at night. Dex always took advantage of any free food that might be about, and now he dipped his fingers into the bowl of various-coloured crisps and fetched out a handful. He had noticed the woman called June looking at him and now she said, "Your hand is very dirty. Now you've touched those crisps no one else will want to eat them."

Dex didn't mind if no one else ate them, there would be all the more for him. He made an effort to answer. "I like them. I'll eat them."

"Well, really," said June. She raised the matter of a theatre visit but no one seemed interested.

Henry's other business concerned residents of neighbouring streets parking their cars in Hexam Place so that sometimes there was no room for Lord Studley's car. "His lordship has to walk round the corner to find me."

"Won't hurt him," said June, in radical mode.

Jimmy, whose kind employer would have walked half a mile to get into his car without complaining, said he couldn't see any way this occupying of the Hexam Place parking spaces could be stopped. It was perfectly legal. Dex drained his Guinness glass and moved away to a small table to be by himself. He pressed some keys at random as he always did but starting with the London code of 020. Some notes of music came out and a woman's voice saying the number had not been recognised. Dex knew this meant his God was busy and couldn't speak to him now. That was all right, it often happened. He would try again later. He picked up the crisps bowl in his dirty left hand and poured its contents into his even dirtier right hand with a sigh of satisfaction.

Thea, redheaded, blue-eyed, wearing a red-and-blue-patterned dress instead of trousers, wasn't quite warm enough, but she thought she looked more attractive than any other woman in the pub. Bored stiff during the meeting after her squabble with June, she had made shy attempts to catch men's eyes, but the only response had been from Jimmy. She couldn't really think of Jimmy as in the same category as previous boyfriends, then she decided this was outrageous snobbery and caught his eye again, smiling this time. But Jimmy, without smiling back, went off to pick up Dr. Jefferson and Thea went home alone, where Damian met her in the hall to tell her they had run out of dishwasher tablets.

5

THEA FILLED THE role of the gay men's woman friend, yet she always felt that Damian and Roland didn't like her much. She was useful to them and that was all. They liked men, gay and straight, and men's company was sufficient for them. Considering how often she shopped for them, even cooked for them when they had guests for dinner, she thought they might have reduced her rent, but she couldn't bring herself to ask.

She had a part-time job, teaching IT and basic word processing in an office-skills school over the top of a dry cleaner's in the Fulham Road, and she also taught an evening class called Internet Literacy. Considering the number of people over sixty who couldn't use a computer and barely knew what *going online* meant, for whom the class was designed, it was surprising how ill-attended it was. No doubt it would soon close down because of cuts and her income be correspondingly cut. It made her cross that neither Damian nor Roland had ever asked her what she did for a living. Perhaps they thought she was like their mothers, had private means and did nothing. Perhaps they thought that when she went out, it was to play bridge or have lunch with other ladies, also like their mothers. They were not interested in her and were only nice to her when they wanted to ask a favour or had a reason to be particularly cheerful.

Neither of them took any notice of Miss Grieves—if she had a given name no one knew it—the ninety-year-old who lived below them. It was Thea who shopped for her, fetched her a Sunday paper, and helped her up the area steps when she was specially troubled by her rheumatoid arthritis. Damian called her the last maiden aunt left in London, but if she had any nieces, no one ever saw them. She looked old enough to be June's mother, and June really was a maiden aunt.

The house belonged to Roland Albert, who came from a wealthy family. To buy it, in the early nineties he had sold an object called the Kamensky Medal to a Russian collector of Russian insignia. The medal, quite small and in Thea's opinion ugly, had been given to an ancestor of Roland's by the then tsar, had been handed down among his descendants, and finally fetched the amazing sum of £104,000. This he had used as the deposit on a mortgage to buy number eight Hexam Place. Even so he could afford it only because the basement flat had a sitting tenant in the shape of Miss Grieves, who had been there for longer than Roland's lifetime. Over the years Roland and Damian had offered her, through their solicitor, various increasingly large sums to get out and so leave them with another floor to their home or else a lucrative property for rent. Miss Grieves, who had a racy manner, said in the words of Eliza Doolittle, "Not bloody likely."

In addition to being so kind and helpful, Thea tried to ingratiate herself with her neighbours. This she did with Damian and Roland in an attempt to make number eight the most attractive house in the street by persuading Damian, the kinder and more easygoing of the pair, to buy window boxes for the second-floor windows and urns for the balcony that extended across the front of the first floor, and filling them with bulbs in spring and annuals in summer.

Not that she did the planting herself. Now two weeks into October, she was awaiting the arrival of the Belgrave Nursery's van, driven by their outdoor-plant adviser. Thea expected a small, rather weedy man called Keith, but when the dark green van turned up, a picture of a mimosa in full bloom on its side, the outdoor-plant adviser was a tall, well-built man with a black beard, the badge on his dark green uniform jacket informing her that he was Khalid.

The urns were to have red and purple hyacinths and white multiflower narcissi, he told her, the window boxes dwarf tulips. A new variety that the Belgrave Nursery was proud to stock was a peach-coloured double called Shalimar. He would put some of those in, mingled with a fringed, dark red tulip and a yellow-leaved miniature ivy. What was the squirrel situation in Hexam Place?

"Pardon?" said Thea.

"Do you have squirrels? Only let a squirrel smell a tulip bulb a mile off and he will be here, rooting in your pots for his breakfast." His mild facetiousness made Khalid laugh at his own joke, though it had no effect on Thea. "Oh, no doubt about it."

"Then don't put them in," said Thea, sour-faced.

"Rather we plant them and supply you with our anti-squirrel pot guards, the latest thing only come on the market in the past month."

When it came to haggling, Thea found herself no match for Khalid. She was unaware that though a British citizen since the age of twelve, he came from a long line of Islamabad market stallholders, and after only ten minutes she had agreed to the anti-squirrel pot guards and Khalid was planting tulips in the window boxes. An hour later he had moved the van, made another parking-permission phone call to Westminster City Council, and was ringing the front doorbell of number seven. No servants' entrances for him. Montserrat let him in and took him straight up to the drawing-room floor with his bag of tools and bag of bulbs, having first glanced at his feet as if she expected to see them encased in mud-encrusted boots.

Khalid, who wore elegant, highly polished footwear, said in a sarcastic tone, "Perhaps you would like me to remove my shoes as is the rule at UK airports."

"Oh, no, your shoes are spotless."

Lucy had gone out to lunch at Le Rossignol. Preston Still was of course in the city. The girls were both at school, and Thomas was upstairs with Rabia, having his nappy changed and being dressed in a new navy blue jumpsuit and new camel-coloured cashmere coat with brass buttons. One thing Lucy enjoyed doing for her children, Rabia had noticed, was choosing their clothes, the more expensive the better. But she appreciated her employer's taste. Nothing was too good for Thomas, who looked so gorgeous that she couldn't help hugging him. The hugging over, Thomas was gently lifted into his sumptuous baby carriage, and Rabia, in her hijab, was pushing him along the gallery when Montserrat came up the stairs and with her a man she recognised as a member of her father's plant team. She recognised too the name on his dark green jacket and knew why he was there and the principal purpose of his visit. This tall, black-bearded, and admittedly handsome man was her father's choice for her as a second husband.

"Good morning," said Rabia.

"Good morning, Miss Siddiqui."

"Thank you, but it's Mrs. Ali."

A gratified smile appeared on Khalid's face. "Let me assist you to carry the perambulator to the ground floor."

Rabia had never come across the word *perambulator* before and it silenced her. An obviously strong man, Khalid picked up the pushchair with Thomas in it and carried both single-handedly down the stairs. Rabia followed, said a rather subdued "Thank you," and hurriedly began pushing Thomas towards the front door.

"How will you manage the steps outside?" Khalid called after her.

"I will manage as I always do," said Rabia, and closed the front door with a soft but firm click.

"A lovely-looking woman," said Khalid.

Montserrat, who disliked hearing any woman praised but herself, said it was a matter of taste and would Khalid like to start on the planting of the nursery window boxes. An argument over which was the nursery, this room or his place of work, ensued. Having refused his offer of squirrel pot guards with a toughness Thea had been unable to achieve, Montserrat decided to leave him to it. She went downstairs to the basement flat, where she called her mother on her new iPhone, bought with gratuities from Lucy and Rad Sothern, to tell her she'd like to come to Barcelona for a couple of days before driving up to the Jura. Montserrat's mother was Spanish, her father an Englishman living in Doncaster. Señora Vega Garcia sounded less than pleased to hear from her daughter, but when Montserrat made no request for a loan or even indicated that she might be short of money, she softened and they had the pleasantest conversation they had had for months.

The "couple of days" would be at the beginning of December or a little later, depending on the weather and the state of the snow. In Colmar she would meet a French friend from schooldays whose brother she had always rather fancied. She wondered what Lucy and Rad Sothern would do when their conductor had taken off the month to which she was entitled. Go without, she supposed.

Khalid, in the manner of every British plumber, electrician, gardener, or other tradesperson, called out, "Hallo? Are you there?" and Montserrat ran up to escort him out.

"These stairs are dangerously steep," said Khalid in a severe tone. Montserrat had never noticed before. "The floor down there is made of tiles, very hard, and this banister requires fixing. It could become detached as a person descends, and then what happens?"

"God knows," said Montserrat.

"Also human beings know. I would call it a death trap."

She let him out and watched him climb the area steps to the street.

———

THE HOUSE OF LORDS car park would fill up in the afternoon, but now, just before noon, it was half-empty. Henry had shampooed the Beemer in the mews behind Hexam Place that morning, and now he parked it in the slot he always used next to the space where the government chief whip left his shabby old Volvo. The difference between the Beemer and the Volvo, one so smart and glossy, the other so scarred and dusty, brought him a lot of pleasure, though he was disappointed that Lord Studley had made no comment on the contrast. Henry got out, opened the nearside rear door for Huguette, then the passenger door for her father. He wasn't rid of them yet.

It was the first time he had driven father and daughter together, and he was afraid all the time Huguette would speak out of turn, like saying to him "See you on Friday" or "Why didn't you text me?" She was capable of it. From the moment Lord Studley had said, "I'm giving my daughter lunch at the House," Henry had been nervous. First, for instance, he had to pretend he didn't know where Huguette lived, though, oddly enough, he had never before been to her street by car. Then he had to say, "Good morning, Miss Studley," not sure if this was all right or whether it ought to be "Good morning, the Honourable Huguette." But apparently he had got it right as neither of them complained. Huguette was in a sulky mood, not speaking much, while Lord Studley talked at length about the oral question he had to answer when the House sat at two thirty. It seemed to be about Brazil, a debt or loan and the International Monetary Fund, and Henry was none the wiser when he had driven round Parliament Square and turned in through the security lane. Huguette looked as if she had gone to sleep. Lord Studley broke off at this point to show his red-and-white-striped pass with photograph to the policeman on duty, though the officer had seen him pass this way daily for years.

His employer wanted Henry to carry into the House and up to his office his briefcase and a large cardboard box full of papers. They went through the Peers' Entrance, where Henry had to have his photograph taken to go on a pass and then go through the scrutiny like at Heathrow. Lord Studley shared an office with a minister of state who was in charge of Southern Hemisphere Development, a man whose driver Henry knew and now talked to about the St. Zita Society, which Robert unfortunately couldn't join owing to his not being a resident of Hexam Place. Lord Studley had gone off somewhere to fetch a file he wanted Henry to take back to number eleven, and in his absence Henry kept up a busy conversation with Robert to deter Huguette from making an indiscreet remark or kissing his cheek or something.

Things went from bad to worse when the phone rang, the Southern Hemisphere Development minister answered, and Henry heard him say, "Oh, Oceane, how are you? . . . Fine, thanks. Clifford just popped out for a minute. I'm sure he won't be long."

There couldn't be more than one woman called Oceane phoning the House of Lords. Don't make me speak to her, Henry prayed silently. Huguette was mouthing *Leave me out of it* when her father came back. He took the receiver with a sigh and, while handing the file to Henry, said, "Come back for Miss Studley at two thirty, will you?" Henry fled. He had got out of that by the skin of his teeth, a useful if old-fashioned phrase he had picked up which seemed applicable to much of his life these days.

The Beemer left on the Residents' Parking outside number eleven, he went down the area steps and into the house by the basement door. Why not pop out to the Dugong for a glass of their alcohol-free wine and a ploughman's and take the file upstairs when he came back? He didn't even bother to put the passage light on but opened the door to his bedsit. The light was on in there all right, and Lady Studley was sitting on his bed, smoking a cigarette.

"Oh, Henry darling, didn't I time it absolutely right? I've been here just two minutes waiting for you. Do say you haven't got to go back for my naughty girl."

"Not till half two," said Henry in a gloomy tone.

———————

THE VOICE SAID, "How can I help you?" and Dex knew he had struck lucky. His God was not always so responsive. He could try number after number and only get that woman saying they were not recognisable or else a high-pitched ringing tone. But this time he got that pleasant, gentle voice wanting to help him.

"Make the sun shine, please," he said.

There was no answer. There never was, and Dex didn't expect it. With the ways of gods he was acquainted since early childhood and knew they moved in mysterious ways. His first foster mother had taken him to her church at every possible opportunity and between visits taught him how to pray at home. She explained that his prayers weren't always answered because he was often bad. God liked prayers but only answered those of good people. He must have got a lot better because Peach quite often did what he asked— stopped the rain, made the sun shine, got him a job. His voice never said yes, he would do it or, no, not this time, but in his mysterious, dark way he did whatever it was or else he didn't.

This time he did it, he made the sun shine, and Dex set off for Hexam Place with the big cloth bag in which he carried his small gardening tools. The large ones Dr. Jefferson let him keep in the area cupboard at number three. It was late in the year for mowing the lawns at number three and number five, but Dex thought it dry enough to attempt it. He called Peach for help as he was walking down the Buckingham Palace Road because a bunch of evil spirits passed him, all of them young, all of them blank-faced and one with red hair. They laughed at him and clutched each other and he was afraid. Instead of answering, Peach made a *brrr-brrr* sound that went on and on. Dex stopped it, though he disliked doing this because it seemed rude. But perhaps Peach knew what the trouble was because the evil spirits didn't touch him but ran away over Ebury Bridge. The sun was strong now, shining brightly out of a deep blue sky.

6

THE MEETING OF the St. Zita Society took place at lunchtime and mainly concerned a particularly horrible habit increasingly indulged in by dog walkers, though not of course June and Gussie. While these offenders obeyed the requirement to scrape up their animal's excrement into a plastic bag, instead of taking the bag home with them, they tied a knot in the top of it and left it at the roots of one of the trees in the pavement. Such nasty little bags were sometimes to be seen at the roots of every tree in Hexam Place.

This subject aroused a lot of anger in St. Zita members, of whom Henry, Beacon, Sondra, Thea, and Jimmy were present round the table in the Dugong. It was unanimously decided to write a letter to Westminster City Council and another, slightly differently worded, to the *Guardian*. Thea was chosen to write the letters, rather to Beacon's resentment. She might have a degree, but he was positive it wasn't as good as his nor obtained from as good a university as the University of Lagos. Could he have been rejected or even not considered for the job because he was African? However, he said nothing—for now, he thought—and walked along Hexam Place a few paces behind June instead of accompanying her.

Making sure Beacon was looking, June went up the steps of

number six to the front door and let herself in, taking her time about it. Zinnia was clearing up after the Princess's lunch.

"Are you drunk?" said the Princess.

"Of course not. At my age!"

"I don't know what difference age makes. My grandmother drank more heavily the older she got. She was paralytic in her seventies and unconscious in her eighties. Have you done whatever it is you have to do on the computer to fix us in for our flight?"

"*Check* us in, madam," said June. "It's too early. We're not going till Sunday."

"I'd have thought the earlier you did it the better."

"Then you'd have thought wrong. They won't let you do it till twenty-four hours before the flight."

"How ridiculous," said the Princess. "When we get back, I'm thinking of getting myself a wheelchair. I could get out then. I'm dying of boredom stuck in here. You could push me."

"No, I couldn't, madam. I'm too old to push other old people about. If you want a wheelchair, you'll have to get one you drive yourself."

"Well, when you chart us in for the flight, could you look up wheelchairs on dongle?"

Zinnia was giggling. She had the Caribbean ready sense of humour and irrepressible laugh. June frowned at her and said she would see. She couldn't be bothered to correct her employer's two new errors, but maybe next time such a mistake was made she'd ask the Princess if she'd like a computer lesson from Thea next door. Imagine how that would go down! June hunted around for Gussie, found him asleep under the piano, and put him on the lead. The two of them carried out a survey of the tree roots in Hexam Place and adjacent streets. Even when composing the relevant item on the agenda, June hadn't suspected there were quite so many of those disgusting little bags. Gussie enjoyed his part in the research, amazed at being allowed to sniff the excrement repositories as much as he liked. June counted twelve in Hexam Place alone. While she was photographing the most obtrusive on her mobile, her activities were watched by a passing dog walker, who stared at June in horror, picked up his Pekingese, and ran off towards Eaton Square.

They were going to Florence. They always went to Florence for a week in October and to Verona for a week in May. From these fortnights in Italy June had picked up a little Italian and had bought herself an Italian dictionary and a phrasebook. HSH the Princess Susan Hapsburg spoke no Italian despite her year and a half living with Luciano. That evening, over drinks, they described to Rad Sothern how they would pass their week.

"She thinks she's an egghead," said the Princess, "goes to museums and churches and whatever."

Rad was too young to know what *egghead* meant. "So what do you do, Your Highness?"

"Well, Mr. Fortescue, since you ask, I manage to get about on foot a little. It's the sunshine, you know, it does me good. I go to dress shops and jewellery shops and spend money and sit outside cafés and watch the world go by. She's happy enough to join me when there's any drink going, I can tell you."

Not deigning to rebut this, June went to the window and looked up and down Hexam Place. The only car parked in the street was Montserrat's VW. "Your friend taking you out for a drive, is she?"

"Not so far as I know." Rad sounded rather uncomfortable.

"I thought you might be going over to Wimbledon Common. It's a fine night. Maybe it's more cosy at home."

Rad said a hasty good-bye, wished them a nice holiday, and made his way across the street to number seven, where he went down the area steps and for a moment disappeared from view. It looked to Miss Grieves on the basement stairs of number eight as if he must have retreated into the cupboard which faced the basement door. That dark girl who was a friend of Thea's soon appeared, flooding the area with light from the basement. In her day and for a good many days afterwards, no girl would have met her boyfriend dressed in dirty jeans with their bottoms turned up, an old biker's jacket, and a man's vest. Rad emerged from where he had been hiding and followed her in. They didn't kiss. Weird, thought Miss Grieves. Not to say bloody mad.

Maybe he'd stay the night. There was no reason why he shouldn't. The Stills seemed easygoing with their staff. Miss Grieves went back to her evening drink, half English breakfast tea and half whisky, and lit a cigarette. Back at the window an hour later she saw Beacon arriving in the Audi, turning the car, parking behind that girl's car. By the light from a streetlamp she could quite clearly see him slip on a headset and move his right thumb round the circle on an iPod. Even the colour of the iPod could be seen, an iridescent peach.

Now if he gets a call to go and get Preston Still from Victoria or Euston or somewhere, thought Miss Grieves, what's the betting that as soon as the car moves off, that girl will have Rad out of there before you can say *mystery*. But why? Maybe Lucy Still doesn't mind that girl having a lover in her room but Preston does. A far cry it was, all of it, from the days when she had been maid of all work to Lady Pimble in Elystan Place. She dragged a chair to the window so that she could keep on looking in comfort. Whatever Beacon was listening to, it seemed to be keeping him in rapture, his head back against the Audi's headrest, his lips parted in a beatific half-smile. Gossip was that he only had hymns on his iPod, "Abide with Me" and "Lead Us, Heavenly Father, Lead Us," and all that stuff. Bloody insane. It could go on all night. . . .

But suddenly the headset was pulled off, the iPod discarded, and Beacon was talking on his mobile. Seconds later the Audi was moving off southwards. Victoria it must be, thought Miss Grieves. And sure enough, Montserrat must have been watching—wasn't there any sex going on with those two?—for Beacon hadn't been gone five minutes when the basement door opened and Rad emerged, shoved by the girl, her hand in the middle of his back.

He ran up those stairs as if all the devils in hell were after him and legged it up the street. Miss Grieves wondered what he'd do if she went out there and asked him what the hurry was. But she didn't go. It took her a good ten minutes to climb those stairs.

Thea decided to have a second cigarette while she was out there. She was sitting on the third from the top of the steps up to the front door of number eight. It was either that or to stand shivering in the wet back garden. She picked another Marlboro from the pack and lit it, inhaling deeply. The only "staff" in Hexam Place to smoke were Henry (in his room with the window wide open and him hanging half out of it), Zinnia (in her own home and in the street), and Miss Grieves (as much and as often as she liked in her own flat with all the windows shut). Damian and Roland were antismoking fanatics. That was the way Thea put it, or sometimes "antismoking fascists." If they had ever had anything to do with Miss Grieves, they would have known about her smoking and done their best to stop it with threats and maybe promises, but they didn't know because they had never been inside her flat or smelt her. Miss Grieves reeked of stale cigarette smoke, providing a lesson to Thea. Before going into Damian and Roland's part of the house, she took the dress or suit she had been wearing to the dry cleaner's, had a hot bath, and washed her hair.

They had gone to work an hour before or Thea wouldn't have dared sit here to smoke her cigarette. She watched Beacon sitting in the Audi, waiting for Preston Still. He was late this morning. Perhaps he wasn't going to his office in Old Broad Street but off to another of those eternal conferences in Birmingham or Cardiff. Henry had departed with Lord Studley before she had started on her first cigarette. The only interesting thing to happen this morning was the departure of the Princess and June for Heathrow and somewhere in Italy. Their taxi was due at ten thirty, June had told her, and it duly arrived, five minutes early, which was par for the course with that company. From where she sat, Thea couldn't see the front door of number six, but she could just see the bottom steps, the driver go up them, and June appear with him after a couple of minutes. The amount of baggage those two old women took with them! June was hauling some of it along behind her, bump, bump, bump, down the steps with her, the driver balancing a huge suitcase on his right shoulder like a furniture remover. The Princess never carried anything except her handbag. She minced down the steps in high heels and on two sticks. Thea thought they must be the only pair of heels she owned, red snakeskin with toes pointed enough to stab someone. June went back for the rest of the bags and they got into the taxi.

Thea was watching it disappear northwards, sucking on the stub of her cigarette, when Damian appeared from nowhere, opened the gate, and advanced to the foot of the steps.

"When the cat is away," he said in his snooty accent, "the mice will play. I thought I caught a whiff on you the other day."

"I can't give up. I *have* tried."

"It's not so much the smoking, though if you'll forgive the cliché, it *is* a filthy habit. No, it's sitting on the steps I mind. Like some slag on a council estate. Still, since you're here, perhaps you'll go inside and find my briefcase for me. Unaccountably I forgot it."

Thea could have said it wasn't unaccountable, he was always forgetting things, but she didn't. She found the briefcase on the table just inside the front door and brought it to him.

"Thank you. You do have your uses."

He walked off to pick up a taxi in Ebury Bridge Road.

Thea lit a third cigarette and walked round the house into the back garden, where the paths and the lawn were invisible under a thick, wet layer of fallen leaves. Unidentifiable toadstools that looked like hunks of purple liver poked their heads through the brown mush. It had begun to rain again. Thea sheltered under the ginkgo tree, scraped the mud off her shoes on its trunk, and thought she might get smoking or "the smoking question" put down as an item on the agenda of the next St. Zita meeting. Where were smokers to smoke, for instance? In the street? Surely not. Perhaps someone's flat or studio room might be turned into a smoking room like you got at certain airports. That reminded her that she couldn't put anything on the agenda as June had departed on her holidays.

"Never pass a weed," said Abram Siddiqui, stooping down to pull up a dandelion growing among the chrysanthemums. He explained to his daughter, who in any case had heard it before, "This means not to walk past it but to pull it out so that you *do not actually* pass it."

"Yes, Father, I remember. We have so many weeds in our garden—well, Mr. Still's garden—that you could not help passing them. There are only weeds and not any plants."

Thomas, in his pushchair, was making friendly overtures to a customer's German shepherd, holding out his arms and shouting, "Doggy, doggy."

Rabia picked him up, and his cajoling turned to screams of protest. She carried him towards the temperate house where the café was while pushing the buggy with her free hand and said, "Thomas, be quiet now. Stop screaming and stop kicking or you will have no chocolate biscuit with your drink."

Abram looked on approvingly but waiting, Rabia knew, to see if she carried out her threat. Orange juice came for the still-yelling Thomas and coffee for Rabia and her father. The biscuits on offer today were a particularly delicious variety. Seated in what Rabia called a "grown-up chair," Thomas was now sobbing and reaching out for the biscuit plate. The woman with the German shepherd passed by on the other side of the glass wall.

"No, Thomas. Drink your juice."

Rabia moved the plate out of his reach but otherwise ignored his pleas. Abram, pleased with her handling of the biscuit crisis, said, "Khalid told me he saw you when he came to take the Christmas-tree booking. He said, but very respectfully, Rabia, that you are beautiful and dressed like a good Muslim lady."

"It is not his business, Father, to talk about how I am dressed."

"It was very respectful. I am your father and I know what is proper. I could not object. There are not many like Khalid, I can tell you, Rabia."

"There may be ten thousand for all I know. They are nothing to me. And now Thomas is behaving like a good boy, and there are not *any* like him, he is so good"—she reached over, took his face in her hands, and kissed his fat pink cheek—"now we will go home. And on the way home we shall buy some biscuits just like those and you shall have one at teatime."

"It is good to hear you do not let him eat in the street," said Abram rather sourly. "Children must not be allowed to eat in the street in any circumstances."

7

MONTSERRAT SAW IN the mirror a petite young woman, slim but not thin, with beautiful breasts and rounded hips, shapely legs and fine ankles. The face she saw was oval, the skin very white, the eyes large and dark brown, the features symmetrical, and the hair a dense mass of black curls. Did she know anyone with as fine a head of hair as hers?

Thea and Henry and Beacon saw a short young woman, about twelve pounds overweight, with oversize breasts (Thea), quite good legs (Henry), far too pale, looked ill (Beacon), and nothing special about her features except that the eyes were attractive, if too starey. All agreed that her hair was her best feature, a true black, Beacon said, glossy as ebony, but he only admired the looks of his own ethnic group. Unfortunately, he said, she hadn't a very nice nature.

"On the make," said June. "You know how they say of people— mostly dead people, I must say—that she'd have done anything for anybody. Well, that Montsy wouldn't do anything for anybody unless it was to her advantage. You'll see."

Montserrat's father and Lucy Still's father had been at school together and remained friends, though Charles Tresser had lost all his money in some banking scandal, while Robert Sanderson got richer and richer. Charles mentioned that his daughter had dropped out of the university he had got her into with some difficulty, and Robert suggested the problem of where she was to go and how to earn her living would be solved by her going to work for his daughter, who was expecting her third child. That was how Montserrat came to be an au pair and called Lucy by her first name. What she was supposed to do she had never been told. Zinnia did the housework, Rabia looked after the new baby and the girls when they needed looking after, Beacon drove the Audi. Lucy had no car but took taxis everywhere. Montserrat had the one-bedroom basement flat, which would have been Beacon's if he had chosen to live in it instead of with Dorothee, William, and Solomon.

If Montserrat's duties had never been specified, she soon knew that she would be expected to perform those vaguely secretarial tasks that weren't to Lucy's taste. Sending for a plumber when one was required, informing credit card companies that a card was lost, asking for help from the provider when Lucy's computer failed. Much the same as the "little jobs" that Thea carried out for Damian and Roland for free. Montserrat found this tedious but she mostly did it. Her conscience had never troubled her when she found she was expected to admit, escort upstairs, and eventually dismiss Lucy's lover. While living with her mother in Barcelona when she wasn't living with her father in Bath, she saw her mother's lovers come and go, and in some cases a secret was made of their visits. This was normal, she thought. She never thought it beneath her dignity or degrading to take the twenty-pound note Lucy tucked into her jeans pocket when she brought Rad along to the bedroom or the fifty-pound note he thrust into her hand when she saw him out of the basement door.

Now, on a morning in October, she found herself asked, not by Lucy who cared nothing for such things, but by Mr. Still, on his way to get into the Audi, if she would find someone to mend the loose banister at the top of the basement stairs.

"Some sort of builder, d'you mean?"

"Try the yellow pages," said Preston Still, sounding impatient. "I don't know. Just do it."

Montserrat couldn't find the yellow pages. For one thing, she didn't know where to look, so she opened every drawer and cupboard she came to and was emerging from one of the spare rooms when she met Lucy coming out of her bedroom. Lucy was wearing a pale yellow suit the same colour as her hair with a skirt some eight inches above her knees, lacy tights, and shoes with five-inch heels. Montserrat asked her if she knew where the yellow pages were.

"No one uses phone directories anymore," said Lucy. "This is the age of the cell phone, or hadn't you noticed?"

"Mr. Still wants someone to mend the banister."

"Oh, I shouldn't bother. He's probably forgotten all about it by now. He's a chronic amnesiac."

Lucy tottered downstairs, waved once, and slammed the front door behind her. Her bedroom was in its usual chaotic state before Zinnia got to work on it, the bed a sprawl of discarded clothes, the sheets scattered with ash and crumbs, the breakfast tray she had taken up two hours before cluttered with smeary plates and coffee dregs in which fag ends floated. Montserrat, no believer herself in the virtues of cleanliness, almost admired Lucy's ability to turn a neatly laid tray of prettily packaged foodstuffs into a filthy tip like the contents of a wastebin ravaged by urban foxes. She looked in vain inside the clothes cupboards and the drawers for the yellow pages, abandoned the room to Zinnia, and went on up to the nursery floor.

Rabia was teaching Thomas to feed himself. He sat in his high chair with a spoon in each hand, digging away at a bowl of goo. The spoon in his right hand was used to transfer the goo to his mouth, more or less haphazardly, the other to fling its contents onto the floor or as far across the room as he could reach. Montserrat, who disliked children, had seldom seen a more disgusting sight.

"He is so clever and good, aren't you, my sweetheart?" Rabia was kept busy, crawling about, wiping up messes on floor, wall, and skirting board.

Thomas laughed, goo leaking out of his open mouth. "Love Rab," he said, wiping a spoon on his nanny's hair.

Montserrat could have sworn tears of joy had come into Rabia's eyes.

"Where can I get someone to mend the banister, Rabia?"

"Maybe yellow pages."

"Yeah, but I can't find them."

"My cousin Mohammed, he is very, very good carpenter. Better than carpenter, *joiner.*"

"How can I find him? You know his mobile number?"

"Of course, Montsy. I have it by heart." Rabia gave it to Montserrat, then, expecting her to forget, wrote it down on the shopping-list pad. "I have all relations' and friends' numbers in my memory."

"Wow, I wish I had."

"Yes, it is a gift." Rabia smiled modestly, picked up Thomas, and hugged him, contriving to smear his mouth all across her blouse. "Now we shall both have to put clean clothes on, my darling. Will that be fun?"

Evidently it would, for Thomas roared with laughter.

A message had to be left on Mohammed's voice mail. He called back when Montserrat was in the Dugong, having a drink with Jimmy and Henry.

"I am coming on Saturday the sixth," said Mohammed.

"The sixth of *November?*"

"That is the next sixth, isn't it? Between nine a.m. and five p.m."

"You mean someone's got to be in all day?" Montserrat knew that someone would be her. "Can't you say morning or after-noon?"

"You take it or leave it, my dear. You will get top-class job."

"Oh, OK, if I must," said Montserrat.

The paediatrician at number three would require Jimmy no more that day, so his driver was having a stiff gin and tonic. Henry, needed by Lord Studley in Whitehall at five thirty, thought it best to stick to elderflower water. He could have a real drink with Huguette that evening, possibly a few glasses of burgundy and a nip or two of Campari, which was what Montserrat was having with orange now.

"If anything goes wrong at number seven," she was saying, "and Rabia is separated from that child, she'll break her heart."

"What d'you mean, goes wrong?" Henry thought the elderflower water would be improved by a spot of gin but he dared not.

"Well, if they split up. You never know, do you? Lucy wouldn't think twice about getting rid of Rabia."

"She'll be all right," said Jimmy. "I hear she's getting married to that guy who drives the flower-pot van."

Montserrat didn't like her news to be capped, especially by something more positive and dramatic. She got up, said she'd see them at the next St. Zita Society meeting, which couldn't be long delayed now that June and the Princess were back from Florence. And there they were, their taxi drawing up outside number six. It was one of those big taxis, like a little bus with sliding doors, and obviously needful for the quantity of luggage which began to spill out onto the pavement. Montserrat hurried down the area steps in case she would be asked to help with carrying it in.

IN COMMON WITH Damian and Roland, the Princess, and the noble family of Studleys, neither Lucy nor Preston Still ever did anything in the house which could be categorised as a menial or horny-handed task. The paediatrician, on the other hand, much to Jimmy's disgust, rather enjoyed knocking a nail in here and there, mending a fuse, or putting a washer on a tap. Jimmy would have agreed with the sentiments in Belloc's verse:

Lord Finchley tried to mend the Electric Light
Himself. It struck him dead: And serve him right!
It is the business of the wealthy man
To give employment to the artisan.

There were of course exceptions to this rule, and on Saturday morning Preston Still, having twice grabbed at the faulty banister, felt it wobble in his hands and nearly let him fall down the basement stairs, carefully examined the structure of banisters and rail with a view to doing a temporary repair. November sixth! Couldn't something better than that have been arranged?

Montserrat said it couldn't and stood by, watching him. He had always supposed, he said, that the banister, wooden, probably walnut, pale gray-brown and polished, was a solid piece, the length of a tree's height, but of course it wasn't; it was cunningly put together by some kind of interlocking system, maybe consisting of four pieces in all. You could only see the joins if you looked closely. This construction, he said to Montserrat, made mending a loose rail much easier. As if to prove it, he took hold of the banister itself and began tugging on it.

By this time Lucy had appeared. Instead of the yellow suit, she was dressed in white shorts, a white T-shirt, and white trainers, the smooth brown skin of her long legs making a nice contrast. With her, looking disgruntled, were her daughters, similarly attired.

"We're all going for a run round the park, aren't we, girls?" The girls made no reply but Hero pulled a face. "So we thought we'd come and see what Daddy was doing on our way."

"Now you've seen," said Preston sourly, "you can get going."

"No, but, darling, what *are* you doing?"

"Trying to mend the banister," said Rabia, who had appeared behind Lucy with Thomas in his pushchair. "Better to wait for my cousin Mohammed, who is coming very kindly on a Saturday and therefore giving up his day of rest."

Preston ignored her. He was vigorously shaking the banister. With a noise halfway between a groan and a crunch, the whole section of polished wood came away in his hands. He nearly fell over backwards, uttering an expletive which made Matilda say in the tone listeners thought would one day land her a job as headmistress of a girls' public school, "Daddy, you're not supposed to say words like that in front of *us*. You should remember Thomas is only sixteen months old."

"I'm sorry, kids," said Preston, still clutching the section of banister. "I really am. I shouldn't have said that." His eyes turned to his son and rested there, growing anxious. "Is that a rash I can see on his neck, Rabia?"

"I am sure it is not, Mr. Still."

"What's that redness, then?"

"It is because his scarf is red. Now see when I move it?"

Thomas began to chortle because he thought he was being tickled. His neck appeared white as milk away from the scarf.

"Oh, well, you know best. If there's any doubt about it, you'll run him along to Dr. Jefferson, won't you?"

All but Montserrat melted away, Lucy driving her daughters before her like an aggressive shepherd with a flock. Rabia had to carry the pushchair down the steps on her own. It was rather cold, and rain was forecast. But indoors the habitual heat prevailed, and Preston, sitting on the stairs where he had wrenched the loose rail out of the section of banister, said irritably, "All it needs is some glue. Have we got any glue?"

"I don't know. I shouldn't think so."

"Well, have a look, will you? And, Montserrat, would you make me a cup of coffee?"

"It'll have to be instant."

She made the coffee. Zinnia never came on Saturdays. Perhaps Preston would have forgotten about the glue by this time. There was none in any of the cupboards under the kitchen's two sinks.

He had moved, was now sitting in a (reproduction) eighteenth-century French chair halfway along the gallery, the banister and its one intact rail on his lap, the other in his right hand. Montserrat, walking slowly to avoid spilling the coffee, wondered why Lucy had married him, he was so hairy. At ten in the morning—she had heard him shaving at eight—he already had a five o'clock shadow, seven hours early. His body and his legs must be a sight to behold. Like a gorilla! And he had a small but increasing belly. No wonder Lucy preferred Rad Sothern, even if he was about six inches shorter.

"Now you've done that," he said, letting her put the coffee cup on the floor, "perhaps you'll go out and buy some glue."

Montserrat knew that *perhaps* meant nothing. "Go where?"

"You must know where there are some shops. I don't. I have a job which takes up all my time, in case you've forgotten. Ask people. Look in the phone book."

She had been there before. She'd just go and she'd ask. Preston emptied his pockets of notes and coins and handed them to her. The rain had started and she took one of the large umbrellas from the stand in the hall. The whole exercise would have been insupportable had she not been able to picture Lucy and the girls umbrella-less and getting wet. Rabia wouldn't care, while Thomas had a hood on his carriage to keep him dry. Montserrat counted the money Preston had given her for the glue, nearly thirty pounds. He must be mad. She found an ironmonger's in the Pimlico Road and, just to be on the safe side, bought two kinds of glue that the man behind the counter recommended. She didn't want to be sent out again.

It appeared that Preston had given up. Her trip had been in vain, and what to do with two useless tubes of adhesive?

"Oh, put it somewhere. Maybe that Mohammed will have a use for it."

Montserrat knew he wouldn't. She waited till Preston had disappeared along the gallery and up the big curving staircase, then she examined the shakily replaced section of banister and the two rails. Before he'd started, both rails had been undamaged. Now the top end of one of them was jagged enough to reveal the raw wood. Montserrat shook her head and laughed silently. He had left his coffee cup on the carpet by that chair he had sat in. She went back and fetched it, not too resentful. After all, he hadn't asked for his change back, and she was the better off by twenty-five pounds. By this time she was feeling so cheerful that she forgot her usual carefulness and started to run down the basement stairs, grabbing the banister as she went. He had left it so shaky, much worse than before he'd messed about with it, that she fell over and only just managed to save herself by clutching at the edge of the stair carpet.

BEGINNING WORK ON the agenda for the October St. Zita meeting the same day as she returned from Florence, June included in the matters to be discussed the revolting question of the little plastic bags of dog excrement and the problem of noise in Hexam Place after 11:00 p.m. Various notes from members had come while she was away. She had no objection to an item requesting a debate on the smoking habits of members and where they should be able to indulge it. June already agreed that if an employer might smoke indoors, why should an employee not do likewise? A request from Thea for permission to be granted to sit on the front steps of *one's own home* (this heavily underlined) especially when *one was not a servant*, June decided to exclude. Let her raise it under "Any Other Business." The date of the meeting was to be lunchtime on October 29. June quickly made the first item "Rules to Be Formulated."

The Princess was watching *Avalon Clinic*, this evening's episode heavily featuring Rad as Mr. Fortescue. June joined her on the sofa, bringing with her two stiff gin and tonics and a bowl of pistachios. Until now, apart from various minor flirtations, Mr. Fortescue had mostly been presented in his role as hardworking gynaecologist,

RUTH RENDELL

but now he was embarking on a love affair with the glamourous sister from Estonia. Both were married to other people, which complicated matters delightfully.

"Thea told me you can get a boxed set of the first series," whispered June when Mr. Fortescue was off the screen for fifteen seconds. "Shall I?"

"Yes. Tomorrow. Don't talk, please. How many times do I have to tell you? He's just coming back."

Gussie, fetched from the boarding kennels in a taxi, snuggled up on the Princess's lap, from where June had to dislodge him for his evening walk round the block. Descending the steps, whom should she see on the other side of the street but Mr. Fortescue himself, sneaking out of the basement door at number seven. June waved to her great-nephew, seeing no reason why she should conspire with them in their intrigue. Rad just raised one hand in a feeble wave. From the basement window of number eight Miss Grieves also watched Rad leave. Two hours before, she had watched him arrive.

Studying wheelchair advertisements in the newspaper, the Princess turned briefly from the page to June, who had returned with the dog. "Don't forget to get that canned set tomorrow, will you? You won't remember if you don't write it down."

"Boxed," said June absently.

FOR RABIA A WEEKEND at the Stills' country house was always something to look forward to. Until they took her to Gallowmill Hall, she had never seen anything of the English countryside, let alone stayed there, *slept* there. She had discovered in herself a rapturous love of the fields and woods, the little stream which ran through the grounds with its ducks and moorhens, sometimes a swan and once an otter. Butterflies, red and black and white,

58

abounded. Thomas could lie on a blanket on the lawn while the sun shone above and fluffy clouds drifted across a pearly blue sky.

It was some weeks since her first visit, but now they were going again, and Lucy told Rabia such a stay would be impossible without her. Who else could manage the children? So indispensable was she that in the car going down—a rented minibus so that all could be accommodated—Lucy apologised to her nanny for the house being so near to London and in *Essex*.

"It wouldn't be so bad if it was only Hertfordshire, but Essex makes people laugh as soon as you utter the name, doesn't it, Press?"

"Not the people I utter it to," said Preston.

Rabia didn't know what they were talking about so she just smiled. Thomas had fallen asleep next to her. If she could only be with him until he grew up or they sent him away to one of those wicked boarding schools, if only she could be with Thomas, she would want nothing else, no second husband, no home of her own. If only. The girls were bickering. They had been made to wear trainers for the country instead of their new shoes and had shuffled their feet out of them as soon as the minibus was off.

"Your shoes stink," said Matilda.

Hero pinched her on the arm. "It's yours that stink. My sweat doesn't smell, I'm not old enough. You are."

"If you pinch me again, I'll kick you."

"Now that is enough," Rabia admonished them because their mother never bothered. "We want none of that while we go away to enjoy ourselves."

They obeyed her; they usually did. It took half an hour to get out of London and onto the M25, then along a turning through Epping Forest, where there was little traffic and the air smelt fresh. The day was bright and cold, the woods golden, leaves falling or blowing off in the gusts of wind. Gallowmill Hall was approached by a long drive between yellow trees, half of whose leaves lay underfoot. In the meadow on the left-hand side a stag and three or four hinds, property of the deer farmer who rented a few of Preston's acres, grazed on the lush green grass. A hawk hovered overhead.

Thomas woke up, whimpering, and put his arms round Rabia's neck as Preston drew up on the sweep in front of the house. If Lucy described it to her friends as "nothing much to look at, one of those two-a-penny late-eighteenth-century places," to Rabia it was a gorgeous palace. That one family could live in such a place, and not even live but just come there sometimes to stay a couple of nights, was to her unbelievable, a dream. But it was real. The previous time they had been there, when the children were in bed, she had crept downstairs and come outside to touch the gray-gold stonework, half expecting it to dissolve in her hand. It was real. The rooms with their high ceilings and pale green or ivory walls were real, and the sweeping staircase, twice as wide as the one in Hexam Place, its banisters filagreed silver, that too was real. The paintings were real and of real people in silk and satin, grandfathers and grandmothers of Mr. Still and *their* grandfathers and grandmothers. And to think that when her father took her back to Pakistan when she was sixteen to meet her future husband, relatives had asked her if it was true that everyone in the United Kingdom was equal.

They had brought all the food for the weekend with them, bags and crates and cool boxes of it, all delivered by M and S and Ocado the day before. Rabia helped Mr. Still carry it in. She got the girls to help too because Lucy couldn't, she said she was tired, being driven out here always exhausted her. Rabia had plenty to do, lunch to be got for one thing, then Thomas put down for his afternoon nap, but she went out later for a walk in the grounds. The girls refused to come with her; their quarrel in the past now, they preferred to play computer games in the bedroom they shared. They might as well have been in London. Rabia saw rabbits and a squirrel, something in the distance that might have been a badger but she couldn't be sure, she had never before seen one. The gardener she had encountered on her previous visit. He had stared then at her long black gown and her hijab, but this time he was used to her appearance and seemed to understand that she spoke English and wasn't crazy or fierce and greeted her with an "Afternoon, missus."

"Good afternoon," said Rabia. "Are you digging that up to plant flowers?"

"That's right. Preparing the flowerbed. We'll have some bulbs in there for the spring and then some annuals for the summer."

"That will be very beautiful." Rabia told him about her father, who was the manager of a nursery that sold flowers and plants and trees, and the man seemed interested.

Her walk had taken her to look at the stream and the little wood and a little maze she didn't go in because you could get lost. The worry that had been with her for months now, whether she should speak out in the matter of Lucy's immoral, and to Rabia criminal, behaviour, she could put to the back of her mind while she was out in the fresh air and under the trees. She went back to the house, feeling cheerful and ready to think about what to give them all for their dinners.

8

T HE WEEKEND PASSED pleasantly enough for Montserrat, all alone at number seven. She celebrated the departure of the Stills by drinking too much in the Dugong on Saturday night. Walking home was not to be contemplated without assistance. This was given by a rather good-looking man, a newcomer to the Dugong, who she thought—insofar as she was able to think—would leave her at the basement door once she had managed to turn her key in the lock. He had different ideas, came in with her, came into her flat with her, and in her bedroom undressed her without her permission. She was too weak to resist and, once naked, had no wish to resist. He stayed all night, departing at eight in the morning after taking her mobile number. He also took a gold bracelet from Lucy's jewel box, discovered during the hurried tour he made of the house before leaving.

Montserrat only discovered this a week later, or guessed at a week later, when Lucy couldn't find the bracelet. Of course Montserrat said nothing. The rather good-looking man hadn't called her, so how was she supposed to know who he was or where he lived? It had been on the tip of her tongue to tell Thea about her experience, blaming her insensible state on his dropping Rohypnol into her drink, but later she was glad she hadn't mentioned it. She and

Thea went out on the Sunday and Montserrat hadn't felt too bad, enjoying the sunshine on Wimbledon Common and later sharing a bottle of wine in a pizza place.

The bit of banister seemed more shaky than ever, so, feeling very responsible, she made a notice out of a sheet of cardboard, wrote on it in block capitals DANGER. DO NOT TOUCH, and hung it on the rail by a piece of string.

THE QUESTION OF Lucy's conduct with the wicked man who was a TV actor continued to worry Rabia, but since it had first come to her notice several months ago now, she had set it against her love for Thomas. It was wrong to think this way, but if she told Lucy what she knew, no doubt Lucy would dismiss her, and if she told Mr. Still, Lucy would know she had told him and still dismiss her. She would never see Thomas again. Her heart would break. Rabia was no fool and was well aware that Thomas had taken the place of Assad and Nasreen, her dead children, and that she gave him twice the love she had given to each one of them.

There was nothing to be done except hope the wicked TV man would tire of Lucy or she of him. Such things happened. Rabia knew this, not from experience but from the kind of TV dramas the wicked man took part in. These had no characters like herself or like Beacon, who was also possessed of a strong moral sense. She knew this because Montserrat had told her that her own task would be considerably helped if only Beacon would call her when the boss was getting into the Audi in Old Broad Street. That would give her twenty minutes at least to hustle Rad Sothern out of the house before Mr. Still walked in the front door. She hadn't actually asked Beacon, but she had given him what she called a "hypothetical scenario" she translated for Rabia as "the kind of thing that might happen." A friend of hers, she had said, was in that particular situation. The driver might have helped her out, didn't Beacon think? Beacon did not.

"That driver should tell his boss," said Beacon, giving Montserrat a nasty, suspicious look.

Rabia made no comment. She was hugging Thomas at the time and Thomas was lovingly kissing her cheek.

"I just have to rely on guesswork," said Montserrat.

Preston Still took a week's holiday in October, and he and Lucy went off to stay in a fashionable hotel on the Cornish coast. The children were left at home with Rabia and Montserrat. Zinnia was also roped in to stay in a room on the nursery floor.

"He'll sort of miss his kids," said Zinnia. "She won't. Don't know why she had them. Mind you, the only notice he takes of them is to ask if they're ill."

Rabia agreed but said nothing. She rather enjoyed being the most important one of the three left in charge and discovered in herself a talent for organisation. Montserrat was to see to the girls' tea and make sure they did their little bit of homework, while Zinnia attended to their clothes and the laundry. Rabia took Thomas over to the *other* nursery, the plant one, and rather regretted paying the visit when her father said that Khalid Iqbal was to be found in the tropical house and she should go along and say good afternoon to him.

"No, Father, if Mr. Iqbal wishes to speak to me, he must come to me. I am going to take Thomas to see the white mice and the ferret." For the nursery offered for sale small mammals as well as tropical fish and a multiplicity of plants.

The mice were even more popular with Thomas than the fish. He put out his hands to their cage, trying to grasp one of them through the bars. Moving his pushchair away, though ever so gently, provoked yells and a storm of tears, so that when Khalid Iqbal approached along the path from the arboretum, Rabia was holding the weeping Thomas close, his wet cheek against her cheek.

The sight of the woman a man hopes to marry lovingly carrying a child adds to the attraction she has for him. This may specially be true of a man from a culture where children are much prized. Khalid greeted Rabia with a fulsome smile and a request after her health.

"Mr. Siddiqui has kindly invited me to take tea with him on Saturday afternoon and said he hoped you too would be there."

To herself Rabia said, Oh, has he? We'll see about that. Aloud: "My father should have told me first. Saturday afternoon will be impossible, I am afraid. I am in charge of the household at number seven until my employers return from holiday."

His disappointment was plain. "Perhaps another time."

"Perhaps," said Rabia, putting Thomas back in his pushchair.

She was rather annoyed with her father. The more he went on like this, the more she would resist. He had arranged one marriage for her, and though she had come to love her husband, no one could say that things had turned out well for her. Very much the reverse. She wouldn't let him do it again. She was a British citizen, used to British ways, unacceptable as some of them might be. As she began the walk back to Hexam Place, the idea of British ways turned her thoughts to the problem of Lucy and the TV man, not to consider any longer whether to tell Mr. Still—that would have such terrible consequences as not to be contemplated—but simply to think about the situation and how different it would be if Lucy were not herself British-born but a member of a family hailing from Pakistan. Her own, for instance. Why, if any of her female relatives had behaved like that, if not subjected to an honour killing, she would at least have been shut up somewhere and probably beaten. Rabia, gentle and loving with children, generally subservient to male relatives, thought this kind of violence on the whole a good idea.

THE ST. ZITA SOCIETY met in the Dugong at lunchtime to discuss the items on a very full agenda. Present—June made a note of the names—were Thea herself, Montserrat, Jimmy, Henry, and Sondra. Apologies were from Richard, Beacon, Rabia, and Zinnia. No alcohol was drunk while the business was under discussion.

June made an eloquent speech on the revolting evils of packaging up one's dog's excrement in a plastic bag and leaving it under a tree. An unsatisfactory letter had come from the council, extolling its own street-cleaning plan and hygiene consciousness. It was unanimously decided that Thea should write again. June thought she should have been asked to write, but she said nothing, merely looked sulky. Noise in the street was dismissed as being mostly caused by employers, not employees. Smoking and sitting on doorsteps was raised under "Any Other Business," along with cats squealing in back gardens at night and pigeons fouling doorsteps. It was unanimously agreed that asking householders to keep their cats in at night would have no effect, besides that no one at the meeting could recall any resident of Hexam Place having a cat. The squealers must have come in from Eaton Square or Sloane Gardens. Much the same applied to pigeons.

Sondra wanted to know if Thea had meant smoking *while* one was sitting on a doorstep, to which Thea replied, "Whatever," and had to be told by June that all responses should be addressed to the meeting through the chair. By the time the date had been fixed for the next meeting, tempers had run rather high, but everyone calmed down when Henry fetched glasses of wine for all. Montserrat and Jimmy were the last to leave, Montserrat's thoughts much concerned with the new man she had met in a club two nights before. Ciaran had spent that night and last night with her in her flat at number seven and seemed keener than any man had for a couple of years. No question of Rohypnol there and no fear of Ciaran O'Hara's stealing Lucy's jewellery. But she was in a dilemma. To tell him about the arrangement she had with Lucy and Rad Sothern or to say nothing? But suppose she said nothing and he saw her admitting or letting Rad out by the basement door? It was quite possible he might, and then it would be too late to explain about the arrangement and that Rad was Lucy's lover, not hers. Lucy and Preston would soon be back on Sunday, and Rad would certainly expect to pay a visit in the coming week, if not two visits. What was she to do?

THOUGH NOW twenty-five years old, Henry kept up his childhood fondness for Hallowe'en and all that entailed. He would have liked to knock on doors, offering trick or treat, but feared the likelihood of a rebuff from his employer, who would certainly find out about it. Eventually, all he could come up with was to get into Hallowe'en fancy dress on the evening of October 31 and, attired in a black robe bought in an Asian shop, his face painted in black and white to look like a skull, walk up to the Dugong for a drink with Jimmy at eight.

He met no child celebrants on the way, but seeing Damian and Roland approaching, he jumped out on them from behind a tree, groaning appropriately and flapping his hands. Roland swore but Damian jumped and took a step back.

"Isn't it time you grew up?" said Roland.

Henry laughed. Perhaps he could persuade Jimmy to join him in a haunting of Eaton Place and stand with him on the steps of the Royal Court Theatre, collecting for some fictitious charity. But Jimmy was dressed in his normal clothes and interested in traditional high jinks only from the point of view of banning them. Dr. Jefferson, he said, being famously concerned for children in every aspect, believed they were endangered by wandering the streets and ringing strangers' doorbells. After a couple of beers (Jimmy) and two glasses of red wine (Henry), they moved out into the street, looking for offenders, but the squares and crescents and streets of Belgravia were empty of children and it had begun to rain.

For Dex the evening was full of fear and strange sights. He had forgotten why he had gone out in the first place, perhaps to buy a bottle of Guinness or a Thai takeaway. Whatever it was, it had been driven out of his head by the evil spirits to be seen round every corner, for the district where Dex lived was more populated by children and teenagers than Hexam Place and its environs. They were, it seemed to him, everywhere in their cloaks and masks, their face paint and their wigs and helmets. Shouting and dancing and congregating on doorsteps. He recognised them for what they were. What surprised him was that there were so many of them and all together, all of the same sort of age, and not one looking like a real child but disguised as evil spirits will always disguise themselves. Peach would perhaps want him to destroy them, but he couldn't, not so many. They would overpower him.

He was getting soaked, the rain drenching his hair and trickling down his thin jacket. He went home empty-handed, having quite forgotten what he went out for.

9

I LIKE IT HERE," Huguette said. "Why haven't we ever been here before?"

Henry shook his head. "Because it's too near your mum and dad's place."

And too popular with their housekeeper and the butler or whatever he was and a lot of other people who might speak out of turn. He suspected that Huguette wanted them to be caught, the alternative being that he move in with her and they use the pub round the corner in the King's Road.

"What are you going to say if your dad comes in here and sees you with me? Just what?" The much worse possibility was if her mother came in. Henry didn't want even to think about that one.

"He won't, he's out somewhere. I'd just say I was on my way to their place and I ran into you and you said to come and have a drink."

"Anyway, I'm not drinking and I've got to pick your dad up in ten minutes."

"I want you to think about asking him for my hand in marriage."

"You what?"

"We'd have such nice-looking kids. We're a handsome couple. Don't you think? He might say yes because of that."

"I'm not risking it," said Henry.

"Where are you picking him up?"

"At the House of course."

"Then you can take me home first."

It was easier than arguing.

"I'll bring the Beemer round the corner." Henry left her there and went cautiously out into Hexam Place. But not cautiously enough. There, on the pavement outside number three, was Beacon talking to Jimmy. Henry gave them an insouciant sort of wave and got into the driver's seat of the BMW. By the time he had turned round the corner at the Dugong, Beacon had gone to fetch the Audi, and Jimmy, who was the envy of all because he hardly did any work, had gone into Dr. Jefferson's house.

Beacon had caught a glimpse of a head of fuzzy golden hair attached to a slender body emerging from the Dugong. He slightly resented it because his opinion was that this kind of hair was attractive only when black and the skin from which it grew black also. Yellow was ugly anyway, no matter whom it belonged to. Never mind, it was nothing to do with him and tonight he was going to have an early night. For some mysterious reason, Mr. Still was coming home hours sooner than usual, and Beacon would be able to pass the evening in his favourite way, in the bosom of his family.

He had barely turned into Sloane Street when the first firework went off. In words used by half the population of London— excepting those under eighteen—Beacon said to himself that it wasn't even Guy Fawkes Day until tomorrow.

MONTSERRAT AWOKE to a sense of foreboding that had nothing to do with its being November 5. It was hard to say what it was to do with, for the feeling was fairly familiar and even she had to admit that mostly it meant nothing. Perhaps it referred only to this being

Friday, one of the days Zinnia didn't come till the afternoon and Montserrat was supposed to prepare and carry up Lucy's breakfast. She lay in bed half an hour longer, heard Beacon bring the Audi round to the front door and Mr. Still's voice saying good morning to him. Montserrat thought Mr. Still was probably the only person left in London to say *good morning* and not *hi* or *how are you?*

The star-fruit yogurt and plate of ruby grapefruit (covered in cling film) had been left ready in the fridge, the single slice of whole-grain bread was actually in the toaster waiting to be toasted, and the coffee machine had only to be switched on. The tray was set with cutlery and a pot of blueberry conserve—Lucy ate conserve, not jam—and Montserrat had only to wait five minutes. She poured herself the first cup of coffee, then set off with the tray.

Lucy was sitting up in bed, swathed in a lace shawl.

"I thought you'd forgotten me."

In no mood to be rebuked, Montserrat said, "Your clock is five minutes fast."

Her eyes alighted on something that shouldn't have been on Lucy's dressing table, Mr. Still's bunch of keys. Standing between Lucy and the dressing table, Montserrat scooped up the keys and put them in the pocket of her trousers. She couldn't have said why, only that it seemed safer.

"I'm expecting Rad tonight." When Lucy gave this notification, sometimes twice a week, sometimes only once, she put on a sexy drawl and even slightly changed her posture, reclining and raising one arm and letting the hand drop negligently. "About seven. I thought we might have champers. Would you like to bring up a bottle from the fridge at six thirtyish?"

Considering the gesture unsophisticated, Montserrat said she would. There was no reason why the able-bodied Lucy, toned by frequent jogging and gym visits, shouldn't have fetched the champagne herself, but she never did anything. Once Montserrat had seen her drop a pound coin onto the floor and ask Zinnia to pick it up for her. Montserrat went back to the basement with a second cup of coffee, avoiding the loose banister. Rabia's cousin Mohammed was coming tomorrow to fix it. Montserrat supposed she would be expected to stay in all day to let him in. Unless, maybe, she could persuade Rabia to do that. . . .

First there was the problem of Mr. Still's keys. If she did nothing, Beacon would bring Mr. Still home at between ten and ten thirty and Mr. Still would ring the front doorbell. Likely but not inevitably. He was usually late on a Friday except when the family was going down to Gallowmill Hall next day. Were they? She didn't know. No one had said, but they didn't always say. Montserrat decided to call Beacon and find out if Mr. Still had mentioned forgetting his keys. The difficulty was that Beacon was such a moralistic pig of a man, like a vicar or something. She had once asked him on a day Rad was coming if he would let her know when Mr. Still was leaving his office and Beacon had asked, suspiciously, what business it was of hers.

"A wife should be at home waiting for her husband to return from breadwinning."

"That's a bit outdated, isn't it?"

"If everyone behaved themselves like what you call outdated," said Beacon, "the world would be a better place."

Nevertheless, she tried again.

"Mr. Still's keys are his own business."

"I was only trying to be helpful," said Montserrat.

"The best help you can give is to open Mr. Still's front door when he rings *his* bell. If he's forgotten *his* keys, which I personally doubt."

Lunch in a pub with Ciaran, which ended in a row because Montserrat told him he couldn't come that evening, was followed by a walk round the shops in Sloane Street with Rabia and Thomas and a visit to Harrods to buy Thomas a tracksuit.

"Does she give you an American Express card?"

"Just to buy clothes for Thomas and pay for his haircuts."

"I expect you buy bits for yourself as well, don't you? She'd never notice."

"She trusts me," said Rabia, shocked. "I would never do that."

"Pity Beacon's married. You and him were made for each other."

They bought Thomas a pale blue fleecy tracksuit with a white rabbit appliquéd on the breast pocket.

"Could you be at home to let your cousin in when he comes tomorrow?"

"If you like," said Rabia. "A chat with Mohammed would be good. He's my favourite cousin. I shall introduce him to Thomas, he loves children."

As if the child were her own, thought Montserrat.

"YOU WON'T MIND," said June, "if Her Highness and me watch our recording of *Avalon Clinic* series one, episode one, while you're here, will you?"

Rad made a face, pretending to be shy, but June knew he was secretly delighted. She looked critically at him, wondering why women found men with long hair attractive. Her own tastes in that area had been fixed in the 1950s when a man would only have worn his hair in a ponytail if he had been acting in a film about the French Revolution. She operated the remote with swift skill in a way the Princess had never learnt, and *Avalon*'s nationwide introductory music blasted into the room, vying with the fireworks, which were now well under way. Both women were rather deaf. The Princess sighed her appreciation as handsome Rad in his white coat, bristling with stethoscopes, a sphygmomanometer dangling from one hand, strode into the room. The real-live Rad was sitting next to her on the sofa. She reached for his real-live hand and squeezed it.

"Let's have a bottle of TDTINW," she said to June.

June recognised these initial letters as The Drink That Is Never

Wrong and fetched in a bottle of champagne, thus missing a vital part of the plot. Rad wasn't going to open it, not he, so he sat tight, periodically squeezing the Princess's hand in turn, while June filled the glasses.

"Going to see Montserrat, are you?" She asked because she knew that for some reason he disliked being asked. It was such a comedown for him after that model and that socialite divorcée.

"Not tonight," he said.

June couldn't tell if he was telling the truth. The commercial break she didn't know how to cut out of the recording came to an end, and they all watched till it finished just before seven.

"Have another one before you go," said the Princess.

Rad said he wouldn't but gave her a kiss, which was more than he was inclined to do to June. Neither woman watched him go. His association with Montserrat, if indeed it existed, lacked glamour. Next door but one, in the area of number eight, Miss Grieves had come out of the basement door to shoo the urban fox away. A chicken carcase in its jaws, it scooted up the steps with Miss Grieves in pursuit. Not hot pursuit but a cold, slower variety, a clumsy plodding which succeeded in getting to the top in the end, by which time the fox and the chicken had disappeared. A brilliant flare burst in the front garden of number five, illuminating the whole front as well as the area of number seven. The fox was revealed tucking into the chicken in the front garden and Rad Sothern in his hidey-hole, just stepping out of it as Montserrat opened the basement door. Miss Grieves turned away and lumbered back down the stairs.

Montserrat had also run downstairs, the basement stairs, avoiding the faulty banister. She let Rad in and said a not very cordial "Hi." Having his hair tied back like that made his face look thin. He wasn't as tall as Ciaran and his front teeth needed crowning. That must be why he smiled so seldom in his role as Mr. Fortescue. She stepped back for him to pass along the passage.

"Look out for the loose banister," she said.

He took no notice, cursing when it wobbled in his hand. She didn't knock on Lucy's door but opened it, pushed Rad inside, then ran upstairs to Rabia. Hero and Matilda had eaten their dinner in the nursery kitchen and were now playing computer games in their shared bedroom. Having completely changed his sleeping habits as small children will, Thomas was fast asleep and Rabia was ironing the white blouses and navy blue pleated skirts the girls would wear for school on Monday.

"Why aren't they out at someone's bonfire party?"

"Mr. Still says it's dangerous," said Rabia.

"Lucy's got company this evening," said Montserrat, "so keep the girls up here, will you?"

Rabia said she didn't want to hear and put her fingers in her ears.

THE FIREWORKS reached a zenith of explosive noise at about eight. The flashes of light, zigzags and branches, the pyrotechnic displays of feathers and banners and fountains, red, white, emerald-green, and sapphire-blue, achieved their maximum brilliance on the far side of the river half an hour later, then gradually began to subside. By nine when Beacon drew up in the Audi outside number seven Hexam Place, the occasional rocket still split the sky, but most of the celebrations were over, to begin again the following night with equal force.

Beacon got out of the car to open the nearside rear door for Mr. Still. It was his habit to stand there courteously until his employer had let himself in by the front door. Mr. Still mounted the first four steps before he started feeling in his pockets. A puzzled frown on his face, he came down the steps again, said, "I didn't drop my keys on the backseat, did I, Beacon?"

"Can't see them, sir. Let me look."

Preston Still also looked. No keys.

"Montserrat will be there to let you in, sir."

"No, no, not necessary. I've got my key to the area gate and the one to the basement door."

The gate in the area railings was never locked, as far as Beacon knew. He watched Mr. Still descend the stairs, cast his eyes up to watch a rocket explode above the roof of number four, and caught sight of Montserrat's face at a window on the ground floor. Time to go home, with luck getting there just as *Avalon Clinic* started.

From the window it was impossible for anyone to see more than the six lowest steps. Montserrat could no longer see Mr. Still, but she guessed that he must be climbing the remaining stairs to the front door, where he would ring the bell. He was earlier than she expected and she had no time to waste. She called Lucy on her mobile, then ran up to the first floor, where Rad Sothern was just coming out of Lucy's room. "He's on the doorstep," she whispered. "He'll ring the bell any minute."

"Oh, God."

"It'll be OK. Come with me and you can wait in my flat while I let him in."

This was never to happen, but a lot of other things did. Montserrat led Rad down the staircase from the first floor and along the passage towards the basement stairs. A light was on in the passage but not at the foot of the stairs. As Rad with Montserrat behind him came within a yard or so, Preston Still appeared at the top of the basement stairs, first his head, then his chest, the whole of him quite rapidly emerging. Montserrat had never before noticed what a big man he was, tall, broad, and heavy. She gave a sort of hoarse gasp. Rad said, "Oh, God," for the second time, and stopped.

Mr. Still advanced towards him, said, "Who the hell are you?" and then "I've seen you before."

Considering that the whole country had seen Rad before, that half of them were watching him on their screens at that moment, the remark meant little. Montserrat could see it had a different meaning for Preston Still, who was seldom at home in time to watch television. "At the Princess's party," he said, "making unwelcome advances to my wife."

It apparently dawned on him before the words were out that the advances had been anything but unwelcome, and as Rad tried to push past him and reach the stairs, Mr. Still seized him from behind, gripping him by the shoulders. Things happened fast after that. Montserrat would never have believed Preston Still capable of such athletic feats. He slammed his foot into the small of Rad's back and, lurching forward with a grunt, shoved with all his force. It was a kicking downstairs, the classic violent way of expelling a man from a house.

Rad might have slithered forward, bumping down the stairs, if he hadn't clutched at the faulty banister. It came away in his hand with a grinding crunch of splintered wood, and he toppled over, shouting out, plunging headfirst down the dark well of the staircase to land on his head on the tiled floor. It was like a dive into water that wasn't there. The crash the impact made was drowned by the noisiest explosion of the evening, a firework let off in Eaton Square.

10

T HE FIREWORKS WERE over and no sound came from the children's rooms on the second floor. It seemed from her silence that Lucy had heard nothing. Montserrat stood listening to that silence before following Preston Still down the stairs. Rad Sothern's head lay in a pool of blood that was spreading across the black and white tiles. If anyone had told Montserrat that she would react to such a scene as this not with horror and fear but with mounting excitement, she would not have believed them. But so it was. Whatever happened next, she wanted to be involved in it. Everything would all come out now, Lucy's affair with a TV personality, a celebrity; the part she, Montserrat, had played and was forced into to keep her job and her accommodation; Preston Still, insurance magnate in the City, millionaire, driven to madness by his wife's infidelity . . .

He was kneeling by Rad. He said in a small, thin voice, quite unlike his own, "I think he's dead."

"He can't be," she said. "He can't be."

"He's not breathing, he's got no pulse."

In creating her scenario, she hadn't thought for a moment Rad Sothern could be dead. People don't die from falling downstairs.

The excitement was still there, but mixed now with awe. "What shall we do?"

"Get the police, of course."

She said inconsequentially, "He doesn't look very heavy."

"What does that mean?"

"We could wrap him up in something and pull him into my flat. We can't leave him here."

"My God," said Preston Still, "I can't believe he's dead. I feel as if I'm asleep, I'm going to wake up in a minute."

"People always feel like that when something horrendous happens."

Montserrat went into her flat and came out with a blanket. She knelt down and began easing Rad Sothern's body onto the blanket and gradually to roll him over.

"How can you?" Preston Still's voice rose an octave. "Stop it. Stop doing that. You're never supposed to move someone who's been—well, who's met a violent death. We have to get the police."

The idea of that frightened her more than that Rad was dead. "You want to be arrested, do you? They'll say it's murder."

"For God's sake. I only gave him a push. It was that banister that was responsible for his death."

"Help me get him through that door."

Montserrat could tell that Mr. Still, whom she was already in her thoughts calling Preston, was far more squeamish than she was. He had to look away as she pushed and he pulled Rad Sothern's body into her flat. He would have closed the door if she hadn't said, "We can't leave that blood there like that."

"It has to be left there for the police."

She said nothing but cast up her eyes. He'd probably never in his life mopped a floor, he wouldn't know how to do it. He was a man. Montserrat was no housewife, but she hadn't reached the age of twenty-two without, at any rate once, washing a tiled floor. A bucket was in the cupboard under the sink. It had never been used as far as she knew, but it was capable of holding water and it had a handle. With a sponge from the bathroom and a bottle of washing-up liquid, she set to work. When Preston saw the red water, itself like foaming blood, he shuddered and once more turned away.

"I think I've got it all up. It wouldn't do for a real police examination, tests and all that, but we aren't going to have that, are we? We're not getting the police." She drew a deep breath. "You haven't got any blood on you, have you?"

"You are like Lady Macbeth," he said in a slow, level voice like a zombie. "Wash your hands, put on your nightgown . . ."

"Come on now. Get yourself together. I'm going to get us a drink. There's some whisky in the drawing room."

They hadn't really done anything, she thought, as she went upstairs to fetch the whisky. All Preston had done was give that TV guy a hard push. Rad would be alive now if the people she'd called to mend the banister had come immediately. Try telling the police that, though. The trouble with Preston was that, big insurance tycoon he might be, he'd led a sheltered life. Didn't know he was born, as her father might say. His natural solution to anything that smacked of the illegal was to call the police. Never mind that they'd take it for granted he'd killed Rad because Rad was his wife's lover. No question. Of course Preston was so naïve that he still didn't realise this. She would tell him, she had to. He was sitting in one of the two armchairs when she went into the flat, lying back with his hands hanging, staring into space.

She had already had a swig of whisky from the bottle. She handed him a glass, set her own down on the coffee table. He spoke without looking at her. "I suppose that man had been visiting Lucy." She nodded, took a gulp of the whisky. "Where did you come into it?"

"We weren't a threesome if that's what you're thinking. I always let him in by the basement door and took him along to her room."

Now Mr. Still turned his eyes on her and she saw anger there. She also saw that he was quite good-looking and his voice was beautiful.

"You were the psychopomp," he said.

"The what?"

"A conductor of souls to hell."

Montserrat, who was rather superstitious, found herself shuddering. She touched the body in its concealing blanket with the tip of her toe. "What are we going to do with him?"

"Oh, well, nothing. He's in here now and you obviously won't want to sleep here yourself. You take one of the spare rooms for the night, and in the morning I'll call the police. After all, it was an accident. All that forensic stuff won't be necessary. Once they've heard what I have to say and you have to say and they've seen the broken banister, everything will be cleared up."

"Don't forget they'll have to know Lucy was in a relationship with Rad Sothern. That's what makes all the difference. And he's famous, *was* famous. Whoever's boyfriend he was, it'd still be enormous in the media. Don't you see?"

The word *boyfriend* brought a dark flush to Preston's face. "It was an accident."

"I know that and you know that, but they won't."

Did she know it? Did he? He had pushed the man downstairs about as hard as anyone could. She felt like saying that he lived out of the world in a land of figures and statistics, stocks and shares and markets, while *she* knew well what the media were and how they would react. Her earlier excitement returned when she thought of the pictures in the papers, the excerpts from *Avalon Clinic* on Sky News, the pictures of number seven Hexam Place and of Lucy with her children, of Preston getting into his car, Beacon holding the door open—and that was only if Rad had vanished, nothing to what it would be if he was found dead. "Best if he disappears, even better if he's never found."

"We can't do that, Montserrat." It was the first time—the first time ever?—he had used her given name.

"We have to do that. It's the only way. Think about it. Think what happens to Lucy and your children and your business and everything connected with you if you tell the police you pushed Rad Sothern down the stairs. They'll arrest you and the media will eat you alive."

There was a long silence. Then he said, "You really are Lady Macbeth. Give me some more of that Scotch, will you?"

She refilled his glass. "That's enough. You've got to be all bright-eyed and bushy-tailed in the morning."

"What does that mean?"

A recollection of the only time she had seen *Macbeth* came back to her. On TV it had been. It was all about a woman telling her weak husband how to behave when he'd murdered someone, wasn't it? Appropriate. "You go to bed. Lucy'll be asleep. It's Saturday tomorrow. Tell her you've got to work all day. I've known you do that, she won't wonder—"

"I don't give a shit if she does!" he said violently.

"I'll sleep here—with that." She waved her hand in the direction of Rad's body. "You come back here and we'll put the body into something and take it away." Her glance fell on the car-roof box. "Into that thing. I got it to carry my skis on holiday but we can use it."

"Take it where?"

"You've got a place in the country, haven't you? Not far?"

"In Essex. I can't take the Audi. Beacon will have put it away for the weekend. We usually rent a car to go to Gallowmill Hall, but that's obviously not possible. . . . Look, Montserrat, the whole thing's not possible."

"We can go in my car," she said.

"It's best if I call the police first thing in the morning. I won't mention you. I'll bring the body out again and lay it on the floor and tell them I was coming in the basement door when I saw—what's his name? Rad something?—come to the top of the basement stairs and fall when he grabbed hold of the banister. I'll say I came that way because I mislaid my keys—which is true—and you were out so couldn't let me in. I'll say I had no idea who this Rad person was and he was dead before I could find out. It all hangs together."

"That's the most hopeless scenario I've ever heard," said Montserrat. "Talk about 'hangs together.' If there was still capital punishment, it's you who'd hang. We may as well put the body into the case now, get it over with, and we can leave in the morning when Lucy's gone to the gym. Don't you say a word to Lucy, mind."

THOMAS WOKE UP CRYING, his right cheek bright red and wet with tears. Rabia gave him slightly warmed orange juice (freshly squeezed) to drink and an ivory teething ring (freshly sterilised) to bite on. It had been hers when she was a baby, and giving it to Thomas made her feel that he was really her child, using his mother's infant things as small children often do. It made her happy that he liked the ring and smiled at her and said his new word *sweetheart*.

"Love Rab."

"And Rab loves you lots, Thomas."

"Say 'sweetheart,'" said Thomas.

So Rabia did and changed his napkin and kissed him and laid him tenderly back in his new grown-up bed.

Along the street in the basement of number eleven, Henry and the Honourable Huguette slept in each other's arms or had done so until they got too hot and rolled apart. It was the first time Huguette had shared his bed in her father's house, and delightful as it was in many ways, especially not to have to leave her flat for the cold night outside, he was nervous and his sleep was fitful. It would have been better if there had been a key to his door, but there wasn't, only a keyhole. Henry thought perhaps he might buy a bolt for the door, which would provide them with great privacy. As it was, every creak, tap, and squeak in the house made him fear someone was approaching down the basement stairs.

A few houses along at number three, Jimmy was sleeping in for a change. Dr. Jefferson had no idea how to manage servants. Jimmy was well aware of this and instead of despising him for it, rather liked him. Of course he could detect from Dr. Jefferson's accent, superficially refined—an inner-London comprehensive school before Oxford—his working-class origins. That was why he wouldn't let Jimmy call him sir or open the car door for him, and although Jimmy didn't "officially" live in, a nice bedroom in the basement of number three was at his disposal. This was where he was sleeping on Bonfire Night and, in spite of his being newly in love, was sleeping alone. There was no night bus to where he lived, and although Dr. Jefferson wouldn't have objected for a moment to his driving home in the Lexus to his flat in Kennington, Jimmy had been drinking with Thea and drinking far too much to drive anything anywhere.

For it was Thea that he was in love with. It was extraordinary. He had known her for such a long time. She was over thirty and not particularly good-looking and he had known her for years. Nor had he been aware of liking her much. But the evening before in the Dugong, sitting next to June on one side and Richard on the other, he looked up from his half of lager and his eyes met Thea's across the table. In that moment he had the curious sensation of his heart tilting, stopping still, then righting itself. He thought, I love you, Thea. Then he wanted to shout it aloud. I'm in love with you, I'm in love with you. Their eyes held each other's and she smiled at him, a wonderful, radiant smile that transformed her rather ordinary little face into a raving beauty's.

He said nothing, did nothing, but went again to the Dugong the following night. She was there as he knew she would be, sitting at the same table alone. Was any hair colour lovelier on a woman than that natural red? Nasturtium-red, conker-red. It was too early for any of the others to be there. Half the night and most of the day he had been thinking about what had happened to him, and he wasn't going to waste time on small talk now. He went up to Ted Goldsworth at the bar and asked for two glasses of champagne, aware that Thea's eyes were on him.

As he set the glasses down, she said, "Hallo, Jimmy," in a voice that seemed to him full of meaning, and he said, "Hallo, Thea." All he had wanted to say the evening before and during the night and all day while he was driving Dr. Jefferson, he now said. "I've fallen in love with you. I know it's mad but I think you feel the same."

No one had ever spoken to Thea like that before. Lonely and fretful, she was overcome by Jimmy's declaration. "I do," she said as if they were getting married.

"Then let's drink this and go on somewhere else, just you and me." He raised his glass. "Here's to us."

"To us," she said, and gave an incredulous laugh.

They had not really drunk too much, just too much for Jimmy to think of driving. The evening passed in a wine bar in Ranelagh Grove to the rumble of fireworks and the hiss of rockets. A sign of love, Jimmy had heard, is that it deprives you of appetite, and they ate little. She laid her hand on the table and he laid his over it. The kiss he would postpone till their parting later on, for he had no idea of their spending the night together, not yet, not for a while. A feeling he half knew to be ridiculous was that their love had a holiness it would be wrong to "spoil" at this early stage. The consummation would come, though, and both of them accepted it with peace and joy and a smiling taking for granted.

They walked back to Hexam Place, hand in hand, it wasn't far. A light was still on in Damian and Roland's drawing room, but Miss Grieves's flat was dark and in a pool of darkness out of the range of Roland and Damian's light and the light from the streetlamp,

Jimmy kissed Thea. Thea held him in her arms a long time, asking herself what she was doing.

"Phone me in the morning," she said.

"Of course. That's a matter of course. I shall want to hear your voice."

Inside her own bedroom, in the silence, Thea wondered what she had meant by that "I do." Had she only said it to please him, not to hurt his feelings? Was it that she was flattered, or again just a case of her trying to please someone but this time landing herself in a great deal of trouble? No one had ever before said he was in love with her. She had never been in such a romantic situation. Perhaps she could teach herself to love him by telling herself how handsome he was and how kind.

As Jimmy let himself into number three and that bedroom he was at last making use of, the lights in the houses gradually went out until the whole street was in darkness.

MONTSERRAT WAS WAKENED in the night by Preston's tapping on the door and hissing at the keyhole, "Open the door, Montserrat. We have to talk."

If anyone heard him, she thought, they'd think he and she were lovers. That might do very well one day, but not yet. She opened the door. "There's nothing to talk about. We've said it all. All we have to do now is find a way to get that case thing on top of the car without anyone suspecting what's inside it. Where are you sleeping?"

"I was in her room. I can't go back there, it's horrible."

"Oh, well, there are four spare bedrooms in the house. You find one of them and come back here about seven."

She went back to sleep, but first she thought that one good thing to come out of this was that now she wouldn't have to explain Rad's visits to Ciaran. Preston was in her room again at six thirty, fully dressed in his weekend go-to-the-countryside clothes, sports jacket, gray flannels, brown brogues. For God's sake, she thought, he can't be more than forty. She had nothing on under the bedclothes.

"Go away, will you, while I get up? You can make yourself some coffee while I have a shower," she said. "Meanwhile, listen to me. We do nothing till Lucy's gone out. She'll go early, she always does when it's workout time, and she'll take the girls with her. Never too soon to train them to be toned-up ladies." She saw him wince and crease up his mouth. "My car's in that garage block in St. Barnabas Mews, number twelve. Your garden more or less backs onto it. We can carry the roof-rack box out into the mews and attach it to the roof rack *inside the garage*. If anyone sees, they'll just think you're helping me do it in advance of my holidays. We tell them it's skis. Right?"

The morning, when he was going to call the police, had come. He seemed to have forgotten all about it. "Right," he said.

"How long does it take to get to your country place?"

"About an hour or less."

"Is it really country? *Essex?*"

He didn't answer, just looked sullen.

"I do Lucy's breakfast at the weekends," she said, "so I'd better get on with it. You'll just have to be patient."

11

W HERE'S MY DADDY?" Hero peered behind the sofa on the gallery as if she were likely to find him there.

"He came in very late," said Lucy in a tone of extravagant boredom. "I expect he left again very early. It's what he does."

"I'm never going to work as hard as him," said Matilda. "I don't see the point."

Montserrat thought, but of course didn't say, that Matilda would marry a rich man and probably wouldn't have to work at all. She watched them prance downstairs, all dressed to match in scarlet jackets over white leotards and black leggings with yellow-and-silver Chanel trainers. The girls were pushed first, Lucy following and slamming the door. Rabia had already departed with Thomas.

The garden at number seven Hexam Place was seldom used. When the Stills first moved in, Montserrat had heard, it had been neat with a lawn and flowerbeds, but in the four years since then the trees and shrubs and weeds had taken over and now it was a wilderness. All the better for their enterprise, though it really mattered little whether they were seen by the Wallaces and Cavendishes at number nine or the Neville-Smiths at number five. The body in the case was heavier than Montserrat had expected,

Rad Sothern being such a thin little shrimp of a man, but she and Preston Still managed. No one was about in the mews. Montserrat unlocked the garage door. She thought she saw a glance of contempt on Preston's face when he saw her blue VW, gray with dirt and pigeon droppings, but maybe she had imagined it. Heaving the case up onto the roof rack was a much harder job than carting it up the basement stairs and through the garden. A pair of steps at the back of the garage she had never before noticed came in handy—indeed were indispensable—and after fifteen minutes of struggling, the case was at last bolted into place. When he had finished, Preston's hands were trembling.

"I shall drive," said Montserrat.

He didn't argue.

"We'll make a detour to avoid passing along Hexam Place. It doesn't matter about people seeing me, but they mustn't see you with me. It would look strange." Preston nodded. "To be on the safe side, though, you'd better get on the floor in the back."

"Now, look, wait a minute. Surely that's not necessary—"

"Of course it's necessary. You should have thought of that before you pushed a TV star down the stairs."

"I'll give you my postcode for the sat-nav."

"Useful if I had sat-nav but I don't. You'll have to direct me."

He said he would. Montserrat got into the car and Preston into the back, struggling to squeeze himself into the space between the back of her seat and the rear seat. Once they were well on the way to the North Circular, she stopped for him to climb out and get into the passenger seat beside her. Fear and perhaps guilt made him bad-tempered.

"It goes against the grain with me to have a woman drive me."

"Too bad," said Montserrat. "Tell you what, when we've disposed of Mr. Fortescue, I'll let you drive us back."

THE MAGAZINE SECTION of a quality newspaper always carried an interview with a media celebrity on Saturdays, and Thea was in the habit of reading it while eating her breakfast. She shared the paper with Damian and Roland, they interested only in politics and business, she keeping the magazine, media, and arts sections, though she would have liked the news too. Today the interview was with Rad Sothern, and the cover was a full-page colour photograph of him in his guise as Mr. Fortescue, but Thea, who would not long ago have been enthralled by revelations about Rad's past love life, that June was his aunt or great-aunt and that he had once been the guitarist in a pop group, found it impossible to keep her attention on the article. Her thoughts were dominated by Jimmy, but they were not perhaps the thoughts he would have liked her to have. Today she must begin teaching herself to love him. She had taught herself to do so many things to please other people that she could surely do this. She and he were going out for the day in Simon Jefferson's car, and she expected Jimmy to call for her at ten. Awake since six and up since seven, she had dressed with the greatest care in her new jeans, pristine white shirt, and rose-pink heavy-knit cardigan. Her hair was newly washed, her eye makeup taking a quarter of an hour to get right, although she somehow knew, with no real experience in this area, that what she looked like no longer mattered much to Jimmy. What has mascara to do with love?

At a quarter to ten she took the three sections of the paper down to Damian and Roland. "You may as well have them. I'm going out for the day."

"You know, I think I've seen this guy coming out of next door," said Roland. "Someone said he was the Princess's grandson."

"According to this he's June's nephew."

"Wonders will never cease." Damian took the magazine and shook his head over the portrait of Rad. "Leave the arts and media bits with us. Even if we don't read them, which is most probable, we'll put them in the recycling. By the way, we're thinking of getting married."

"Oh, cool," said Thea. Had they taught themselves to love each other or had it come naturally?

"Roly proposed over breakfast. He said, 'Will you civil partner with me?' Don't you think that was neat?"

"Oh, I do. Can I come?"

"I expect so." Roland's tone was cool in the old-fashioned sense of the word.

From the window where she had stationed herself, Thea saw Simon Jefferson's custard-coloured Lexus pull up at the kerb. This was her own dream scenario come true! Learning enthusiasm, she ran off to the front door without saying good-bye.

TIDYING THE DRAWING room, June found an object which might have been something designed to play music or speak into or both, down the back of the sofa cushions. The inadvertent pressure of her thumb stimulated it to chant the first line of "God Save the Queen" and display a dozen little brightly coloured pictures.

"It must be Rad's," she said, showing it to the Princess when June took up her breakfast.

"It's what they call a Raspberry. You'd better phone him. But not on that thing, even supposing you know how. Do it on the real phone."

June tried the landline but got no reply. The alternative number she had for him, which she had never before used, set off the national anthem again on the thing she held in her hand, making her jump. It asked her to leave a message but she saw no point in that. "He'll turn up when he wants it," she said to herself.

THEY PASSED THROUGH the village of Theydon Wold, Montserrat noticing that the pub called the Devereux Arms did three-course lunches. Maybe she could persuade Preston to take her there once they had unloaded Rad Sothern's body. It amazed her that he had scarcely known how to find Gallowmill Hall, in spite of owning the place. His directions had gone wrong three times, and once they had nearly found themselves on the M25, heading for the Dartford Crossing. When he had driven, he had to use the sat-nav because he knew the postcode but not the rest of the address.

Montserrat had been nearly but not quite as impressed by the place as Rabia. She, after all, had seen such houses before, in reality and in pictures. How must it be to own a house like this? Not only to have number seven Hexam Place but this Gallowmill Hall as well.

"Why's it called that?"

"There's a watermill on the river and there used to be a gallows somewhere near here."

She noticed he winced when mentioning this instrument of punishment for capital crimes. "You can take the car through the archway. There shouldn't be any callers, but you can't be sure and it's best if no one sees us."

There went her chance of a good lunch in the Devereux Arms. "Now we've got him here, what are we going to do with him?"

"I don't know."

"We don't take the case off the car till we're sure. It's too heavy to keep lugging about." She noticed how pale he looked. "Not carsick, are you?"

He shook his head. "Let's get some fresh air."

The archway led into a kind of courtyard. They left the car and walked back through the arch to where lawns sloped away from the broad gravel expanse. Everywhere was carpeted in fallen leaves, red, brown, and yellow, and the trees from which they had come had almost returned to their state of bare, skeletal branches. Above the shallow, wooded hills the sky was a pale milky blue, streaked with strips of pale gray cloud.

"Has this place been in your family for hundreds and hundreds of years?"

"About two centuries," he said.

"Why don't you live here?"

He didn't answer the question. "My parents did and my grandparents and ancestors all the way back to the beginning of the nineteenth century when my great-great-great-grandfather built this place."

The view enlarged as they rounded the house and came to what Preston called the garden front, opening up to show all sorts of details in the landscape, a biggish house on the crest of a shallow hill, village roofs, ugly barns around a farmhouse, a church spire. It brought back to Montserrat recollections of period dramas on television, women in bonnets setting forth from houses like this one, Regency bucks on horseback, doffing hats to the ladies.

"Did those ancestors go to that church?"

"St. Michael and All Angels," said Preston as if that were what she had asked him. "I suppose they did. Hardly anyone goes there now, I'm told. Ancestors of mine are buried in a kind of family mausoleum in the churchyard."

What a lot of keys a man of property such as him had to have or mislay or leave behind. He hadn't mislaid the key to this front door. He unlocked it and they went in. Once she had got used to the idea of the kind of house Preston owned, the interior was just what she expected: oil paintings framed in curlicued gilt, Oriental rugs, polished dark furniture, Chinese porcelain, pink and green and black with birds and flowers. It surprised her that the interior was so warm.

"We keep the heating on low from October to April."

"Who's 'we'?"

"The caretaker and his wife. Oh, don't worry. They won't be here."

She hadn't been worried, only amazed that a man of no more than forty would still talk in terms of a man and his wife.

"I'm hungry," she said. "Is there anything to eat?"

The kitchen was enormous and quite modern—well, if you called twenty years old modern. Sliced bread was in the freezer and cans in a cupboard. "We could have beans on toast." Maybe he didn't know what that was.

"I couldn't eat a thing," he said. "If you feel up to driving back, I'd like a drink."

"You said you didn't like being driven by a woman."

He said with unbelievable ungraciousness, "I can put up with it."

A derisive laugh was her answer. "We have to put our celebrity somewhere before we think about that."

She thawed out two slices of bread by toasting them, opened a can of salmon, and made herself a sandwich. He was sitting at the table with his head in his hands. Opening cupboards, she found a half bottle of brandy, a half-used bottle of Cointreau, and some dregs of red wine. The measure of brandy she poured for him was generous, and she was about to add water when he covered the glass with his hand. He drank half and colour came back into his face, a dark red flush. "I've decided," he said. "We should never have done that, put him in that box. We should never have come here—or anywhere. When you've finished that, we'll go back to London and take his body to the nearest police station."

"Don't be ridiculous. It'll be dark in two or three hours and then we can hide him somewhere and no one will see. Take a dead body to a police station? They'll get you to a psychiatrist and have you sectioned. It'll be worse than charging you with murder, putting you in a bin will, and that's what they'll do." She rinsed the glass and the plate under the tap and put them away. "You said it's best if no one knows we've been here, so we have to be careful not to be seen. Now I'd like to look round the place, find somewhere to put him."

More keys. He picked three bunches off hooks on the wall and stuffed them into his pockets. There were all kinds of outbuildings, there were stables. He showed her a summerhouse and something that looked like a temple with a dome and pillars that he called a folly. At the end of a long drive was a small house, built in what she recognised as the Gothic style, but now abandoned, its windows boarded up.

"That's the lodge," he said. "Caretakers used to live there, but the present ones have a flat we had made for them in the house."

The place looked forlorn, in need of painting, several tiles fallen off the roof. One of the doors to the garage sagged off its hinges.

"I'll have to have this place seen to," said Preston. "I don't know why I've let it get into this state."

Not for want of cash, thought Montserrat. "What's that?" She pointed to a mound overgrown with long grass and weeds in which was a wooden door approached by a descending flight of six steps. A book she had loved as a child, a series of films came back to her. "It looks like something a hobbit would live in."

"It's an Anderson shelter," said Preston.

"I don't know what that means."

"In the war—World War Two, that is—there were two kinds of air-raid shelter, the Morrison, which was like a sort of metal table, and the Anderson, which is that one. You dug a pit for it in your garden and put turf on the top."

"But did you have air raids out here?"

"There was a bomb in the village. A cow was killed."

"How do you know all this? You weren't born. Your dad would have been a little kid."

"My grandfather told me."

"Can we see inside?"

The door was locked but Preston had a key on one of the bunches. Inside were two bunks, their mattresses green with mould, a table with a mould-overgrown book lying on it, a bare bulb hanging from the roof.

"It's something like this we want," Montserrat said, "but this won't do. If you do the place up, this might get—well, dismantled. A cave or something—are there any caves?"

"Of course not. Not in Essex."

She walked up the steps, let him lock the door, and stood in the lane which led to the church. Its tower loomed up close to them. A hundred yards along was a gate in the hedge that was the boundary of a little cemetery. The gray stone church looked solid enough, but the churchyard appeared to be quietly decaying in an unnatural darkness. All the trees which grew among the gravestones were dark, two or three evergreens were far from green but had leaves that appeared to be made of black leather, the yews extravagantly large, the holly luxuriant. Ivy climbed over everything. Even some of the gravestones were canopied with ivy. All of this vegetation seemed to be mouldering, perhaps because these leaves never fell but wore out with time.

Most of the monuments were slabs and upright stones, many leaning over, but there were three tombs, shaped like large boxes of stone. All were coated in yellow-green lichen and darker green stonecrop. At half past two it was still light out in the lane. Only in here, dusk had come or had never been absent.

"There's never anyone about," said Preston. "You may see four or five old people come to matins on Sunday. The vicar looks after three local parishes, and tomorrow morning may not be one of his Sundays."

Montserrat put her hand out to touch the lichen on the biggest of the tombs. "It's an Anderson shelter for the dead," she said in a ghoulish voice, and read the the three words incised on its base: "THE STILL FAMILY."

"It's not been used since my grandfather was laid to rest." Preston's tone was both pious and reproving. But he had brought the wrong key and they had to go back.

THEY WENT FOR a walk in Holland Park, holding hands, and when lunchtime came had their lunch in a restaurant there. A lot of people were about. Jimmy liked to be seen with Thea, and Thea was training herself to like being seen with Jimmy. Each of them thought they would be an object of envy, and each told the other. This wasn't difficult for Thea on account of Jimmy's being so good-looking, tall and well built and with a fine head of dark hair.

"Those men would like to be in my shoes."

"All those women would like it to be your hand they're holding." She couldn't think of much to say, but that would do.

Though dry, it was too late in the year to sit on the grass, and the seats were uncomfortable. The restaurant had a bar area, and there they sat with their drinks (tonic water and Angostura for Jimmy, pinot grigio for Thea) and told each other about their past lives. Jimmy had been married for five years back in the nineties, but his wife had run away with a chimney sweep.

"I didn't know there were such things anymore," said Thea.

"He didn't actually go up chimneys. He had a chimney-cleaning company. They've got three children now."

Thea had been to a polytechnic which became a university, where she got her degree in computer studies.

"You're a clever woman," said Jimmy.

He had been a driving instructor, a driving examiner, a car salesman, and had met Simon Jefferson when giving his wife a driving lesson. Dr. Jefferson, noticing from the window Jimmy's skill at parallel parking, took him on as his driver two years after his divorce and Jimmy's, which by coincidence happened at much the same time. Thea recounted her first meeting with Damian and Roland while escorting Miss Grieves and her shopping trolley to the corner shop in St. Barnabas Street.

Jimmy paid the bill. "Your place or mine?"

Thea felt guilty about letting him pay when she didn't really love him yet. "Well . . . we may see Damian and Roland on our way in."

"Dr. Jefferson will be out all day."

"Your place then," said Thea, pushing away the unforgivable thought that it was as well to get it over.

12

B Y THE TIME it got really dark, things had undergone a change. They had removed the box from the roof rack, taken it into the house, and, after some hesitation and gritting of teeth, opened it. Neither of them had much experience of dead bodies. Preston had seen his father after death and two years later his mother. Montserrat had never seen a body except this one, immediately after death. She expected changes to have taken place, though she couldn't have said of what kind. She unwrapped the blanket. There was no stiffness, the limbs felt limp, and from her wide experience of reading and watching thrillers, she supposed that rigor mortis had come on and passed off again.

Rather roughly, Preston pushed her aside and rolled the body back in the blanket. "We'll carry it inside the car," he said. "It will be impossible to cope with it in the case. If you don't need it, I'll put it in the luggage room."

Proud of not shrinking, in contrast to his squeamishness, Montserrat wasn't going to say she couldn't face using the case now. "You have a luggage room? Wow!"

He carried the case away. Would she have the nerve to ask him for what she had paid Henry for it? Or what she could say she had paid? She would. "That box cost me two hundred pounds."

"Very well." It was the first time she'd ever heard anyone say that. "I'll give you a cheque when we get home."

"I'll drive," she said.

If she let him drive, she was afraid he might take them past the churchyard and on out to the major road before she could stop him. But he didn't demur. They heaved Rad Sothern's body onto the backseat of the car, and Preston covered it with sacks he brought from a room off the kitchen.

At five it was dark. Lights were on all over the village of Theydon Wold and in the house on top of the hill, but when the houses stopped, all the lights stopped too. Montserrat asked him why there were no streetlamps, and Preston said that local people had petitioned to maintain the rural darkness they preferred and that the protest had been successful. The best place to park a car for their purposes was a little way along a track that led off the lane they had used before when visiting the churchyard. The clay surface was ridged with deep ruts, but these were hard and firm as there had been no rain for a week.

Hard to believe, Montserrat thought, that they were no more than twenty-five miles from London. The silence was deep, the darkness impenetrable. Preston had said they would need a torch and he had brought one. Above them the black sky was studded with stars, a sight not seen by her since she had last been in Catalonia with her mother. Preston removed the sacks and put them on the floor, then he and she lifted out the body in the blanket and laid it on the ground.

"His death was pure accident," said Preston.

"You've said that before. Quite a few times actually."

"It needs to be said. You're behaving as if I murdered him and you're helping me cover up a crime."

She didn't answer. They walked along the gravel path, carrying the body in the blanket, Preston shining on the ground the torch he had brought. Montserrat wondered about the blanket. Could it be identified as coming from number seven Hexam Place, home of Mr. and Mrs. Preston Still? Not if it was placed inside the Still mausoleum, perhaps inside one of the coffins with its ancient occupant. She doubted if even she, with the iron nerves she was discovering in herself, could face such a task.

Halfway there, Preston lowered the body to the ground, set his end down, and said, as she had half-expected he would, "Let's take it back, Montserrat. Take it to London. There won't be any hue and cry for him yet."

She stood her ground, holding on to Rad's legs. "And do what?"

"I see your point about going to a police station. We can't do that. What we could do is take it to Hampstead Heath, say, and leave it somewhere. Take it out of the case and just leave it in—well, woodland."

She tried sarcasm. "And no one would see us, of course. Have you been up on the Heath lately? Have you? It's like Piccadilly Circus up there on a Saturday night."

He lifted his shoulders, shook his head. Her eyes growing used to the darkness, she could see him clearly enough. "If I do this," he said, "I don't think I can go back to Lucy and the kids as if nothing had happened."

"Well, something has happened. A lot. Once we get rid of the body, you'll feel better. You'll see."

"You talk as if you've done this before."

She made no answer. Let him think that way if he liked. She edged forward, and after a moment's hesitation he lifted Rad's head and shoulders once more. They set the body down on the shaggy grass beside the Still Family mausoleum, and Preston went down the steps to the door, lighting his way with the torch.

"I don't for a moment suppose the key will turn. No one's opened this door since my grandfather was—laid to rest here."

Of all the soppy ways to put it. "And when was that?"

"Nineteen ninety-two."

"You can only try."

The crippled old door opened. It trembled and creaked but it came open. Montserrat expected a horrible smell in the form of a stinking fog to come rolling out of it, but there was nothing, only a dense darkness. Torchlight showed an interior very much like the inside of the Anderson shelter, but with shelves instead of bunks, and coffins on the shelves. She had noticed no cobwebs in the shelter, but in this small, shabby mausoleum spiders had spun lavishly, and some of the threads looked to her like dusty ropes, they were so thick. It was a cavern hung with spun and woven tapestries.

"Right," she said. "We'd better get it inside. Someone passing by in a car could see this light and think it was funny."

As she spoke, a car did pass, a hundred yards away, not along the lane, but by the village street. Its headlights were on full beam and blazed momentarily, catching them in blinding light. Montserrat had spoken to him without looking at him. Her gaze had been on the inside of the mausoleum and its contents. But now when he didn't answer, she turned to face him. He was trembling, his face livid in the light from the torch, which was shaking in his hand.

His voice came with difficulty as if his throat had dried. "I can't put this—this thing in there."

"Why not? What do you mean?"

"Those are my ancestors in those coffins. They are my *family*. I can't contaminate them with that, a creature who sneaks after dark to another man's wife . . ."

"They're dead. They won't know."

"I can't and there's an end of it."

"What are we going to do with him then? We can't leave him here. They'll find him and make the connection with you. Of course they will."

He looked as if he was about to kick the door, but thought better of it and closed it almost reverently, turning the key in the lock. "Put him back in the car."

If he wouldn't leave it here, there was no arguing with him. How many times had they gone over it already? They carried it back. The torch battery had expired and the darkness seemed deeper than before. They heaved the body onto the backseat once more, rearranged the blanket, covered it with the sacks. Montserrat got into the driving seat. This was something else there was no point in arguing about. She was resolved only on not returning Rad's body to Hexam Place. Somewhere along the route, down some byway, in some woodland, it must be left. She was starting to wonder why she had helped Preston in the first place. He was nothing to her. Or was he something to her? Was he becoming something to her? Today had brought them together in a curious way, Macbeth and Lady Macbeth. The way they spoke to each other now could never have been contemplated when he was the master of the house—she really had seen him that way—and she was just the au pair. That relationship had changed.

He directed her away from the motorway onto the roads that ran through Epping Forest, and on one of these, leading from Theydon Bois towards Loughton but still in deep woodland, she became aware of the car's wobbling, not quite holding the road surface. The unmistakable sign of a flat tyre. She tried to pretend she was imagining it, but that illusion lasted only a moment. She managed to bump the car into the entrance to a ride that ran off the road.

"Why are you stopping?"

"We've got a flat tyre. Didn't you feel it?"

He got out, said, "It's the nearside rear." He peered at the tyre. "It looks like a nail in it."

She joined him. "Can you change the wheel?"

"I don't know. Certainly not in this darkness. I belong to the RAC of course. I'll call them. It doesn't matter that it's not my car."

"Yeah, sure, you can call them. With a corpse in the back. They won't notice that." She gave a little dry laugh. "Before we call anyone, we have to dump him somewhere or sit here all night till we think of something else."

JUNE CALLED RAD on his landline and was invited to leave a message. "You left your phone here. Down the back of the sofa. The Princess got me to ring because she was anxious." Then she called the other number she had for him and the phone with the little pictures started playing the national anthem, a tune she wouldn't have thought he'd know. Perhaps you didn't have to know it to make it work on a mobile phone. She had left another message before she realised there was no one to receive it but herself.

The Princess had fallen asleep in front of the television, and Gussie had fallen asleep on her lap. She might as well walk up to the Dugong, find someone to have a drink with. June felt vaguely uneasy, though she was the first to admit there was nothing to worry about. He had simply forgotten his phone. It was just rather odd that he hadn't missed it and guessed where it was.

Henry was in the Dugong with Richard and Sondra. June said, "Hallo, strangers," because they hadn't been in there for a long time. They said tomorrow would be their tenth wedding anniversary and they were having a glass of champagne before taking themselves off to the Rossignol for a celebratory dinner.

"Happy tin wedding," said June, raising her glass of chardonnay.

"Is that what it is?" Sondra sounded disappointed.

"Bit dodgy for presents, isn't it?" said Henry. "I suppose you could always ask for some tinned fruit."

Up at number seven, Rabia was letting her cousin Mohammed out of the house by way of the basement door. Instead of ten in the morning, he had arrived to mend the banister seven hours later, full of excuses that his wife had gone into labour. He had had to be at the hospital delivery room until he became the father of a fine boy at 3:00 p.m.

"It is very good of you to come at all, cousin," said Rabia, feeling it would be unkind to mention that she had had to stay indoors all day waiting for him and he might have phoned. Nor did she point out that the new baby was not his first son but his fourth.

She made him tea, brought him a plate of pastries, and sent a loving message to Mumtaz. The banister, as he pointed out, was now as solid as a rock. Coming to the bottom of the basement stairs on their way out, he spotted something shiny lying on the black and white tiles in the corner.

"It is not often you see such an object nowadays," said Mohammed, picking it up. "Smoking is an obsolete habit, wouldn't you say? Silver, I would hazard a guess, and engraved with the initials *RS*. I wonder who has mislaid this valuable object."

In spite of covering her ears when the subject was raised by Montserrat, Rabia had unwillingly picked up enough to know whom the cigarette case belonged to. But what to do with it and whom to tell? Somewhat preoccupied, she let Mohammed out and thanked him for coming.

RAD SOTHERN'S BODY was again taken out of the car and laid on the grass. Montserrat kicked enough fallen leaves over it to cover it. The woman who took Preston's call said their mechanic would be with them in anything up to forty minutes. Montserrat got into the back of the car and checked the seat for stains. The only one she could find was a brown patch, which might be taken for blood but was in fact the result of Thea's spilling a latte. The RAC man took only half an hour to get there, took the flat tyre off, attached the spare wheel, and said not to drive on it at more than fifty miles an hour.

"Chance would be a fine thing," said Preston in a sneering tone, as if it were the RAC man's fault that the roads they would be driving on would be restricted to forty and thirty.

Montserrat thought he was quite a dishy man, so when he handed her a form to fill in commenting on the standard of the service, she filled in all the EXCELLENT boxes and signed it Preston Still. Then she warned Preston that he had better expect a big fuss in the media over the disappearance of Rad Sothern. It wouldn't have started yet and there might be nothing tomorrow—with luck they would be spared the attentions of the *Mail on Sunday*—but once Rad started failing to turn up for appointments, the search for him and the speculation would begin.

"Why would they come to me?" Preston sounded aghast.

"Because people will have seen him come to the basement door." She added brutally, "When he was shagging Lucy."

"Why shouldn't they think he was—er, shagging you?"

"Fucking hell," said Montserrat vigorously. "Thanks a million. I'm to take on your wife's lover, take responsibility for a guy you pushed down the stairs out of jealousy. What for? To save your bloody marriage? Let me tell you, mate, that's buggered already, has been for years."

He made no sound. She saw that he was crying, the tears trickling slowly down his cheeks.

"OK, I'm sorry. But it's true. With a bit of luck if anyone's seen him in Hexam Place, they'll think he was visiting June. Come on, we've still got to get rid of him—remember?"

They had put the body on the backseat and covered it once more with the sacks. There wasn't enough room for it in the boot.

"We've got to take him a long way away from here. We don't want that RAC man making the connection."

Montserrat drove, glad of the darkness. The spare wheel that had been put on was thinner than the one which had the puncture and had a bright yellow hub. Other drivers were less likely to notice it in the dark and so less likely to remember when and where they had seen it. She found her way out onto what Preston said was the Epping New Road and at a roundabout took an unclassified road up to High Beech. Preston kept saying nervously, "We can leave it here, we can leave it here."

"Not yet," she said. "Why don't you shut up and leave it to me?"

It was a bad moment when the driver of the car that was following them began hooting. "It's because I have to go so slowly," Montserrat said. "That's all it is. I'll pull off the road and park."

And it appeared that this was all it was. The pursuing car went on its way, and they were left behind in an empty part of the forest, all tall beech trees and thin birches that shivered in the rising wind. Any car coming down here would have to have its headlights on full beam. Overhead the sky was invisible, a thick, cloudy darkness, without moon or stars. They lifted the body out once more and carried it along a path of rutted clay. Something rustled in the depths of the woodland, a deer perhaps. There were deer in the forest, Preston said.

"I can't carry this any further," he said. "I've come to the end of my tether."

She didn't answer, but dropped Rad's body on the fallen leaves and, tugging on the blanket in which it was wrapped, pulled it under a holly bush. "There. We'll leave it there. It'll do."

"No one could see it from the path."

"I said it'll do," said Montserrat. "Now we'll go home."

THEY HAD THE car back in the St. Barnabas Mews garage in just over half an hour, and there they went their separate ways. Montserrat's parting words were that she'd want paying for the new tyre she'd have to get on Monday. She watched him head for number seven Hexam Place. He had nowhere else to go. She was beginning to wonder why she had got into this in the first place, but now she told herself that perhaps she had some kind of future with Preston Still. If the police closed in on him, she could probably save him and then his gratitude would begin.

Not a good idea to go back to her flat quite yet. She went into the Dugong, asked for a chardonnay, and called Ciaran on her mobile. He'd be with her, he said, in ten minutes. By the time he arrived—nearer forty minutes than ten—June had arrived on her own and Thea had arrived with Jimmy. They were clinging to each other in the rather awkward position a tall man and a short woman must cope with, his arm round her shoulders, hers round his waist. Shortly afterwards Damian and Roland paid a rare visit to the Dugong, Roland shaking his head at the sight of Thea and Jimmy holding hands. Unusually for the regular drinkers of Hexam Place, they all split into separate parties, Montserrat and Ciaran drinking rather a lot of white wine before departing for Montserrat's flat. Dex sat alone in a corner with a Guinness in front of him and, though politely asked by June to join them, only shook his head and said, "Cheers." Damian and Roland shared the smallest table in the room, well away from the others. Montserrat felt strange going into her flat after the events of the night and morning, but there appeared to be no evidence of those events apart from the absence of the blanket. As she told herself, it really didn't matter as you couldn't prove a negative.

13

THERE WAS NOTHING. Nothing in the morning papers—Montserrat scanned them all in the newsagent's in Ebury Bridge Road—and nothing on the radio or the TV news. She had a hangover and went back to bed. Lying there, feeling better now she was not perpendicular, she wondered how Preston was getting on. Had he shared Lucy's bed or moved into a spare bedroom? She decided that, though he was undoubtedly a financial genius, he was a weak man and because she was a strong woman, a weak man rather suited her. Preston was an awful name. She wondered what Macbeth's first name might have been. One of those weird Scottish ones perhaps, Hamish or Lachlan. Perhaps it said in the play. Once her headache had gone away she would have a look, and if she couldn't find *The Complete Works of Shakespeare* in the house she'd see if Thea had it. It was the sort of thing Thea likely would have.

It was a lovely day for November—well, a lovely day for any time of the year. The sky was blue, the sun shining, a little breeze blowing. A text from Thea inviting her over for coffee fetched her out of bed at midday. The house was silent, Rabia spending the day with her family as was customary on a Sunday, the girls off somewhere with their mother at some athletic enterprise. As far as

Montserrat knew. It was quite possible, of course, that Rabia had taken all three children with her, and in their absence Preston had murdered Lucy and then killed himself. Possible but unlikely. She went across the road to number eight. Thea had put two chairs out on her balcony and made real coffee in her espresso machine.

"Did you watch *Crosswind* on Channel Four last night?"

Montserrat said that she had been out with Ciaran.

"Yes, well, I was out with Jimmy. Or, rather, *in* with Jimmy. But I did catch the start of it, and guess what, Rad Sothern was supposed to be on the panel but he didn't turn up. He'd never told them, he just didn't come, and at the last minute they had to get some politician."

"Maybe he's ill or stoned or something."

"Yes, maybe. But I saw June coming back with the papers, and she said he'd been with them on Friday, and when he went, he forgot his cell phone, it was down the back of the sofa, but she tried and tried to get hold of him and she couldn't."

"He'll turn up," said Montserrat, glad she hadn't been asked if she'd seen him on Friday night.

Thea offered her a glass of pinot grigio and Montserrat accepted on the grounds that it would be a hair of the dog. They got through more than a glass each, nearer a bottle, while Thea described in detail how wonderful sex was with Jimmy. This was not really the case, but she had refused to admit her disappointment even to herself. She had heard that the effect of being in love was to see the sky as bluer, the sun brighter, the whole world changed for the better, so of course the sex must be the best she'd ever had.

Fighting just about successfully against sleep, Montserrat hoisted herself from the near-supine position she had sunk into and asked Thea what Macbeth's first name was.

"He didn't have one," said Thea, not too pleased at being distracted from her theme.

"He must have."

"Well, no one knows what it was." Ever helpful, she fetched Montserrat a tattered paperback of *The Complete Works of Shakespeare*.

From the sunny balcony Montserrat watched the front door of number seven open and Preston Still come down the steps. She guessed he had gone to fetch the Sunday papers and waited for him to come back with them, but after half an hour he hadn't returned. Where was her two hundred pounds and the money for the new tyre?

LUCY RARELY MENTIONED Rad Sothern to Montserrat except to say at what time he would present himself at the basement door. So when she tapped on the front door of Montserrat's flat at seven that evening, the au pair thought Lucy had found out she and Preston had spent the previous day together, for experience of life had already taught her that you may still be jealous of your spouse or partner while being unfaithful yourself. But it was the disappearance of Rad Lucy had come about.

"It's so odd never to hear a word from him, darling. Do you know where he went when he left here on Friday?"

Montserrat said that he hadn't said and of course she hadn't asked him.

"He wasn't on his programme last night and they didn't seem to know where he was. It's so unlike him not to call me."

"Have you tried asking June?"

"Well, no, darling, I haven't. Would you like to?"

Montserrat wouldn't like to at all and had no intention of doing so, but if asked, she would say she had and June had said she didn't know. For once she went to bed early. Ciaran phoned seven times but she didn't answer.

HENRY SAT OUTSIDE number eleven for nearly two hours on Monday morning before Lord Studley appeared. When he finally turned up, the under-secretary was in a bad temper because the junior minister called in as a substitute for Rad Sothern on *Crosswind* had while on the air called an Opposition peer a toffee-nosed poof. He had been required to apologise but so far had refused to do so. Unusually for Lord Studley, he recounted all this to Henry on the way to Parliament.

"Shocking language, my lord," said Henry, sensing that this was what he was supposed to say.

He was to pick up Lady Studley and a friend of hers who was staying with them at twelve and bring them in for lunch. Henry wasn't altogether sorry about the presence of the friend as this would prevent Oceane from sitting next to him in the car and touching him in intimate ways while he was negotiating the traffic in Parliament Square. Both women had on hats of the kind usually worn at Ascot.

AN APPEARANCE AT the nursery from Lucy in the middle of the day was so unusual as to make Rabia believe at first that she must have done something wrong in taking Thomas to visit her family on the previous afternoon. But months ago she had asked permission to take him to her father's house, and leave had indifferently been granted. It was soon plain, though, that rebuking her was not the purpose of Lucy's visit. However, it started off on the wrong foot in more ways than one. Thomas, now quite good at walking, was toddling across the floor to pick up a fallen fluffy rabbit when Lucy interposed herself, squatted down, and held out her arms to him.

"Here's Mummy, Thomas," said Rabia. "Say hallo to Mummy."

Lucy was perhaps a formidable sight to any small child with her five-inch-heel knee boots, miniskirt, faux-leopard jacket, and streaming blond hair. The little boy reacted promptly enough.

Screaming, "Rab, Rab," he turned to Rabia and threw himself into her arms.

"Oh my God, what's wrong with the child?" Lucy got to her feet with difficulty, looking bewildered rather than cross, but Rabia was terrified. How would a mother feel if her child seemed to prefer another woman to herself? Of course Thomas couldn't really, all children love their mother best, it only looked that way. But suppose Lucy was so hurt and angry as she might well be that she would think getting rid of the nanny was her only course?

It was only a single moment of horror. Lucy said, "Come and sit down a moment, darling. I want to ask you something. I think of you as the expert, you see."

They sat at the table, Rabia having quietened Thomas with a mug of chocolate milk and a jammy dodger. "Do you think it terribly important for children to have their father living with them?"

"It is what I have always been used to in my community."

"I suppose it is. But then you've been used to arranged marriage and praying God knows how many times a day, haven't you?"

Rabia felt able to say nothing, only to smile.

"A father would never get custody, would he?"

Rabia said she was sorry but she didn't know what this meant.

"If there was a divorce, the mother would always get the children, wouldn't she?"

Momentarily plunged back into fear, Rabia said Lucy would have to ask a lawyer. She wanted to ask if the Stills were going to have a divorce but she dared not. Lucy thanked her and went away, taking no more notice of Thomas. In need of instant comfort, Rabia seized Thomas and hugged him tightly, covering the front of her black gown with smears of jam and chocolate milk. She still hadn't decided what to do with the silver cigarette case.

Downstairs, Montserrat had come home from buying a pair of black leather boots from Marks and Spencer and found an envelope pushed under her front door. Inside was a cheque for 350 pounds drawn on Coutts Bank to Montserrat Tresser and signed P. Q. Still.

"I wonder what the *Q* stands for," she said aloud.

No note was inside the envelope. She didn't exactly expect him to have thanked her for driving him around to dispose of a body, but he might have written something, maybe a few cryptic words acknowledging unspecified help. That was it then, was it? There was to be no more? Lucy's conduct was to be overlooked, they were together again, and all was well? Montserrat poured herself the dregs of the whisky she and he had shared on Friday night. The boots looked rather less attractive than they had in the shop. She had bought them because they were a lot like Lucy's, but Lucy's came from Céline and cost eight hundred pounds. She knew because she'd seen them advertised in the *Sunday Times Style* magazine.

The tap on the door at seven woke her. She had fallen asleep from boredom, nothing to do, and whisky. It had to be Ciaran, except that he had no key and couldn't get in. She opened the door. Preston stood there.

He came in and spoke to her as if they had known each other for years and years. No greeting, no *How are you?* "I've told Lucy I want a divorce."

The logistics of it concerned her more than the law, the personalities, or the emotions involved. "Where will you go?"

"I expect I'll take a flat somewhere near. I'll need to see the kids."

"Is there anything in the paper about Rad?"

"It's too soon."

"I suppose it is," she said. "It's not as if he had a wife or a girlfriend to miss him."

But there, on the following morning, she saw she was wrong. The tabloids, the ones that are called *red top* and never *quality*, all carried a front-page story by a woman called Rocksana Castelli, who said she was Rad Sothern's "partner" and had been sharing his flat in Montagu Square for the past year. The photograph looked a lot like Lucy Still, same emaciated body, long, skinny legs, and blond hair, but about ten years younger. Miss Castelli, Montserrat read, had last seen Rad at the flat on Friday afternoon before she left to visit her mother in Hornsey. They had had a disagreement, so she hadn't been much disturbed when he didn't return that night. On Saturday she phoned him twice on his cell phone and got an answer but no one spoke. It was yesterday, Monday, that she thought things were serious and she told the police.

Montserrat wondered if Lucy had seen it. Quite a shock for her if she had. Would it be a wise move to see June? The severe-weather warning put out the night before had resulted in no more than a light breeze and a drizzle. She ventured across the road with the *Sun* in her hand only to meet June halfway there with the *Daily Mail*. That Rad had a live-in girlfriend interested June more than his disappearance.

"I always knew he couldn't have been going out with you."

"I never said he was," said Montserrat.

"That must have been her that phoned. I heard it ring but of course I didn't answer it. I don't know how to work those contraptions."

"I'm going in, I'm getting wet," said Montserrat, putting the *Sun* over her head and retreating to the area stairs.

The only way to initiate the next stage of the drama, thought June, was to phone the police. On the real phone, of course. Eventually she was put on to a Detective Sergeant Freud. "Mr. Sothern spends a lot of time here with us. That is, the Princess and myself. The Princess is a great admirer of his medical serial. He was here having a drink with us last Friday evening."

"Where did he go when he left you?"

"That I couldn't say," June said virtuously. "It was no business of mine."

Sergeant Freud said he would send someone round to number six Hexam Place. She had a few minutes or perhaps a few hours in which to decide whether to mention Rad's apparent connection with number seven opposite. She had rather liked the look of the girl in the photograph, a pretty girl with lovely colouring and a shy, gentle expression. No need to cause her further upset by telling the police about Montserrat. The Princess couldn't understand how an episode and not a repeat of *Avalon Clinic* could be shown when Rad had disappeared, but she watched it just the same.

Jimmy dropped Dr. Jefferson off, got into a queue of traffic, sat in the butter-coloured Lexus, and phoned Thea, pouring out love words from a full heart and reminding her of the raptures of the previous night. A policeman moved him along and he drove back to Hexam Place, where he had arranged to meet her in the Dugong. Thea had an early copy of the *Evening Standard*.

"This stuff is so sordid," said Jimmy when she insisted on showing him a photograph of Rocksana Castelli in a bikini on the side of a swimming pool, Rad Sothern half-submerged in the water.

"He was seeing someone at number seven."

"Mr. Still's place?"

"Well, he wasn't seeing Mr. Still," said Thea. "He isn't gay. And it wasn't Montserrat, that I do know. Maybe it was Zinnia."

"Can't we forget these squalid people, sweetheart? Let's go back to your place."

"OK, if you want," said Thea.

After lunch, when it was time for Lord Studley to take his seat on the Coalition front bench for prayers, Henry drove Oceane and her friend to Sloane Street to go shopping in Prada and its ilk. They kept him waiting outside so long that he had to evade traffic wardens by driving round and round Lowndes Square. Their conversation on the way back was of such a lubricious nature, punctuated by little screams and breathless gasps, that he wouldn't have been surprised if, on arriving at Hexam Place, they had proposed a threesome before he went to fetch Lord Studley. But nothing like that happened, and having left the Beemer on the Residents' Parking, he went up the road to fetch the *Evening Standard*.

Montserrat was in the newsagent. This later edition had a photograph of Rad Sothern and Rocksana Castelli toasting each other with champagne in a club. The headline said ROCK IN TEARS FOR RAD.

"I bet he never said a word about her."

"I barely knew him," said Montserrat.

Henry spotted the plainclothes officer going up the steps to number six. He'd know one of them anywhere. Why did they bother to disguise themselves? June had been waiting for him for hours. If he didn't hurry up, she was thinking, she'd have to postpone the extraordinary general meeting of the St. Zita Society scheduled for 7:00 p.m. Then the doorbell rang. DC Rickards looked about eighteen, but even people in their thirties and forties looked eighteen to her.

He appeared to believe that the Princess was a member of the royal family and seemed overawed by her. Gussie set up a furious barking and had to be shut in the kitchen. "This is Mr. Sothern's mobile telephone," said June. "Should I have reported it to someone?"

"Just us," said DC Rickards. "You did quite right. Mr. Sothern your grandson, is he?"

"Certainly not. I'm an unmarried woman. He's my great-nephew." She had already told DS Freud about Friday evening's drink and that she didn't know where Rad went after he left number six. To reveal that she had never previously heard of his girlfriend would have betrayed an ignorance of Rad's private life and make him appear less of an intimate friend and kinsman than she would have this young man believe, so she said what a lovely girl Rocksana was and how fond of her were the Princess and herself. "She must be out of her mind with worry."

DC Rickards made no comment. "Do you know if Mr. Sothern was on friendly terms with other residents of Hexam Place?"

Quick thinking brought June to say that she thought not, but that everyone must have recognised him when he called at number six owing to his being the famous face of Mr. Fortescue. DC Rickards thanked her and said to her surprise that she had been very helpful.

She had half an hour in which to give the Princess a stiff drink, make her a plate of smoked salmon and scrambled egg, walk Gussie round the block, and take herself across the road to the Dugong for the St. Zita Society meeting. Henry, Richard, Zinnia, and Thea were already there, but not Jimmy. Jimmy was sitting in the butter-coloured Lexus on the consultants' parking at University College Hospital in the Euston Road. It was probably the first time since he had worked for Simon Jefferson that he had been kept waiting while his employer carried out lifesaving treatment on a six-year-old. He was trying to write a poem to Thea but finding it more difficult than he expected.

The St. Zita meeting had been called specially (not much more than a week after the previous one) to discuss the response from Westminster City Council to the second letter about the bags of dog excrement. The "clean streets" enterprise wrote that they would continue to remove all waste from the streets but, in the light of recession, economy, and "the general tightening of belts," could take no specific steps to curb canine waste litter. June made her little speech and threw the meeting open for opinions and discussion, but it quickly deteriorated into the favoured topic of the evening, the disappearance of Rad Sothern.

"If he doesn't turn up," said Zinnia, "if he's like *dead* and they can't do any more recording, do you think they'll have to kill Mr. Fortescue?"

14

ALL HER LIFE since she had come to London with her father when she was small, Rabia had judged the ways of those she called British Christians as strange. Often wicked. Their morality, or lack of it, shocked her deeply. It had begun to worry her that Thomas, so good, so sweet, so innocent and pure, must grow up among people to whom chastity meant little and marital infidelity was common. She could do nothing, it was not her business—all that she knew—but it worried her.

Now the household itself where she worked was to be disrupted by a breach between the parents. She knew it, she had seen it. Shouts that were still perfectly audible behind the closed bedroom door began it, the obscenities that had dreadful meanings. Pain hurt her physically when she saw Thomas's face crumple at the hateful words, when the tears splashed down his cheeks and he put out his arms for his Rabia. Then Mr. Still moved out of that beautiful big bedroom with its two pairs of long windows, its cherubs on the ceilings, its silk-curtained bed, and took himself up to the top of the house above the nursery floor, where he made a bedroom and a bathroom and a study his own domain.

"They've actually separated," said Montserrat, "except that they're still living under the same roof. There'll be a divorce."

"What will become of the poor children?"

"If it wasn't for them, the whole thing could be over in a matter of weeks. But it can't be a quickie when there are kids. Lucy will get custody of course."

Rabia thought that would be a terrible shame and remembered how Thomas had turned away from his mother and come to her, but she said nothing. Just the same, she thought it no harm to tell Montserrat that Mr. Still came up (down these days) to the nursery at every opportunity he got to ask about his children's health.

"It's no exaggeration to say that the whole country is searching for Rad Sothern. I do wonder what's happened to him. What do you think?"

Rabia didn't know what to think. But she did wonder if she should tell the police that, in addition to arguments between Lucy and Mr. Still, she had once heard the voice of Mr. Fortescue on the floor below. *Avalon Clinic* was one of the few programmes she watched. Thomas was asleep by the time it came on, and Rabia liked sitting with the girls to see it. It was about healing people and doing good. That familiar voice might mean Rad Sothern had been in this house several times. Montserrat might know. She would ask Montserrat before she told the police, of whom she was rather afraid. She took another look at the silver cigarette case, wondering once more what to do about it.

Montserrat was indignant at Rabia's suggestion. She must be mistaken. It was possible that Lucy and Mr. Still met Rad at one of the Princess's parties, but they would never have had reason to invite him to number seven. No, Rabia was wrong. She might have heard Rad's voice on television, but it was an actor's voice, Montserrat said earnestly, a disguised voice, suitable for an upper-class, top-flight consultant, nothing like his normal tone, which, frankly, was nearer estuary English.

She thought she had convinced Rabia. The girl was rather naïve. Montserrat piled on the hard time the police would give her if she mentioned Rad and his voice, and the even harder time Lucy might inflict on her. "She's capable of giving you the push, you know."

"The push?"

"Sacking you."

Preston Still had only once made contact with her since the money had been handed over. Being used in this way and then ignored was hard. She started answering Ciaran's calls again, went to the cinema with him, and once let him stay the night. He asked if he could have a key to the basement door and she didn't see why not. Preston had apparently made a flat for himself on the top floor. Rabia said he generally went out for his meals. Once or twice Montserrat saw Beacon open the car door for him and Preston climb the steps to the front door. He had never mislaid his keys again.

THE PRINCESS HAD always been fonder of Rad than his great-aunt. She told June that she lay awake at night worrying about him. June was to invite Rocksana Castelli round for tea.

"A drink will be more in her line, madam," said June.

"You shouldn't say things like that. The poor girl will be brokenhearted."

June recognised her from her photograph. She came in a taxi and June watched her climb the front steps, looking around her and taking in her surroundings. In skintight jeans, equally tight sweater with a pale gold leather jacket over it, and high-heeled boots, she looked uncannily like Lucy. June wondered if she was wearing a wig, as surely no one could naturally have quite so much hair, striped in various shades of blond and with little braids sprouting out of it.

The Princess told June to open a bottle of The Drink That Is Never Wrong because the poor girl must need cheering up, and Rocksana showed them both an enormous sapphire she said was her engagement ring. Rad's girlfriend drank more champagne than the other two put together, and June had to open a second bottle. Rocksana said she had fallen in love with the house and would June show her over it. Her disappointment showed plainly as, once they had climbed the first flight of stairs, one shabby room succeeded another, the furniture was thick with dust, and the atmosphere smelt of dog and stale French perfume. No one had decorated these rooms since the Princess had moved in over half a century before, and Zinnia repeatedly said they'd have to get a team in to spring-clean the place before she could be expected to take it over.

"You could let the top two floors to someone," said Rocksana.

Got her own eye on it in case Rad doesn't come back, thought June. She took the girl downstairs again and put the champagne back in the fridge. Invisible to June behind the basement window, Montserrat watched Rocksana walking up and down looking for a taxi. There never were taxis, Montserrat had only seen them bringing people home to Hexam Place. After about ten minutes' pacing that became limping, Rocksana took off her shoes and set off to walk in her stockinged feet towards Sloane Square.

"IT'S GOING TO cause a lot of trouble," said Thea, scanning the civil partnership guest list. "You want to have a look at who you've got down here. You tell me what strikes you, there's something stands out a mile."

"What do you mean?" said Damian.

"Just look at the sort of people you've got on the list. Rather, the sort of people you haven't got on the list."

"Come on, don't keep me in suspense."

"Well, you've got the Stills and Simon Jefferson and Lord and Lady Studley and the Princess and me, but you haven't got any of the servants. You haven't got Jimmy or Beacon or Henry or Rabia or Montserrat or Zinnia or Richard or Sondra or *June*."

"It didn't occur to us to ask them."

Thea threw down her ballpoint. "Suit yourselves of course, but whatever happened to equality? Maybe not Rabia, she's a darling but she's a strict Moslem and she wouldn't come. Zinnia—well, she's a bit rough is Zinnia, and anyway she works on Thursdays. But Montserrat? Her dad went to school with Lucy's dad, something like that. And June's more of a lady than the Princess—anyway the Princess wouldn't come without her."

"We've got enough people with those on the list. It's not snobbery, I promise you, Thea. Another ten guests and we won't be able to get them all in this room."

"Well, it's your party, but I'm telling you, there'll be trouble."

In her secretary's role, Thea wrote all the cards as instructed despite her misgivings. She was already wondering if she could keep these omissions dark. If Jimmy found out, there would be hell to pay, and equal hell if she told him. Perhaps, though, she should tell Montserrat. Montserrat of all the people on the list would be least disappointed. Damian and Roland bored her, and she had once told Thea she disliked weddings and would never go to another. A civil partnership was really a wedding, wasn't it, just a wedding under another name? Jimmy would have to do without her this evening. She picked up the phone and called Montserrat.

EVEN IN THE HEART of London gales blow, winds crack their cheeks, and tiles fall off roofs. Even in a little bar round the back of Leicester Square tempestuous shrieks and claps of thunder penetrate the walls when a November storm starts up. This storm had been forecast, but no one believed in it till the first sixty-mile-an-hour gusts started and the rain lashed down out of a black sky.

Thea and Montserrat were sitting in the little bar, drinking chardonnay and eating Pringles crisps and big black olives. Thea's mobile rang the moment they sat down. Of course it was Jimmy, wanting to know if he should come and join them.

"Better stay in on a night like this," said Thea.

Montserrat helped herself to more of what the barman called "nibbles." "I've lost seven pounds in the past month so I think I can treat myself to a crisp or two."

"No one ever eats two crisps," said Thea.

Thin herself, one of those who boast that they don't have to worry about their weight, Thea looked critically at her friend and admitted that her looks had greatly improved recently. The spots were gone and the little roll of fat, the dimension of a bicycle tyre, round her middle had disappeared.

"You're looking good," Thea said. "Ciaran brought that on, has he?" When there was no answer beyond a small smile, she moved on to the question of the guest list. "It's true they've got about a hundred people coming."

Montserrat gulped down the dregs of her wine. "I wouldn't have thought they'd got a hundred friends. They're not very nice people. You won't go, will you?"

"What d'you mean, like make a gesture? If you're not asking my friends, I'm not going? The fact is, Montsy, I don't come in the category, I'm not a servant."

"You're nearly as much a one as I am and they're not asking me."

"I thought you wouldn't mind," said Thea. "I thought you'd be glad. I mean, you don't like them. You wouldn't enjoy yourself."

"It's the principle of the thing. To be perfectly honest with you, I wouldn't mind so much if you'd make a stand with me and not go."

Driven to placating Montserrat, anything rather than give in, Thea picked up their empty glasses and offered her friend another drink. "Have a vodka this time, why don't you. I'll pay."

Montserrat nodded coldly and Thea went up to the bar, wishing she had never said a word about civil partnerships and guest lists. It would have been better to leave it for Montserrat to find out for herself. Jimmy rang again while Thea was waiting for their drinks and she nearly didn't answer it. But even if she hadn't yet succeeded in loving him, she couldn't do that to Jimmy.

"Are you sure you wouldn't like me to join you? The storm's over and it's stopped raining."

"Jimmy, I think it's best for us sometimes to have an evening apart, don't you?"

No true lover has ever been known to make that remark. Jimmy said, "Mind you call me when you're leaving and I'll pick you up."

The vodka elicited a glum thank-you from Montserrat. "I can't just let it go. I shall have to raise it at the next meeting of the St. Zita Society."

"Well, that won't be for ages. We've only just had a meeting."

"That was an *extraordinary* general meeting. We're still due for November's. I shall tell June and put it on the agenda."

Montserrat cheered up a bit after that, and the two of them returned to the chardonnay, of which they drank rather a lot. "We'll have a taxi home," said Thea. "I'll pay."

Another call came from Jimmy, but this time Thea didn't answer. She and Montserrat had to walk all the way to the top of Regent Street because all the cabs were taken. The place had been taken over by drunken teenagers, a revelation to Thea but nothing new to Montserrat. They waited for a bus—or a cab if one came—and one of the boys started shouting abuse at a man with ginger hair.

"It's what they do," Montserrat said. "Ginger hair, red hair, whatever, it's the latest thing. You want to cover up your head in case they start on you."

For the boy, who was now shouting obscenities, had been joined by a Gothic-looking girl. Thea had nothing to cover her head with, and when Montserrat offered her the scarf that was wrapped round her own neck, it was too late. If Montserrat herself had been the target of "fucking carrots" and "ginger shithead," she could have withstood it and returned abuse of her own, but Thea was made of more tender stuff.

"Let's go, let's go." The scarf wound round her head but inadequate to cover all her hair, Thea was almost in tears. "We can walk, let's walk."

"God knows why you didn't accept Jimmy's offer."

Shouts and shrieks pursued them. Just as they set off, determined to walk all the way if necessary, the wind and rain buffeting at them, a taxi stopped at the lights. "Sod's law," said Montserrat. They got in, gasping with relief.

Yesterday's copy of the *Evening Standard* lay on the backseat. Montserrat was too affected by three vodkas and several chardonnays, too tired, she called it, to notice the *Standard*'s front page. Thea found herself trembling from the teenagers' insults, an attack she had never anticipated or considered possible. She read the piece in the paper to distract herself but without much interest in its subject. Bodies found in Epping Forest could be of no concern to her. It looked as if this one had been found by a yellow Labrador. In the absence of a picture of the corpse, the newspaper showed one of the dog.

The fox was sauntering down Hexam Place. As the taxi drew up, it squeezed through the railings at number eight and ran down the area steps of number six in the vain hope of a find comparable to that in Miss Grieves's bin. Bits of twig, plane-tree leaves the size of dinner plates, and torn plastic bags lay all over the roadway, scattered by the storm. Thea paid the driver. She tried to help Montserrat to her door but her offer was indignantly refused. Thea watched her just the same and satisfied herself that her friend was more or less in control of herself.

Number seven was in silence, all the lights off. Montserrat, in a fuddled state but well able to walk, let herself into her flat and fell onto the bed. A raging thirst drove her into the bathroom, where she drank first from the cold tap, then filled an empty wine bottle with water for the night. Funny the things you think of for no reason in the middle of the night. Her mother always said that whatever you did before you went to bed, you must without fail clean your teeth and take off your makeup with cleansing cream and astringent. Montserrat hadn't any astringent, had never possessed any, and the cleansing cream was all used up. She dropped her clothes on the floor and fell onto the bed for the second time, sinking at once into a deep sleep.

According to the green figures on the digital clock, it was 2:37 when she woke up. It might have been thirst that woke her or a footfall in the passage outside. She drank without putting the light on, thought, Must be Ciaran, maybe he said he'd come, and rolled back into half-sleep. The darkness was dense, thick like black velvet. Ciaran got into bed beside her, smelling unlike himself of some expensive male cologne. It made such a pleasant change that she turned over into his arms.

Neither of them spoke for half an hour, during which time Montserrat drifted in and out of sleep. Whatever had happened, and it was quite involved and complicated, it was unlike any previous experience of hers for at least the past year. She felt the face that was close to hers, the arms wrapped round her, then put her hands inside the open neck of his shirt. The skin was thickly furred, a forest of hair, in complete contrast to the smooth chest of Ciaran.

"Oh, my God, Preston," said Montserrat, and fell immediately asleep once more.

15

THE STUDLEYS AT number eleven, the Neville-Smiths at number five, and Arsad Sohrab and Bibi Lambda at number four all had their Sunday and their weekday papers delivered. The others fetched them from Choudhuri's, the newsagent's, known as the corner shop, though it was not on a corner but halfway along Ebury Lane, or went without. Thea fetched the papers (the *Sunday Times* and the *Sunday Telegraph*) for Roland and Damian, June for the Princess and herself (the *Mail on Sunday*), Jimmy for Simon Jefferson (the *Observer* and the *Independent on Sunday*), and Montserrat (also the *Sunday Times*) for the Stills when she was fit to walk up the street.

That Sunday morning Montserrat had a headache but nothing worse than that. She got up, wondering if she had dreamt Preston's visit of the night before. But, no, she could still smell that Hugo Boss scent, and two coarse, dark hairs lay on the pillow next to hers. Hexam Place was deserted as was usual on a Sunday. Winter had come. Frost was on the windscreen of the Neville-Smiths' Mercedes. Gussie, visible on the drawing-room windowsill of number six, was wearing his quilted coat. Montserrat made her way down to Ebury Lane. Mr. Choudhuri had put the papers out onto the street, the quality ones looking discreet on the top shelf of the rack and the red tops blatant below. In spite of her saying she would never look at the *Mirror* or the *Star*, it was one of their headlines that first caught her eye: IS EPPING FOREST BODY MR. FORTESCUE? She stood there, reading it and the story beneath it, turned the page to see a full-page spread of a forest scene with upturned soil, police, and a police car.

"I hope you are buying that paper, Miss Montsy." Mr. Choudhuri had been standing just inside the door, watching her. "Not just having a free look."

"Yes. Sure I am. And the *Sunday Times*."

"If that is for Mr. Still, there is no need. Already he has been here and bought his." Mr. Choudhuri looked at his watch. "It is, after all, ten minutes to midday."

As if it were any business of his what time she got up or came for the paper. The story, which she began to read as soon as she got back, was just like all stories of bodies being found in woodland and open spaces. Foul play was suspected. There would be an inquest. The difference was that most of the other bodies had not been those of celebrities as familiar to the nation's television viewers as their own family members. On an inside page was a photograph of Rad Sothern wearing a white coat with a stethoscope hanging round his neck, although the body had not yet been confirmed as his.

Across the street at number eight Damian and Roland sat having a prelunch sherry and reading about the discovery of the body, the former with the *Sunday Times*, the latter with the *Sunday Telegraph*. Thea had brought them the newspapers and was about to go out with Jimmy in the Lexus.

"Have you ever seen this sitcom or whatever it is this guy Sothern is in?" said Damian to Roland.

"Good heavens, no."

"I may have seen *him*. In the flesh, I mean. He seems to be a family connection or 'loved one,' as we are supposed to say these days, of someone round here. However, if there's any sort of police enquiry, I shall deny it."

"Better to keep entirely out of anything like that," said Roland. "And you should too, Thea. Don't let that friend of yours, Manzanilla or whatever she's called, draw you into it."

"Montserrat," said Thea. "Manzanilla is the sherry."

"So it is. Shall we have another glass?"

Simon Jefferson's musical horn sounded in the street below, a cadence rather like the "Last Post." Thea ran downstairs to Jimmy. No, he hadn't seen a Sunday paper, he never read papers. Why bother when you had the telly? Thea was realising how different a person can turn out to be from what you thought he was when first you tried to fall in love with him. Should she tell him about those teenagers in Regent Street last night? If she was going to get engaged to him, she ought to be able to confide in him, tell him about things that worried her.

"It was because I've got red hair," she said.

His advice disappointed her. "Just ignore it, sweetheart."

The front page of Friday's *Evening Standard*, greasy from Thai takeaway, had floated over the railings during the night and come to rest on top of the bin in the area of number eight. Miss Grieves saw it from her front window and read the headline but waited until the butter-coloured Lexus had gone before putting on her dressing gown and coming out to retrieve it. Missing persons always interested her, especially in the unlikely but possible event of their being celebrities. Newspapers were not among her regular purchases, but she intended to buy one now. It took her, as always, a long time to dress and put on the beaver lamb coat which had been her mother's and the UGG boots she had got Thea to buy for her the previous winter. These boots, reduced in the sales on account of their being pink, she had practically lived in during February and March and was now returning to with relief.

With no Thea to help her up the steps, she had to manage on her own. It was ten years since she had been to the paper shop, and when she got there—it took her a quarter of an hour—she found that it was no longer run by Mr. and Mrs. Davis but had been taken over by an Indian man. She would have found things less bewildering if the shop had been hung with Indian streamers and mass-produced statuettes of many-armed gods, but it was full of Christmas decorations, cards and wrapping paper, and artificial coniferous trees. However, the man called her "madam," which she liked, and fetched the paper of her choice, the *Sunday Telegraph*. The price appalled her but she said nothing. The cost of everything had rocketed since she had been out of the world.

Back at home she read the story, using a magnifying glass as well as her glasses. The photograph of Rad Sothern left her in no doubt. Their saying his identity hadn't been confirmed meant nothing to her. That was who it was, the same man as she had seen on her television and also seen sneaking into the basement of number seven.

NOTHING ON THE TELEVISION said whether the body was that of Rad Sothern. June sat by the phone with Gussie on her lap, waiting for the police to call her, probably Detective Sergeant Freud, to ask her to come down to this or that police station or mortuary and make an identification. They were bound to ask her as Rad's great-aunt. The Princess was spending the evening watching a rerun of the second series of *Avalon Clinic*, the steamy episodes where Mr. Fortescue got sexual with staff nurse Debbie Wilson.

When it got to nine and they hadn't phoned, June went back to the drawing room with two stiff gins. She took off Gussie's coat for the night and the Princess said, "There's no point in doing that. You'll only have to put it on again to take him out."

June sighed. She had decided it was too cold to go out, but the Princess said a dog had to have his walk no matter what the weather. "I don't know why you thought the police would phone you when that girl Rocksana is obviously his next of kin."

"I wouldn't call it next of kin," said June. "That's what I am."

Round the corner in St. Barnabas Mews she met Montserrat putting her car away.

"I'm ever so sorry, June."

"What about?"

"It was on the news just now. It *was* your grandson."

"My great-nephew."

"Comes to the same thing really, doesn't it?"

"We shall have the police round here in droves tomorrow," said June. "You needn't worry. I shan't tell them anything about you and him."

"Me and him? I only spoke to him once."

"That's the best angle to take, my dear. What I think is, it's best for everyone not to know a thing. It's different for me and the Princess of course. We were his *friends*. We're very close to Miss Castelli, as a matter of fact."

June said good-night and walked back, tugged by the now shivering Gussie. A figure descending the area steps at number seven gave her a bit of a shock. It was like seeing a ghost, only in black robes, not white. But the features that turned to her, peeping out of a dark cloth, were not a skull but the pretty face of Rabia returning from her weekend off. The Stills' nanny raised one hand in a polite gesture of greeting, dipped her head, and passed on down the steps to let herself in by the basement door.

On the other side of that door, Montserrat waited for Preston. Would he just arrive again without warning? Would the identification of the body as Rad's make any difference? Just before eleven he phoned. He would like to talk to her on a matter of business. Now? said Montserrat. Yes, now. She had taken her clothes off but she put them on again, leggings—funny how they'd come right back into fashion—and a tight dark red sweater. Waiting for him, she asked herself what he could possibly mean by business but came up with no answer. This time he tapped on the door.

He looked pale and worried. Business or not, she had been sure he would bring a bottle of wine with him but he was empty-handed. Montserrat was sitting on the bed.

"Lucy's in a dreadful state," he said, "screaming and crying over that man."

"You mean she's screaming and crying at you?"

He sat down on the one chair in the room. "Who else has she got? But I didn't come down to tell you that. They know it's Rad Sothern now, as I expect you know. Now you and I won't say a word if the police question us. We didn't know him, never saw him, and that's all it amounts to. But what about Lucy?"

"She's not going to tell them he was shagging her."

"Oh, please. Must you use that word? No, she's not going to say they were having some kind of—well, relationship, but she's afraid *he* may have told someone about *her*. After all, she's a well-known socialite. She had her picture in the *Evening Standard* only a couple of weeks ago. I don't know what you think you're laughing at."

Montserrat composed her features. "Do men do that? I mean, tell their mates?"

"Don't ask me. I don't do that sort of thing."

This time she did laugh and heartily. "Come on. What were you up to here last night, or were you sleepwalking?"

He blushed, the way she had never seen a man of forty blush before. His whole face and neck became the colour of her sweater. She shook her head, smiling at him. "Now listen. You haven't been so crazy as to tell Lucy anything about us taking Rad out to Essex and all that, have you? No? Sure?"

"Of course I haven't."

"Well, don't. If the police come here to talk to any of us, we just say we didn't know him, we never met him. June at number six, she was his great-aunt or his grandma, I don't know, but she says she won't say she saw him speak to me, she wants to keep it looking like he was faithful to that Rocksana woman. Right?"

"Right."

"There's no one else saw anything. You're not getting back with Lucy, are you?"

He shook his head. "It's too late for that. I can never forgive her."

"What's she doing now?"

"Gone to sleep. I gave her a sleeping pill."

"Then why don't you go and find a bottle of wine somewhere and come back here for the night?"

COMING OUT OF Tesco with shopping for Miss Grieves, her regular Monday-morning task before she had her first class at eleven thirty, Thea almost bumped into Henry coming out of Homebase. Henry had been buying a bolt, or rather two bolts, for his room (or studio flat as his employer called it) at number eleven. He smiled, said hi and it was a lovely day, but nothing about the bolts. Convinced that it was a good idea to have the means to make his door secure, he was worried just the same that if Lord Studley found out, he might make a fuss about damage to the woodwork. All the doors on the upper floors of number eleven were made of beautiful tropical hardwoods, and even those in the basement were similarly panelled, painted ivory, and had brass fingerplates. But for his peace of mind he could no longer risk Huguette coming to his room or, come to that, her mother coming to his room while Huguette was there, without adequate safety measures being taken.

It would do no harm for Thea to know, but still, *better safe than sorry* was an excellent maxim. He had walked to the shops from Hexam Place, leaving the Beemer on the Residents' Parking. Another thing Lord Studley made a fuss about was his car being used for anything but fetching and carrying himself and his family. He was no Simon Jefferson, Henry often thought ruefully. He might just as well use the few hours before returning to pick up his lordship from the Peers' Entrance in putting the new bolts on his door. Then, later on, there was yet another extraordinary general meeting of the St. Zita Society.

Its purpose, Thea was recalling as she banged hard on the basement door, was to discuss what was to be done about the exclusion of the "staff" from Damian and Roland's guest list. Miss Grieves came, shuffling along in the UGG boots she wouldn't take off again till the spring, maybe not even at night, Thea thought. She handed over the lighter bag of shopping and brought the other in herself.

As was often the case, Miss Grieves was ready with a question expecting the answer no. "You don't want a cup of tea, do you?"

The state of the cups, chipped, cracked, and, when the home help had paid a rare visit, stained with dark crimson lipstick, always ensured Thea's refusal. She sat down briefly on the edge of a chair. "Didn't you once tell me you'd been in service, Miss Grieves?"

"Nothing wrong in that, I hope. They're a bunch of bloody snobs round here."

"Nothing wrong at all. Quite the reverse. I thought I'd propose you for the St. Zita Society." Thea explained, describing it as a kind of combination of a union and social club. Miss Grieves said she didn't mind, her usual rejoinder when she liked the idea of something very much. Then she said, "How d'you get hold of the police? I want to complain about the bloody foxes."

Thea knew she was lying. "Look in the phone book," Thea said because she couldn't exactly not answer. She even fetched the directory for Miss Grieves, rooting it out from under a stack of old magazines. The date on the top one was April 1947.

16

THE CONSPIRACY IN Hexam Place that none of the "staff" would say a word about seeing Rad Sothern make his secret way into number seven gave Montserrat confidence. If there were no untoward developments, if no police interest was shown in the Still household, Preston would go ahead with the divorce, not as speedily of course as if there were no children, but helped on its way by his being a rich man. Money always expedited these things. It would be a no-fault divorce so that Rad's name need not be brought into it.

It would be best for Preston to move out and into that flat he had talked about. She didn't quite trust him so near to Lucy. While he had said last night that he could never forgive Lucy, he had shown signs of sympathy for her. Montserrat had decided that she would marry him. She didn't love him or even like him very much. He was too hairy to be attractive to her and too pompous as well, too stuffy with his long words and his *Macbeth* quotes. But she would marry him. He must be grateful to her, she had saved his life or saved him from years of jail. Lucy was thought beautiful by a lot of people, but she was beginning to look worn. Besides, she was thirty-six and Montserrat was twenty-two.

Lucy had money of her own from her rich father so Preston wouldn't have to give her so much. She would get the children, a good idea as far as Montserrat was concerned. She'd let Preston see them whenever he liked. It was best to look facts in the face, and this marriage she contemplated would hardly last long. She might even fix a period of time for it—say four years. She would still only be twenty-six and be as beautiful as Lucy by that time what with all the cosmetic surgery and facials and body toning and designer clothes she'd have paid for with Preston's money.

Her next step was to make a change in the kind of meetings they had. Permanent relationships were not grounded on sneaking into a girl's bedroom after dark and disappearing again at dawn. She would have to get him to take her out to expensive restaurants and, later, away for weekends. One place they would never go to was Gallowmill Hall.

Her friendship with Thea, once so enriching (as Thea had put it) for both, had now dwindled to almost nonexistence. Her friend was always somewhere with Jimmy. If Jimmy and Thea's relationship became a permanency, Montserrat decided that she and Preston would not number them among their friends. Preston wouldn't want to know someone's driver, or "chauffeur" as he called it. The day was fine and bright if cold, and Montserrat was making up her mind to go shopping to Kensington High Street—Sloane Street being beyond her means at present—to get her hair done, buy some clothes and makeup, when the landline rang. Not Preston then. He would have used her mobile. Another of those premonitions she knew meant nothing came to her.

The voice, very unlike Preston's or that of any man she intended to associate with in future, said, "Miss Tresser?"

"Yes."

"This is Detective Constable Colin Rickards. I'd like to come and see you if I may."

Montserrat asked what this was about, disgusted with herself for speaking in a small, squeaky voice. Why don't we leave that till I get to see you, said Rickards, and Montserrat hadn't quite the nerve to say she'd like to know now. But she did try to get in touch with Preston. The woman who answered his phone knew she wasn't Lucy; with Lucy's voice she seemed familiar. Mr. Still was in a meeting, she said, and when Montserrat said it was urgent, she told her it was a *board* meeting. She wouldn't have believed this Rickards could have got here so quickly and come to the front door, though she'd asked him to the basement. The chance of Lucy answering the front door was highly unlikely, but Rabia might, and though Montserrat raced up the basement stairs, Rabia *had* answered it. Thomas was in her arms, and Rickards, a small, thin, ginger-haired man, was praising him to the skies.

"Your youngster?" he said to Montserrat.

Her headshake was almost a shudder. But it was a natural mistake. He could hardly have thought Thomas, with his golden curls and milk-white skin, was Rabia's. But now he would know about Lucy's existence. Did that matter? She took him down to her flat.

"You the tenant of this flat?" was the first thing he asked.

"I'm the au pair," said Montserrat, "and a friend of the family."

He looked in his notebook. "And also a friend of Mr. Rad Sothern, I understand."

"Who told you that?" She was sure none of the "staff" in the street would have said a word. Thea had promised they wouldn't. Surely Lucy wouldn't be so treacherous when it was she whose lover Rad had been. . . .

"I can't tell you that," said Rickards. "I can say you've been seen speaking to him and admitting him to this house."

Outright denial was what it had to be. "I spoke to him once," said Montserrat firmly. "I was coming out of the basement door"—

she waved her hand in that direction—"and he was passing and he asked me the way to Sloane Square."

"Really?"

"Yes, really. And if that's all . . ."

"That's not all, Miss Tresser. What's your first name, by the way?" She told him.

"That's a name I've never heard before. Where's that come from? Asia, is it?"

"It's Spanish. I'm half-Spanish."

"Amazing, isn't it? People come from all over now, don't they? All four corners of the earth, you might say. When did this meeting with Mr. Sothern take place then? When he asked you the way?"

"I don't know. I can't remember something like that."

"Let me help you. Would it have been November fifth, Bonfire Night?"

"It might have been," said Montserrat, using the phrase favoured by petty crooks of all kinds.

"I'm asking, you see," said Rickards, a sudden burst of sunshine breaking through the window turning his ginger hair to red-gold, "because that was the last time Mr. Sothern was seen alive. He had visited his great-auntie at number six and then came across here. That's why it seems strange to me that he had to ask you where Sloane Square was instead of his auntie." Momentarily, he shut his eyes against the bright light and shifted his chair out of the sun. "It seems even stranger to me that Mr. Sothern didn't know where Sloane Square was when before he moved to Montagu Square, he lived for two years in the King's Road."

Montserrat said defiantly that she couldn't help that. That was what he said.

"Now, are you sure you wouldn't like to think about it for a few minutes and then tell me what really happened between you and Mr. Sothern?"

"I've told you what really happened."

"Because, you see, Mr. Sothern was never seen by anyone after he spoke to you and, according to our information, came into this house by the basement door."

"I can't help that."

"Then perhaps you can tell me if Mr. Sothern was friendly with anyone else living here."

"I don't know any more than I've told you," said Montserrat. "Can I ask you something?"

"That depends on what it is."

She asked if people got at him, *mocked* was the word she used, because of his ginger hair.

"Of course not," he said stiffly, and left, saying in an ominous sort of way that he would want to see her again.

Montserrat tried once more to call Preston, and this time he came to the phone. "You didn't tell him anything, did you?"

"I told him I'd spoken to Rad once but he didn't believe me. Who d'you think can have told him they saw me talking to him and letting him into the house?"

"I don't know why you ever agreed to do what Lucy wanted and conduct him through the house to her room. It was treachery to me."

"Being a psychopomp," said Montserrat, who had recalled the word. "Lucy was my friend, not you. Before you start blaming me, you want to remember that I haven't done anything wrong. I didn't push anyone down the stairs, I just helped you."

"All right, Montsy, all right. I know. Are the police going to talk to me?"

"They didn't say. I didn't mention you, of course I didn't. I hope I know the meaning of loyalty."

Preston said he knew that. He hardly knew how he could have managed without her. "You'll want to know that I'm moving out this evening and into my new flat in Westminster. Meet me there, will you? We'll go out to eat. It's twenty-five Medway Manor Court."

LUCY CRIED A LOT. She spent a large part of every day howling and sobbing. Rabia heard it from the nursery floor and worried because Thomas also heard it and said so. "Mummy cry."

What could she say? "Poor Mummy cut her finger."

After it had gone on intermittently for days, Rabia went downstairs while Thomas was having his afternoon sleep and found Lucy in the drawing room. She looked quite unlike herself. Tears had washed away her makeup and her hair hadn't been washed at all.

"Can I bring you a cup of tea?" Or provide something more needful. "Maybe run you a nice bath?"

"I don't want anything. My heart is broken."

"Thomas was unhappy. I have told him you cut your finger."

"He has nothing to be unhappy about. I'm the unhappy one." Lucy scrubbed her eyes with her fists. "My husband has moved out. He means to sell the house. What am I going to live on?"

Rabia felt something turn over inside her, an upheaval like a child shifting in the womb. She said the reverse of what she thought and believed: "Everything will be all right. The children will be yours whatever happens."

"How can I look after them on my own?"

Rabia dared say, "I shall be with you," and added, "Shan't I?"

"How do I know? Maybe I can't afford you. All he tells me is that I have betrayed him and he can never trust me again. He never thinks how he was out night after night, never at home with me. What did he expect me to do?"

Rabia knew the answer but couldn't utter it. She heard the school bus draw up outside and excused herself to run out into the hall and let Hero and Matilda in. Nausea had risen in her throat, and with it a dreadful feeling of fullness, though she had eaten nothing all day but a sandwich with Thomas at lunchtime. She was conscious all the time of the weight of that cigarette case in her pocket.

Matilda glared at the drawing-room door. "Thank God she's stopped that racket," she said like a woman three times her age.

WHEN SHE WAS the second Mrs. Preston Still, thought Montserrat, as she came up the escalator at St. James's Park station, she would never travel in the tube again. Taxis for her or even a replacement for the VW if they lived in a place where the Residents' Parking was satisfactory. She caught a glimpse of herself reflected in a shop window in Victoria Street and felt pleased with what she saw. What beautiful hair she had, a glossy dark cloak of it falling in ripples over her shoulders. There was no doubt she should wear makeup more often, especially crimson lip-gloss. Who would believe her eyelashes were her own, entirely natural? But no harm in that. Her weight loss showed. She must keep up the noneating and the shunning of spirits. Passing a stack of *Evening Standard*s, she picked up one and walked along reading the front page and smoking a cigarette. Another picture of Rad with Rocksana, a new picture of Rad with his previous girlfriend, but nothing, luckily, of or about Rad and Lucy.

The expected kiss from Preston never came. His "Hi, there" was offhand in the extreme, but after a moment or two of looking her up and down, he did say, "You look very nice." The flat was minimalist, not to say stark, the floor part laminated wood, part marble. It felt hot but looked cold. Preston had already laid in a stock of spirits and aperitifs, and in spite of her resolution she accepted a Campari-soda. Campari wasn't spirits, was it?

"I got in touch with the police. I thought it wise. In fact it was. They were very courteous. I said I would be happy to talk to them and they came here. A carrot-topped fellow. He's not long gone, as a matter of fact."

"What did you say about Rad?"

"That I'd never met him. He'd never been in the house. I knew

142

nothing about your friends, I said. Your father was a friend of my wife's father, I said, and that was all I knew of you."

"Thanks a bunch," said Montserrat.

"Surely there was no harm in that. Isn't it best if we seem hardly to know each other? Especially now I'm living over here. This chap Rickards didn't seem to want to talk to me again. It may well be that by this time they've talked to other people who claimed to have talked to Sothern after you did."

"But they didn't," said Montserrat. "Nobody could have talked to him. He never came out of your house alive, right? Remember? You kicked him downstairs and it killed him."

"For heaven's sake," said Preston, looking this way and that as if he feared police spies lurking behind the floor-length iridescent curtains. "What's the point of saying things like that? It was an accident anyway, you know that. Shall we go out and eat?"

Not to Shepherd's in Marsham Street, as she had hoped, but a poky little Italian restaurant off the Horseferry Road. There was no temptation to eat much. Once they had exhausted the subject of Rad Sothern's disappearance and the newspapers' verdict on it, Montserrat realised they had nothing to say to each other. She hadn't been in love with Ciaran or any of his predecessors, but they could communicate, have a bit of a giggle, talk about a film they'd seen or music they liked. Preston just sat there, his expression set, unsmiling, his mouth turned down at the corners. She'd read the term *po-faced* somewhere and hadn't known what it meant. She knew now. But she would marry him. The process had begun and would continue every day. Outide the restaurant she was afraid he would suggest she go home and put her into a taxi, but, no, she'd come back with him, wouldn't she? When they got there, he opened a bottle of wine and put on a CD. She didn't recognise the music but, by its turgid tunelessness and lack of any sort of beat, she could tell it was classical. He started talking again about the police and what they might suspect and whether they would come back, but when she asked him about Lucy and if she had confessed to the affair with Rad, he snubbed her.

"We don't have to discuss that."

On the dot of eleven he said that if she would like to get into bed, he would join her in ten minutes. No man had ever before spoken to her like that. She wanted to tell him she didn't believe it and what planet was he living on, but instead she told herself yet again that she would marry him, and off she went meekly enough. In the night he woke up, sat up, and began talking to himself. Most of what he said was a mumble except for one clear sentence.

"It was an accident!"

17

APART FROM THANKSGIVING dinner for the Kleins, who were Americans, at the last house in the street, it was otherwise not a special day in Hexam Place except for the November meeting of the St. Zita Society in the Dugong. The principal item on the agenda was the absence from Damian and Roland's guest list of any member of the "staff." Thea had of course been asked.

"But I'm not a servant," said Thea.

Jimmy had proposed to her earlier in the day while having lunch with her, but Thea had said she didn't know, she would have to think about it. He appeared to have taken it for granted that she would rush to accept and was accordingly enormously upset. He had brought his late mother's engagement ring with him rather like Prince William, and now he would have to take it away again.

"It's no use you getting in a state. I don't like the idea of marriage. But I'll think about it and now you'll have to go because I've got to go downstairs and see about Miss Grieves."

Proud of what she had done, Miss Grieves, lighting a cigarette for herself and one for Thea, told her how she had given the police an account of the times she had seen Montserrat talking to Rad Sothern and admitting him to number seven. She agreed to come with Thea to the St. Zita meeting and seemed to regard it as a reward for her achievement as a police informer. June took the chair and Montserrat was also there, unaware of Miss Grieves's part in the discovery of Rad's running to earth in the area of number seven. Beacon hadn't come, being occupied in driving Mr. Still home to Medway Manor Court. Sondra was there and Henry, and Dex, silent in a corner, the only member of the society to drink Guinness, the tall black glass with its crown of creamy foam particularly appropriate this evening when his head and face, furred with luxuriant dark hair and beard, were topped with a whitish knitted tam-o'-shanter.

When Thea had given the society an enthusiastic account of Miss Grieves's early years as a maid-of-all-work in the Elystan Place home of Lady Pimble and the new member had unanimously been accepted, they discussed what June called "the sorry business" of Damian and Roland's snobbish and exclusive conduct.

"You could boycott the event," Jimmy said to Thea. "You and Montserrat."

"Boycotting it won't make them ask all the rest of you." Thea spoke roughly and as if she wanted to add, *you fool*, though she didn't. Jimmy was hurt, a familiar feeling now. He was thinking about the early days of their courtship, no more than weeks away, and wondering what he had done wrong apart from being himself. Perhaps it was that which was wrong and she was just realising it. She was a lot cleverer than he was. He thought of her as an intellectual.

"Even if we were a union," said June in a rather sad voice, "we couldn't make people ask other people to a party." She brought out the phrase she had carefully learnt. "And if we could, it would only create a precedent."

The agenda was going nowhere. "Any Other Business" was sometimes a fruitful area for discussion, but today the only item of any interest was Dex's declining work. He was too shy to raise the subject himself but had made a prearrangement for Jimmy to tell the meeting how Dex had been threatened with dismissal by the Neville-Smiths and turned away by Mr. Sohrab and Ms. Lambda. Nothing was wrong with his work, but the recession had bitten so hard that everyone was short of money these days.

"Me too," Dex interrupted. "Aren't I short?"

June intervened to say that the St. Zita Society wasn't a union. With a frown that furrowed his forehead into ridges and ruts like a ploughed field, Jimmy went on to say that Dexter also had a "gentleman's agreement" with the would-be vendors of number ten, empty now for six months, to keep the garden and lawn tidy, "which they reneged on," said Jimmy.

"Well, you know what I always say," said Richard, "a gentleman's agreement isn't worth the paper it's written on."

When the laughter from those who hadn't heard the old joke before subsided, it was agreed that Dexter should advertise his services in Mr. Choudhuri's shop window. Meanwhile, Thea proposed that he should do a couple of hours a week for herself and the other residents of number eight. As soon as the words were out, she began worrying what Damian and Roland would say. Suppose they refused to pay him and left it down to her?

When the society members came out into Hexam Place, the Thanksgiving guests were leaving in taxis or their own cars. Walking a few paces behind, Dex followed Montserrat to the nearest tube station. Montserrat ought to have waited for him so that they could walk together, but she didn't want to, she didn't want passersby to see her with him and maybe think they were friends or even worse.

Preston hadn't invited her. She had invited herself and he had said, "I suppose so." She wanted him to give her a key. "In case you're not back."

"I expect I shall be," he said. "You don't need a key."

Not long and he would ask her to move in with him. Then she

would have a key. Perhaps she ought to ask Preston if he'd have Dex work for him—well, work for Lucy and the kids, do the garden at number seven. He and Lucy always said the garden was a mess but never did anything about it.

"Why should I?" was Preston's initial response. "I'm not even living there anymore. I don't care if it looks like a hayfield. Besides, he's mad. Someone told me he tried to kill his mother."

"He was let off," said Montserrat. "He was unfit to plead or something." She thought it would be unwise to say that Preston had not only tried but succeeded in killing Rad Sothern.

His face turned away from her, Preston studied the *Evening Standard*, which he had brought in with him. For several days there had been nothing about Rad Sothern except an article predicting the producers of *Avalon Clinic*'s plans for the future. But tonight there was a further rehash of Sothern's past, it looked like from where she sat, an examination of his childhood and early youth, his previous television roles.

"He had a harem of women," Preston said suddenly. "It was you brought him into my house. You'd been one of them, I suppose. And you brought him into my house. To meet my wife."

"Lucy met him at a party at the Princess's."

"That's your story."

Montserrat said nothing. Quarrelling with him must be avoided. He got up and poured himself another glass of wine, then, as if on second thought, refilled her glass. "Aren't you soon going to Barcelona?"

"I was. I've changed my mind." She wasn't going to tell him it would be unwise to go when things had got to this stage between them. "Do you think the police will leave you alone now?"

"I hope so. I haven't done anything and they know that very well."

Any minute now and he would ask her to go to bed and say

he would follow her. It was hardly romantic, but you can't expect romance from someone you'd been associated with the way they had. She waited, half-smiling, sweeping back her long, dark curls with one carefully manicured hand. Instead he said, "You must give me an undertaking you won't talk to the police if they come again."

"I don't want to talk to them."

"Don't." He folded up the paper. "If they ask you, just say you know nothing. You've told them everything you know." He got up, took a step towards her. Was he going to *kiss* her? He wasn't. "I'll call you a taxi. I don't suppose you want to get in the tube at this time of night."

CHRISTMAS TREES FROM the Belgrave Nursery were a little more than twice as expensive as those from a typical garden centre, but most of the residents of Hexam Place were untroubled by matters such as that. This year Mr. Siddiqui was taking orders in early November and promising his daughter that Khalid would personally be delivering the tree for number seven.

"It's nothing to me, Father, who delivers the tree. It is just that Mrs. Still would like a fine big one to make fun for the children. No one else in the street has small children so she should have the best."

In truth, Lucy had expressed no opinion on the size or quality of the Christmas tree or even said she wanted one. Rabia had asked her if she should buy one of these festive conifers and Lucy had said, "Oh, do as you like. I don't care."

Why Christian children enjoyed looking at a Norway spruce hung with glass ornaments and packed around with presents, silver strings woven through its branches and a fairy doll on top, Rabia had never understood. That was of no importance. All that mattered was that Thomas should gaze and clap his hands and laugh.

Lucy had followed up her indifferent comment on the Christmas tree by one equally dismissive. "It will be the last one they ever have, I expect. The kind of flat we shall be able to afford won't have room for luxuries like that."

Rabia pushed Thomas in his buggy up to look at his favourite tropical fish. Khalid was there, setting out on display pots full of red and white poinsettias. In spite of what she had just said to her father, she found herself looking properly at Khalid for perhaps the first time. He was good-looking, and more than that to her, he had a kind face, the firm, red mouth always ready with a smile. His eyes were bright and keen.

"Good morning to you, Mrs. Ali, and how are you today?"

There was no need to snub him. What harm had he done her? "Good morning, Mr. Iqbal."

Her thoughts she could never put into words, but she could think them. If I were to marry and have a baby boy of my own, a healthy one with no troubles that would take him to an early death, would I be able to forget Thomas? Were there any substitutes for someone much loved? Perhaps. But not if the substitute didn't yet exist, if it was only a doubtful dream.

She need commit herself to nothing. To become friends with a man—in one's father's presence, of course—was a long way from promising to be his wife. As she began pushing Thomas back to the main building where her father was, she thought of Nazir, her husband, who had been kind if demanding, but the memory of him was already growing vague while she could see her children before her eyes as if they were there, walking along the path ahead of her—her two dead children with Thomas between them now he could walk so well. Lucy had always been kind to her, but while she knew that Khalid was reliable and honest and Mr. Still too probably, Lucy might say to her on a Tuesday that Rabia was so good with the children they couldn't get on without her, and on a Wednesday, "Oh, darling, we're moving out tomorrow and you'll have to leave."

Would Lucy? She might. Outside the door to her father's office, she picked Thomas up, hugged him tightly, then carried him inside to where Abram Siddiqui sat behind his desk.

"This big boy is too heavy for you, my daughter. Put him down. Let him walk about the room."

"We shall not stay long, Father," said Rabia, but she put Thomas down and watched him make his still-unsteady way across the carpet to a display of violently coloured seed packets, fortunately just out of his reach. "I came to ask you to invite Mr. Iqbal to tea when I come next Sunday. No, you must not look like that. It is nothing, it is just getting to know someone a little better."

The newspapers had carried no mention of interviews held with suspects "helping the police with their enquiries." Perhaps there were no enquiries. Sondra maintained that she had seen Detective Sergeant Freud and Detective Constable Rickards twice call at Miss Grieves's flat, but these calls had no perceptible consequences. Asking Montserrat's guidance as to whether she should accept Jimmy (to which she received a very positive "Don't you dare!"), Thea, perhaps not liking to be so violently dictated to, said that Miss Grieves had once again seen the redheaded detective talking to Montserrat on the basement doorstep of number seven.

"That's a lie for a fucking start," said Montserrat, more savagely than the statement warranted.

"All right. Calm down. You want to watch your mouth. I must have been mistaken. No doubt you know dozens of guys of about thirty with orange hair."

"No doubt that old bat's a mental case. She must be a hundred years old."

So relations between the two became strained. Thea might have accepted her friend's advice and said no to Jimmy, but Montserrat's violent reaction to a simple observation made her change her mind, and during an outing in the Lexus that afternoon, Thea told him rather grudgingly that she wouldn't mind getting engaged. The ring that Jimmy had been carrying about for days in his pocket was much prettier than she had expected.

She needed a boost after the snub she had received from Roland. Telling him that she had suggested to Dex that he might do some work at number eight met with a chilly "You did what?"

"He's really quite good at what he does and he does need the money."

"Damian and I are not a charitable trust," said Roland, and Thea lacked the nerve to remind him that at present she did the gardening for nothing.

But what Miss Grieves had said was not a lie. DC Rickards had been at number seven and not just on the doorstep but inside. Montserrat remembered what Preston had said and told the policeman she knew no more and had nothing more to say.

"Tell me something," said Rickards as if she hadn't spoken. "If Mr. Sothern came in this house and it wasn't to see you, why did he use the basement door?"

"To get in," she said, forgetting he wasn't supposed to have come in at all but only to have stood outside and asked the way to Sloane Square.

"So he did come in, but not to see you. If he came to see someone else, why not use the front door?"

"He didn't come in and he didn't use any door and I'm not saying any more."

She realised that she had gone too far, said too much, when she had promised Preston to say nothing. It was four days since she had seen him or even heard from him. Was she to see him now? Perhaps it would be a good idea to tell him of the conversation she had just had with Colin Rickards. It might frighten him. He had to learn he couldn't treat her like this, sleep with her when it suited him, take her out for a crappy meal, then ignore her for days.

She had to leave a message with him on his voice mail. How many other people would hear it? She didn't care. He took twenty-four hours to call her back.

18

T O BECOME ENGAGED was one thing, to let everyone know
it quite another. As it happened, Jimmy's mother's ring was
far too big for Thea. The woman must have had enormous hands.
Thea said it wouldn't be right for Jimmy to have it made smaller,
surely one's mother's ring was sacred and shouldn't be tampered
with.

"We don't have to have a ring to be engaged." It was the sort of
thing you said to a child. She had a sense of déjà vu and remembered
when, aged nine, she got a new tea set and said to her friend that
they didn't have to have real tea in the cups.

Jimmy seemed content. "I'll get you a super wedding ring."

Her heart sank a little but moved up a few millimetres when
he said, "I'm really sorry I won't be able to come to Damian and
Roland's civil partnership. I've got a ticket for Arsenal playing at
home."

Along with the other "servants" they hadn't invited him. Now
she wouldn't have to explain. She imagined the future civil partners'
reaction if they heard that he called them by their given names.
Sooner or later one or the other of them (maybe both) would get a
knighthood, men in their position always did, and then woe betide
anyone who didn't call them sir.

Would she ever marry Jimmy? Quite possibly she would, simply to avoid trouble, the way she avoided trouble by doing all Damian and Roland's small chores for them, by getting Miss Grieves's shopping, by paying the Belgrave Nursery to plant all those flowers to make the house look lovely, and getting no reimbursement or thanks for it.

ON SUNDAY PRESTON had his children for the day, and when he brought them back in a taxi at six in the evening, Montserrat, making an intelligent guess as to his timing, was waiting for him. She let him in before he could get his key out, and when he had left the children with their mother, Thomas screaming for Rabia, who was still at her father's, she asked him to come down to her flat.

From the start she handled it badly. She had dressed herself up for him in a miniskirt and low-cut top, too-high heels, and that dark red lipstick she had thought so flattering. With earrings like chandeliers and a triple string of pearls bought in the Portobello Road, she was dressed for a party, not a Sunday night in front of the television. And she was nervous as she waited for him to join her, fidgeting, pacing up and down. He walked in without knocking. But perhaps to knock would have been a sign of formality. She would have liked him to have put his arms round her, called her by some endearment, though she knew better than to expect it.

She opened the bottle of white wine she had forgotten to put in the fridge. "Preston, I think I must have missed your calls. Actually I did get a missed call come up on my mobile, but I didn't recognise the number."

"It wasn't me." He took a sip of his wine, made a face, and pushed it a few inches across the table, a sure sign he wanted to drink no more of it.

She tried to gather up her courage. Although she knew she must always unconsciously have felt this way, she realised she was afraid of him. It took a lot of nerve to say what she had to say. An urge charged through her to take off those stupid pearls, but she squashed it. He would only think she was starting to strip.

"I thought we were having a relationship." There, she had said it. "I thought you sleeping with me was the start of it."

He didn't seem the least embarrassed or indignant or angry or anything at all really. He just looked at her, the pale gray eyes staring. She noticed for the first time that the whites of his eyes showed all the way round the irises. Surely that wasn't common, she didn't know anyone else like that.

"I'm still married," he said.

"You were married when you slept with me. You were married when you asked me to your flat."

"As far as I'm concerned," he said, watching her drink the warm wine, "you and I were associated in a kind of enterprise. You know what I refer to. I was grateful for your help."

"Is that all?"

"What else is there? I don't need to go into details, we both know what happened. There was an accident. You persuaded me—frankly, against my better judgement—not to call the police. No doubt you meant it for the best. I have my own views on that. Any relationship, as you call it, between us must be over if it ever began."

Anger throbbed inside her head. "If it wasn't for me, you'd be in prison by now, d'you realise that?"

"Oh, I doubt it. It was an accident. You seemed to forget that."

Why had he stopped calling her by her first name? The last time they'd met he'd called her Montsy. Somehow she knew he never would again, unless she did something, took positive steps. "It's not too late for me to go to the police now."

He shook his head, got out of his chair, and walked to the window. Once more he looked big, tall, heavily built, strong. Perhaps only in her imagination he had gone pale. "And tell them what? You're as much involved as I am, remember."

"I never touched him. I didn't push him down the stairs. You want to remember I could turn queen's evidence." Could she? Did it even exist anymore? "I could say you forced me, you threatened me. I could make a plea bargain." Was there such a thing outside of America or the movies?

"And just what proof would you have for any of this?"

She had given these details almost no thought, but now they came to her as if they had been lying just below the surface of her mind, waiting for use. "Suppose I told them to go to Gallowmill Hall and in the luggage room to look for a car-roof carrying case. They'd find Rad Sothern's DNA all over the inside, hairs and fibres from his clothes." What a godsend in situations such as this were the detective and mystery dramas on television, teaching one about police procedure and search warrants and forensics. "They'd find blood from where he hit his head and maybe dust and whatever from that floor."

She had drawn him into it against his will. "And how would they know the case was yours?"

"I can prove it. Henry Copley, who drives for Lord Studley, sold it to me."

She was sitting on the bed and he came and sat beside her. "Look, Montsy, you don't mean anything of this, you know you don't. It was a joke, wasn't it?"

It seemed that the positive steps had paid off, yet suddenly she felt near to tears. "It wasn't a joke but it could be one. I don't want to go to the police. I hate the idea." The tears didn't come. She had stopped them without touching her eyes, stopped them by an effort of will. "Take me out to dinner, Preston. Please. We can talk about all this. We've never really talked about it. And then we can come back here afterwards."

"All right," he said, "if that's what you want."

———

SINCE HENRY HAD put the bolts on the door, Huguette had several times come to his room. It was easy for her, almost as easy as to have him come to her flat, for all she had to do was pick a day when she was visiting her parents and, after saying good-bye to them and leaving the house, slip down the area steps and be admitted by Henry. Then he slid the bolts across.

It gave him a severe shock when he heard footsteps on the tiled passage and saw his door handle turn. Whoever it was (as Huguette put it) went away after trying again.

"Doesn't my dad knock on the door? Does he just expect to walk in?"

Henry couldn't say it wasn't her father but her mother.

"If you'd only let me tell him we're engaged."

We're not, thought Henry. "It wouldn't do for him to find you here."

"I don't understand why you can't have your privacy. It's mediaeval just walking in here without knocking, it's treating you like a slave."

Henry started laughing. "That's why he won't let you marry me. Because I'm a slave." His mobile was ringing. He reached for it. "Very good, my lord. Ten minutes' time at the Peers' Entrance."

She seemed not to realise that if it was her father on the phone in the House of Lords, it couldn't have been her father outside the door five minutes before.

THE SEMIDETACHED HOUSE in Acton owned by Abram Siddiqui, his mortgage now paid off, was to Rabia a far more comfortable place to be than number seven Hexam Place. But number seven contained Thomas, and number fifteen Grenville Road, Acton, did not. She worried about Thomas while he was away from her and with his mother or his father. Mr. Still no doubt loved his children, but it seemed to Rabia that the only way he knew to show love was by finding spots on their faces.

She would have disliked it if Khalid Iqbal had shown anything approaching love, but his behaviour had been exemplary. He had arrived at the precise time he said he would, spoken to her with great politeness, and not, of course, attempted to shake hands with her. No man had ever touched her but her father and her late husband. Mr. Iqbal accepted a cup of tea and just one of the sugary cakes provided by Rabia's father, but refused to take a second. Perhaps Abram Siddiqui had told him how much she disliked greed. Mr. Iqbal talked entertainingly about the Christmas-tree trade at the Belgrave Nursery and the new lines they were offering for the first time: pink poinsettias, an innovation; holly wreaths; and amaryllis, tall plants with improbably bold and beautiful flowers borne in pairs on a succulent stem.

The conversation turned to the family, and an explanation was given, quite lucid and easy to follow, of the ramifications of the Siddiqui-Iqbal-Ali clan and exactly what was the precise relationship between Khalid and Rabia. Not too close, she was glad to note, and as she noted it, she asked herself what she was thinking of. It could mean nothing to her if he was her third cousin once removed. He rose to go after three-quarters of an hour, made her a little bow, and left, saying what a pleasure it had been to meet her away from business matters.

"I think you liked him, my daughter," said her father as they watched Khalid's tall, upright figure pass the window, heading for the bus stop.

"He's very nice, Father. I always knew he was very nice."

"I have a feeling he would make a good husband. I have a gift for detecting these things, you know."

"For some other lucky woman," she said, smiling.

As he always did when she had been visiting him at home, her father drove her back to Hexam Place. She went in by way of the basement door and heard Mr. Still's voice coming from Montserrat's flat but she thought nothing of it. Hers was not a suspicious nature. The children were with Lucy, the girls watching television in the morning room, Thomas lying on the sofa, fretfully half-asleep. It was ten o'clock.

It was a good feeling to have four people pleased to see you. Hero and Matilda were tired and bored with their programme. Rabia was someone new to talk to and always interested in their activities. Thomas woke up, jumped off the sofa, and ran to her. Lucy was simply relieved.

"Oh, God, you don't know how pleased I am to see you. It's been a nightmare. This little demon has been giving me hell."

"Never mind," said Rabia. "We'll go upstairs now and leave you in peace."

"There's been a man here wanting a job clearing up the garden. Deck or Dex something. I told him he should ask Mr. Still, but he didn't seem to understand Preston isn't living here."

Rabia said nothing about hearing Mr. Still's voice downstairs. "Yes, I know Dex. Montserrat knows more about him than I do. I'll ask her, shall I?"

"Oh, please do, darling. You're such an angel. What would I do without you? I don't dare think of it."

Those were welcome words. Like a magic spell they banished her fears even though she knew how unreliable Lucy was. "I'll speak to Dex or Montserrat will and give him Mr. Still's address. Would that be the best thing?"

"Of course it would. Absolutely. And now I'm so exhausted I really must rest."

Rabia had felt the weight of the cigarette case all afternoon. She put her hand into her pocket, closed her fingers over it, and brought it out. She handed it to Lucy, said, "This was in the house, at the bottom of the basement stairs."

Holding it in a trembling hand, Lucy looked at it. "What am I supposed to do with it?"

Rabia didn't know. She said nothing but left the room with the children while Lucy stared at the initials on the silver.

Next day, chancing to encounter Mr. Still when he dropped in for the inevitable papers on his way to work, Rabia mentioned Dex to him. He was in a better mood than usual for that time in the morning and said she could pass on his phone number. By coincidence, Montserrat also told him Dex was looking for work when she met him that evening. This plea went down less well. He snapped at her, said he was sick of that man's name, and said he wanted to hear no more about it. If this Dex came to Medway Manor Court, he intended to tell the porter to say he was unavailable.

DEX'S READING AND WRITING skills were not of the first order, and although he could answer his phone when it rang, he didn't know how to put a name and phone number or address into it for future use. He had managed to write down Preston Still's address as Meddymankurt, but he knew what he meant and found Medway Manor Court without trouble. No one was at home, the porter in the lobby told him in a lofty and contemptuous way. It was useless to wait. Mr. Still would not be available. Nevertheless, Dex sat down on the broad flight of steps that mounted to the double glass doors and resigned himself to a long wait, using the time to call numbers that might put him through to Peach. He tried one combination of numbers after another in the hope of getting lucky or, really, of Peach's deciding that this was the one to answer. On the fourth one he tried, a voice which must be Peach's told him to press one if he wanted to speak to an operator, two if he had an enquiry, three if he wanted to discuss his account, or four if he knew the extension he required. Dex didn't know what the last two meant and the second one frightened him, so he pressed one. The phone rang and rang and he was still listening and hoping it would stop or a voice answer when the porter came out of the front doors and told him to move on, it was useless waiting for Mr. Still.

RUTH RENDELL

THE BOLTS THAT were bought and screwed in place to set Henry's mind at rest had failed to do the job. The attempt on his door, though unsuccessful, frightened him just as much—well, almost as much—as if Huguette's mother had opened it and walked in. Driving Huguette to the Palace of Westminster two days later, he told her he would have to come to her in future. It was the only safe way.

"If we were married anywhere would be safe."

"Your dad'll never say yes to that."

"He doesn't have to. I'm over sixteen—I'm over eighteen. If you don't let me ask him—well, *tell* him—he'll get me married to someone else. D'you know why I'm going in there now? It's to have a drink with him and the youngest Tory backbencher in the Commons. Filthy rich and needless to say not married."

"Why didn't you say no then?"

Huguette made no direct reply. "I want to see if he's as good-looking as you or if he's maybe better. D'you know something? You've never said you love me, Henry Copley."

Negotiating the seized-up traffic, the lights and jaywalking pedestrians of Parliament Square, Henry was silent for a moment or two. In the passage that constitutes a police barrier and is known as the security lane, wide enough for one car to get through, when Huguette had shown the woman officer her pass, he said, "Of course I love you. You know I do. I'll come and see you tomorrow afternoon and I'll show you and you can make me jealous about the backbencher, whatever that may be."

"Darling Henry," said Huguette, sounding uncannily like her mother even to a nuance of Oceane's accent.

19

B EACON HAD SEVERAL TIMES in the past done little jobs for
Mr. Still he didn't like doing himself. Speaking to Zinnia, for
instance, when the former cleaning lady left and a replacement was
needed. Mrs. Still never did anything, that was well-known. Beacon
had even found Rabia, though Mr. Still had interviewed her. Now
he was asking Beacon about Dex Flitch.

"He's mental, sir," said Beacon. "He stuck a knife in his mother,
only luckily for him she didn't die."

"Dr. Jefferson employs him and so does Mr. Neville-Smith."

"With all due respect, sir, though Dr. Jefferson's a real saint,
kindness itself to everybody, he does take on people you wouldn't
have set foot in your home."

"All right. I believe you. What is it about this Dex?"

"He looks like a hobgoblin but he hunts evil spirits. He's got a
god lives in his mobile and he does what the god says. He calls it
Peach, like the communications-service people. I call it blasphemy.
I'm sorry, sir, but you did ask."

"Yes," said Mr. Still. "Thank you, Beacon. I'll steer clear of him."

But Mr. Still didn't steer clear of him. Beacon knew that because
while he was giving the Audi a wash in the mews next day, Jimmy

came out of the back garden of number three and said he had heard Dex was coming to do the garden at number seven.

"Not that it doesn't need it," Jimmy said, "and I did tell Mr. Still to think again. He came round while Dr. Jefferson was at work and asked for his mobile number. Dex's, I mean. I had to give it to him, didn't I? I mean, it went against the grain but I had to give it to him."

"I warned Mr. Still myself, I don't mind telling you."

"Maybe I should have told him about Peach."

"I did that," said Beacon. "Disgusting irreligious rubbish."

"CANAPÉS," SAID ROLAND. "Not pineapple and cheese or celery with faux caviare, not rubbish. We had in mind quail eggs and foie gras, that sort of thing."

Thea said, "Have you thought about caterers? It's getting near Christmas."

Glancing out of the window, she saw that the first flakes of the predicted snow were falling. Snow in November! Unheard of.

"You mean they'll all be booked up? Well, my dear, the thing is, we thought you might do it."

Canapés for fifty guests, somehow get all the raw materials in, carry them up the stairs, for no one else would. Marry Jimmy and she'd never have to do it again—except perhaps for her own wedding.

"All right," she said, "if that's what you want."

THE SNOW BEGAN to fall while Dex was working in Dr. Jefferson's garden. Using his narrow trowel with the sharp-pointed tip, he was removing from earthenware tubs the plants the frost had killed, first wilting their leaves, then blackening them. Dex loosened the soil around the dead plants and dropped their roots and shrivelled stems into a black plastic bag supplied by Jimmy. When the last tub was done, the first flakes floated out of a heavy gray sky. First they scattered like petals on the soil, then covered it with a thin white sheet. Dex began packing up. He cleaned off his tools under the outside tap, put them into his toolbag, and knocked on the back door to tell Jimmy no work could be done in this weather.

"You tell Dr. Jefferson I did my best but it snowed. Will he still pay me?"

"He left your money." Jimmy produced an envelope and handed it over. "He *would*. I wouldn't, I don't mind telling you, but he's like that."

Dex's mobile rang when he was turning into Ebury Bridge Road. This happened rarely. He answered it just with his name as Dr. Mettage had taught him was best. Then people knew they had the right number.

"Dex."

"Peach," a voice said. It seemed to come from far away, but it was a beautiful voice, different from any other he had heard before, the voice of a god who lived in the sunset. But Peach had many voices.

Dex said his own name again. He didn't know what else to say. He couldn't go on walking while his God spoke to him. The snow was falling on his hands and on his phone. A bus shelter was a few yards on. He crept into it and crouched on the narrow bench.

"Peach," the voice said again. "Are you still there, Dex?"

Dex nodded, then realising Peach couldn't see him said, "Yes, I am."

"Listen to me. There's an evil spirit you must destroy." When Dex had said yes and what must he do, Peach said, "It's a woman. I mean it looks like a woman. It's about the same height as you and it's got a lot of thick dark hair, long hair. It lives at number seven Hexam Place and you must follow it. Follow it and destroy it. Tell no one."

"I won't tell anyone."

"Do it soon," said Peach. "I will reward you."

Dex wasn't sure what a reward meant, what the *word* meant. Perhaps one of those messages which appeared and said Peach was going to give him ten free calls. He knew better than to tell anyone. He had tried talking about his God in the past, to Beacon for instance, who spoke angrily to him and said a long word beginning with *b* that Dex had never before heard. Jimmy wasn't angry when Dex told him about Peach but said he was mad. Dex knew that already, ever since he went to that place where everyone was mad, so he must be. Neither Beacon nor Jimmy understood. Dex got up and walked out onto the pavement, enjoying the feeling of the cold flakes falling on his face and hands, now his mobile was safely in his pocket.

DECEMBER CAME IN bitterly cold. The pond froze over in St. James's Park and the pelicans all huddled on their island. During a sunny spell while the snow held off and the sky was blue, Rabia pushed Thomas to Harrods along pavements sticky with thaw and red grit and bought him a scarlet quilted coat with a hood. It was trimmed in gray fur, not white, to avoid making him look like a baby Father Christmas.

Having left her car out in Hexam Place overnight, Montserrat found the door handles frozen shut, so she went out on foot to buy snow boots. Unable to afford UGGs, she bought a cheap imitation, pale blue suede with white fleece tops, at a shoe shop in Victoria Street. She took a bus back, climbing to the upper deck, and, looking over her shoulder, saw Dex get on behind her. Perhaps he'd got that gardening job with Preston after all, but he was nowhere to be seen when she got off. Beacon, walking by, said to use a hair dryer on the frozen door handles, only possible of course if she had an extension lead long enough to reach from an electric point inside her flat up the area stairs and out into the street. She asked him what time he expected to bring Mr. Still home that evening.

"That's not your business," he said. "What d'you want to know for, anyway? You ask Mrs. Still if you want to know things like that."

Montserrat went inside to look for an extension lead. Zinnia didn't even know what she meant, Rabia was out with Thomas, and Lucy was out to lunch. Montserrat tried heating up the car key but only succeeded in burning her fingers. Best wait for the thaw and take the tube to Preston's. After that evening when he took her out to dinner at her request and, again at her request, came back to Hexam Place to spend the night with her, she had heard nothing from him. Yet he had been nice to her, had talked to her in quite a cheerful, pleasant way over dinner, and when they were in the taxi going back, he kissed her in a passionate way—well, passionate for him. Only when they were turning into Hexam Place did he start behaving cautiously. He got the driver to drop him outside the Dugong, while the driver took her on to number seven. There she waited for him in the area, but he came into the house via the front steps and the front door. Five minutes later he came to the flat. Montserrat thought they were by now sufficiently close for her to ask him why, but all he said, with a reversion to his old manner, was that it was his house and he'd be damned if he was going in by the servants' entrance. That was the first time she had heard anyone say "damned" since her grandfather had said it when she was a little girl.

She had expected him to phone next day. By this time she ought to be used to his not phoning when anyone else would, but she wasn't. She was scared to call him at work, and when she left messages for him at the flat in Medway Manor Court, he never answered them. It was time he talked to her about his divorce, she thought, and her moving in with him, even mentioned marriage as something to be thought about. She had to see him and preferably tonight. A face-to-face talk was needed. She would steer him towards planning for the future.

Perhaps it was just as well that she hadn't succeeded in thawing out the handles on the car doors because it was snowing again and her mobile told her that a heavy overnight frost was forecast. The car would look like an igloo by the morning. Her new boots were not glamourous or elegant enough for meeting Preston, so she put on black pumps, but leather rather than suede and with a heel only an inch high. Now was no time to break her ankle. Her only thick coat, black wool with faux-baby-lamb lapels, was shabby but the warmest thing she had. The first thing she'd get Preston to buy her when they were living together was a real fur coat.

The pavements between here and Victoria Station had been gritted. The snow falling onto them turned into a kind of reddish soup. Her shoes squelched in the gritty liquid and she regretted the boots. Few people were about, so it was odd that for the second time that day she saw Dex. She had turned round before crossing the road to check nothing was coming, and there he was, apparently following the same route that she had followed. He lived round here somewhere, didn't he? He too must be getting the tube one stop.

Inside the terminus she stopped and phoned Preston on his landline. It had to be his landline because she didn't know his mobile number. Of course he didn't answer, but that meant nothing. He was bound to be at home by now. She went down the escalator and halfway down heard the public address system telling her there were delays on the Circle line. Nothing, though, about trains not running. The platform was crowded, densely packed with people. Montserrat knew it was wise to stand at the extreme left-hand end or the extreme right-hand end because seats were usually available in the first and last carriages.

She struggled along, forcing her way through towards the left-hand end. The sign told her a train was due in one minute. That this part of the platform, like the end of the train, would be less crowded wasn't true this evening. Someone at the platform edge turned round and said to her, "Don't push," and she said, "Sorry," but went on pushing and got to the edge herself, calculating exactly where the double doors in the last carriage would open. The train could be heard quite a long way off, a kind of roaring rattle on the rails just before the gleam of its lights. Something pressed against her back, a light touch, then a heavier pressure. She cried out, stumbled over the edge, but grabbed hold of the man beside her and the woman on the other side, clutching at them and letting out a loud scream. She would have toppled over but for the two of them pulling her, swinging her back.

The train came in, filling in the lethal space where death by electrocution waited. Most people got onto the train, but not the two who had held her back. They supported her to one of the seats, the last one on the platform, and she half-sat, half-lay there, making little whimpering sounds. The man asked her what had happened.

"I don't know. Someone pushed me."

"Did you see who it was?"

"I didn't look." Montserrat turned from one to another. "Thank you. I nearly fell. I would have but for you."

The woman helped her back up the escalator and put her into a cab. Montserrat had told him Hexam Place, but once the cab was moving said to go to Medway Manor Court instead. She badly needed someone to care, to hold her, to sympathise. Really what she needed was someone to love her, though she doubted if Preston would do that.

"You imagined it," he said when he had let her into the flat. "You must have. These things don't happen."

"This one did."

He didn't hold her or show any sympathy, but he did give her brandy, which was a kind of caring.

"Please, Preston, can I stay here? I'll be all right in the morning. It's just that I'm afraid to go out there tonight."

"I wish you wouldn't talk to me as if I were a monster. 'Please, Preston.' 'Can I stay here?' Of course you can stay here."

She said, "Thank you," in a humble way, then, "What does the *Q* in your name stand for?"

"You don't want to know." But he was smiling.

"I do. I really do." She'd be able to say it when they got married.

"Quintilian."

THE SNOW FELL to a depth of about five centimetres. "You mean two inches," said June.

The oldest servant in Hexam Place, she was the only one to sweep the pavement outside the house they occupied or worked in. Zinnia refused to sweep outside anywhere at all, saying to anyone who cared to listen that it wasn't her job. At number eleven Richard and Sondra agreed not to mention the subject unless asked by one or other of their employers. Simon Jefferson told Jimmy he wouldn't dream of expecting him to perform such a chore and swept his bit of pavement himself. Elsewhere the snow lay untouched, was ground down by those pedestrians who ventured outdoors, thawed out one milder day and frozen again overnight, creating sheets of ice.

On a day of renewed cold, June slipped when she was pushing the Princess in her new wheelchair. June fell, the wheelchair overturned, and the Princess toppled out. This mishap was witnessed by Lucy, alighting from a taxi, Roland mounting the steps to number eight, and Thea looking out of her front window. She too saw Lucy and Roland "passing by on the other side," as she phrased it to herself. The Good Samaritan parable was then enacted as she ran downstairs, clutching and talking into her mobile, and doing her best to set both old women on their feet.

The Princess was shouting that she had broken her hip, without much foundation for this claim. June really had broken her wrist, putting her right arm out in a vain effort to break her fall. An ambulance came and took them both away. Thea was asked by a paramedic, under the mistaken impression that she was the Princess's daughter or June's, if she would like to come with them, and though she didn't want to, she said yes, of course.

Life came to something of a standstill. The only work Dex now had was his three hours a week for Dr. Jefferson. Everyone knew that he had it only because of the kindness of Dr. Jefferson's heart. Dex had considered going from door to door, offering to clear snow, for more had fallen at the weekend. But it was only a thin covering that thawed on the mild Saturday afternoon. Beacon had told him that because he had money from the government called something Dex couldn't pronounce, he shouldn't earn other money by working. But Dr. Jefferson gave him the money and so it must be right. Dex was more troubled because he had failed Peach, and he wondered if he should make a second attempt.

THE PRINCESS'S YOGURT PHASE had lasted longer than usual but had faded just at the point when disturbances in the dietary arrangements at number six were least needed. She never wanted another mouthful of yogurt as long as she lived, she said. It was muesli she fancied, having tasted it while at the hotel in Florence and retasted it in one of those dreams with which she regaled June when her breakfast was brought up. In the dream her husband, Luciano, had been given poison in a pot of yogurt by a chambermaid who was under the impression she was giving him a love potion.

No longer able to carry a tray, June transported the coffeepot, the toast, butter and honey, and the no-longer-desirable yogurt in a shopping trolley that had to be humped from stair to stair. The plaster on her right arm extended from her knuckles all the way up to her elbow, so she had had to give up many tasks. She couldn't push the wheelchair or walk Gussie. The Princess had to stay at home, nursing her bruises, and Gussie paced the house, whimpering. If only Rad were still alive, June would have got him to sign her plaster, but Rocksana Castelli was willing to do it and to bring round to number six several more B-class celebrities she had met during her association with June's great-nephew. June's idea was to get enough famous names to turn the plaster into a valuable item, then auction it in the Dugong. Ted Goldsworth, the licensee, ran a charity to raise money for Moldovan orphans, and June realised that if she wanted to receive the approbation of Hexam Place, she would have to give the proceeds to it, though she would much rather have kept them for herself. The doctor who had put the plaster on had promised to cut it off when the time came with the greatest care not to damage the autographs.

BEACON WAS SURPRISED and a little disturbed by Mr. Still's request (command) to him to leave the Audi with him overnight. The bus went door-to-door, so it wouldn't hurt Beacon to take that home in the evening and come back on it in the morning. What, after all, was the point, said Mr. Still, of paying the enormous cost of a resident's parking place if it was never used? Like most drivers employed by rich men, Beacon had come to regard the Audi, if not quite as his own, as a vehicle in which he had more than a half-share. But when it came to giving him orders, Mr. Still had the right and of course Beacon was obedient.

Mr. Still had been going home rather earlier than in former days. Generally disapproving of almost everything done by his employer, his employer's wife, and to some extent his employer's children and their lifestyle, Beacon supposed that getting home to Medway Manor Court was pleasanter than getting home to Hexam Place because Mrs. Still was present in the latter but not in the former. This evening, however, it was to Hexam Place Mr. Still was going at seven, and the car was to be parked in melting snow ruts behind an old VW Golf, the property of Montserrat, the au pair.

She was there, pouring warm water out of a milk jug onto the door handles.

If they had gone into the house together, Beacon told himself, he would have handed Mr. Still his notice next day. To countenance such immorality was more than Beacon could stomach, let alone contaminate Dorothee and Solomon and William by association. But he was spared the necessity of giving up his job in these hard times, for while Montserrat went down the stairs to the area, Mr. Still mounted the steps to the front door. Beacon went off to catch the bus home.

Montserrat poured two glasses of wine, sat down to wait for Preston, and contemplated her reflection in the mirror. It was an image to be admired, the low-cut, dark red maxidress—bought with the five twenty-pound notes he had unexpectedly pressed into her hand—her hair done by Thea's sister, and the dark red lipstick that matched the dress. The money, she supposed, was a reward for not telling the police or anyone else about his "accident." Why should she tell them? There was nothing in it for her.

He walked in five minutes later. She no longer minded his failing to knock. They had reached too intimate a stage in their relationship for her to care about things like that. He kissed her, said, "No more taxis tonight. I can drive us."

She liked that "us," but the idea of driving to some distant restaurant was less acceptable. "There's going to be freezing fog, darling." He no longer protested when she called him that. "We could buy our dinner and take it back to your place or here."

"I hate takeaway," he said with a reversion to his old manner.

"OK, if you're sure. I'll just put my car away."

He got up. "Let me do that for you."

Such offers, *any* offers, were new. "Thank you, darling." She handed him the car key.

"Perhaps you'll open the garage doors."

She went out by way of the basement door after she had seen

him go back up to the ground floor and the front door. The fog was starting, white and cold, hanging in the windless air. No one was about but Thea, going into number six to attend to June and the Princess. Montserrat waved to her, slipped, and nearly fell over on a sheet of melting ice that covered half the pavement. Preston was already sitting in her car, the engine running and the lights on. He took no notice of Thea, though he must have seen her. He was a strange man, cold and hard, like the weather. But she would marry him. Earlier, on the phone, he had talked about his coming divorce, the sale of this house and what he called "a division of the spoils." She would marry him and have some of those spoils as compensation for what living with him would be like.

She unlocked the doors and opened them. The light switch was inside on the left, but when she pressed it, the light failed to come on. The lights on the car would be adequate. She went to stand at the back of the garage and began to beckon him in. The standard-size garage was made narrower by stuff stacked along the walls on either side, a folding bed she was storing for a friend of her father's, four suitcases of various sizes, plastic sacks containing bedding.

She hadn't expected him to turn the lights up to full beam as he drove towards her. Beckoning with both hands, she flinched and retreated a step or two, blinded by those lights, the dazzle forcing her to close her eyes. She tried to make a patting-down movement with both hands, but cried out when instead of braking, he accelerated. She threw herself spread-eagled across the bonnet of the car, clutching at the windscreen wipers.

There was no longer any need to scream. She was alive. But she went on screaming for the relief of it, letting out the aftermath of terror in short, sharp cries and whimpers.

20

THE FIRST THING he did was put her in the wrong.

"You've only yourself to blame. What possessed you to stand there gesticulating at me? Do you think I don't know how to drive a car into a garage?"

If she tried to speak, she would start crying. She slid as best she could off the bonnet of the car, slipping down over the grid and those blazing lights and tearing her dress. He went on haranguing her.

"I've always made it a principle not to have anything to do with women who assert themselves too much. And when I go against it, this is what happens. I told you I'd put the car away for you, and instead of letting me get on with this perfectly simple and straightforward task, you interfere and half-kill yourself."

Rubbing her arms and thighs, twisting her neck this way and that, Montserrat came to stand so close in front of him that her forehead almost touched his chin. She tilted her head up, said, "You almost killed me, is what you mean."

He shouted at her then. "Don't be a fool!"

"Is that what you meant to do?"

They were standing between the end of the folding bed and a plastic sack of blankets and sheets. He took hold of her by the shoulders and began to shake her. Montserrat struggled, shouting and yelling into his face, and in that moment a man walked in through the open garage doors, squeezing along between the car and the suitcases. It was Ciaran.

"What's going on here?"

"Mind your own business," said Preston.

"If you're assaulting a woman, it's anyone's business. Primarily it's the business of the police. Now take your hands off her."

To Montserrat's surprise, Preston did. "All right, Montsy. Let's go."

"She's not going anywhere with you," Ciaran said.

"Who is this person, Montsy?"

Preston had called her by that diminutive twice in succession. Maybe what had happened in the garage had been her fault, after all. "A friend of mine," she said.

"I'm her boyfriend."

"Is that true?"

"What if it is? It's nothing to you."

"You know where I am if you need me," Ciaran said to Montserrat. "Just call me and I'll come. Anytime. Happy to be of help." He walked off down the mews.

Montserrat followed him for a few yards, then stopped while Preston shut the garage doors. He tried to take her arm. "You're not actually seeing that fellow, are you?"

"I used to be. I could be again. I'm going home now and maybe I'll give him a call. I need someone to protect me from people like you."

"Now, Montsy, what have I done? If you'd had a light that worked in that garage, I wouldn't have had to have the beam on. I'd have been able to see you, not been blinded by the glare. It was an accident, you know that."

"Accident is what you always say. I know you tried to hurt me. You did, Preston. I'm not saying tried to kill me, but hurt me so's I know who's the master, not assert myself. You said that yourself, it must be what you mean."

He took her arm, not gently but in a hard grip. "Come along, we'll get into my car and I'll take you back to Medway Manor Court. There's a nice little Italian place round the corner, we'll go there."

"No, we won't." She shook him off. "I'm going to be covered in bruises. I know your nice little Italian places. I'm going home."

SHUT UP TOGETHER all day, the Princess and June bickered incessantly. Gussie had no walks until Rocksana appeared with chocolates and flowers and offered to take him out. She had turned out to be a kind girl, after all. She signed June's cast in green ink and next day brought with her a pop singer whose name and photograph had lately been in all the papers and magazines. Rocksana told June that if she got online, the first image she would see was this singer plugging her new autobiography and giving advice on losing weight without pain. The singer also signed the cast and promised that her new husband, a famous TV presenter, would come next day and autograph it in purple ink. This was everything June most desired, but it went against the grain with the Princess, who complained that all these visitors were hoovering up her gin.

While they were quarrelling, Thea arrived with Chinese takeaway, Dr. Karg's crispbread, and a piece of Shropshire Blue. She admired the signatures, was sufficiently overawed by some of the particularly celebrated names, and made a request.

"Can I sign it?"

This was what June had feared. "I'm afraid not. You see, it's only for celebrities, TV personalities, and people like that. Yes, I know the Princess has signed it, but she *is* a princess." The two of them had settled their differences and for the time being appeared the best of friends. "I think that makes her an exception, don't you?"

Thea didn't. She was hurt, far more hurt than she would have expected to be if she could have imagined this situation. But she said nothing, simply standing there watching the Princess peering into the various little plastic pots of rice, pork, chicken, and vegetables.

"Actually I don't care for Chinese food."

"Oh, I thought you did."

"We can eat the biscuits and cheese," said June. "Would you mind taking Gussie round the block?"

Thea didn't see how she could say no. She seldom did. They would be asking her to push the Princess's wheelchair next. Gussie had to have his coat put on, an exercise which often resulted in his dresser being bitten. Carrying the takeaway in the knowledge that she would have to eat it herself—Damian and Roland certainly would not—Thea took the little dog up to Ebury Bridge Road and back again, noticing the single thing to be pleased about: it was a lot less cold than it had been.

THE BELGRAVE NURSERY was unlike most other garden centres in that it potted up its Christmas trees before delivering them. The pots, as Abram Siddiqui said, were works of art in themselves, Santa Clauses, reindeer, fairies in tutus, all painted on a background of snowy mountains and navy blue skies, glittering with stars. Khalid took on the task of delivering them himself, mainly to convey the one he considered the most beautiful to number seven Hexam Place and thereby see Rabia.

True, Christmas and Christmas trees meant nothing to Rabia and himself. The paintings on the pots, though he admired them for the skill of the artist and also as a commercial success, he saw as near-blasphemous; they portrayed animals and, worse, the human figure in various forms. Nevertheless, those painted pots were a great selling point and would lead to an increase in orders for next Christmas.

From the nursery window, Rabia saw his van draw up outside. She was sitting in an armchair upholstered in blue linen with white spots, and Thomas, in a blue-and-white-striped jumpsuit, was standing on her lap while she held him up to the window. A pretty sight. "Look, Thomas, here is Mr. Iqbal's van, and here is Mr. Iqbal getting out of it to bring our Christmas tree."

This sight was a cause of great excitement. Thomas jumped up and down heavily on Rabia's thighs, but she gave no sign that he had hurt her, his pleasure far outweighing her pain. The Christmas tree in its painted pot was a beautiful object even before it was dressed. Khalid Iqbal was coming up the steps to the front door. To go down herself to let him in was unnecessary, Rabia decided, it would give him too much encouragement. Zinnia could do that. But still, as Rabia hastily covered her head, lifting Thomas down and teaching him the polite things to say when Khalid came to the nursery door, she tried in vain to restrain herself from feeling a small surge of not quite excitement, happy anticipation rather, that this kind, handsome man who admired her was paying them a visit.

Thomas, whose language skills had come on by leaps and bounds, burst into speech the moment the door was opened. "Hallo, Mr. Iqbal, how are you?"

Khalid said he was fine, thank you, and he hoped Thomas was, but his expressive dark eyes were on Rabia as he set the tree down and asked her where she would like it. Thomas danced about, pointing to one spot after another. "Here, here, here—no, here!"

"Mrs. Ali?"

"I think between the windows, Mr. Iqbal. Then when the curtains are drawn, they will make a fine background for it."

"You are right," he said in the sort of tone that implied she would always be right. "Do you like the tree? Are you pleased with it?"

It wouldn't do to give him too much encouragement. "I am sure Mrs. Still will be very delighted. It is just what she wants."

With that he had to be satisfied. She picked Thomas up and held

179

him so that he could reach one hand to the topmost branch of the fir. "That is where the fairy doll will go. Last year you were too young to understand."

"Old now," Thomas shouted. "Grown-up!"

Khalid said in his gentle, respectful tone, "My mother has written you a note and asked me to give it to you, Mrs. Ali. I believe it is an invitation."

Rabia took the pale pink envelope, conscious that she was blushing deeply. Black-eyed but as fair-skinned as a white woman, she knew he must notice how the blood mounted into her pale cheeks. The card in the envelope which she opened when he had gone invited her to tea on the following Sunday, her father would also be there, and was signed Khadiya Iqbal. Rabia wrote a polite little note accepting. It would be Mr. Still's weekend to have the children, and he wanted her to accompany them to Gallowmill Hall on Saturday. Of course he couldn't manage them on his own, she understood that. She plucked up her courage and asked him if it would be possible to be back by Sunday afternoon as she had been invited out to tea. It looked to her as if Mr. Still was quite pleased to return early. It would be no problem, he said, they would be back by lunchtime, and he was aware that Rabia would be giving up her day off to come with them.

IT REMAINED COLD but no more snow had fallen in London. Dry days went by, then came a wet day to wash away the last of the snow that lay on the cars and on the pavements. Thea avoided Oxford Street at the weekend but took a morning off work to do June's and the Princess's Christmas shopping. The presents they wanted were for each other, slippers for June from the Princess, and a gift box of cologne and body lotion produced by an expensive perfumer from June to the Princess. June put on a big show of incredulity when Thea told her what it cost and, paying Thea in twenty-pound notes, gave her three instead of four and afterwards denied it. It was no use arguing and Thea resigned herself to going short. She bought Jimmy a scarf, which, since he sat at the wheel of a car most of the time, he would never wear.

Teaching her last class before the Christmas holiday began, Thea ventured out at 7:00 p.m. into the West End crowds. She had forgotten Thursday was late-night shopping, but she still had small gifts to buy for Damian and Roland. They were bound to give her something. She was looking in windows, seeking inspiration, when she was caught in the midst of a group of teenage boys in hoods emerging from a pub. Like her previous tormentors, they were bent on taunting her about her red hair, one of them pulling off the scarf which half-covered it. In tears, partly from exhaustion, Thea escaped onto a bus and phoned her sister, the hairdresser. Would she come round and tint her hair dark brown or black?

"But your hair's a beautiful colour."

Thea was reluctant to tell Chloe her reason. "I'm sick of it. I want a change."

Chloe would come. That evening if Thea wanted it. "But it won't suit you."

Who cared about that? Again Jimmy had to be told they would benefit from an evening apart.

HAVING A CUP of tea with Rabia on Saturday morning, Montserrat said it was a funny idea to take the kids to Gallowmill Hall in this weather. What were they going to do there? The fields would still be covered with snow. She had forgotten for a moment that she wasn't supposed to have been there or even to know where the house was, but Rabia seemed not to notice. Rabia was packing suitcases, one for each child, and was anxious to be ready with everything done when Mr. Still arrived at ten o'clock.

"I wonder why he asked you," said Montserrat.

"To look after the children. That is my job."

"I suppose." She thought she would be a more appropriate choice, especially when he had apologised over and over since the incident with her car. And explained and said repeatedly that he didn't know what had come over him. After all, if things worked out, and surely they would, the children would have to get to know her and she them. "Oh, well, I hope you don't freeze to death."

Rabia washed up their cups, politely sent Montserrat away, and went down to fetch the girls from Lucy's room, where they were playing with their mother's makeup. "I'm so relieved I don't have to go" was Lucy's parting shot.

Beacon had been persuaded to bring the Audi round to Medway Manor Court and return home, much to his chagrin, on the bus. A good many of his neighbours thought the car was his own, and although he was himself too upright to have lied about it, Dorothee didn't deny it when people talked about "your car." Mr. Still got to number seven Hexam Place at five past ten, bringing with him a hamper from Harrods to avoid stopping at a supermarket on the way. Rabia smiled and said it was a good idea, though her real fear was that the food would be of the most unsuitable kind for children, game pie and roast partridge and peaches in brandy among other things, and she hoped the caretaker at Gallowmill Hall would have stocked the fridge with simple basics.

Much as he wanted to make himself comfortable on Rabia's lap, Thomas had to sit in his baby-seat. That was the law, Mr. Still said. There were tears and rage and much kicking of the seat in front, but once they were going and Thomas had seen and heard a fire engine on its howling way to a fire, he calmed down and began to enjoy himself. Mr. Still was in a good mood or perhaps just putting on a good show, not so much for his children as for Rabia. Before they set off, he asked her for Dex's phone number. He had had it once but had lost it, and he'd heard she had a wonderful memory for numbers. She might have that one in her head. Rabia had and wrote it down for him. He smiled, thanked her, and had insisted she sit in the front next to him, though Matilda claimed that place as the eldest child. But, no, it must be Rabia.

"It's very good of Rabia to give up her day off to come with us," he said. "Now we wouldn't manage very well without her, would we?"

The girls were both sulking. Thomas said, "Want Rab, want to sit on her," and started making a noise like a fire engine.

It was cold, though inside the car it was soon warm. The fields, as Montserrat had predicted, lay under sheets of snow. Deer stood huddled together under the bare trees, feeding on bundles of hay. A light was on in the hall of Gallowmill Hall, evidence of the recent presence of the caretaker, as was the warmth which rolled out to meet them when Mr. Still opened the front door. Rabia expected to carry the cases in herself, but Mr. Still said a commanding "Here, let me do that" and became quite an efficient porter while she carried Thomas inside.

The Still children were not the kind who enjoyed playing in the snow. Perhaps Thomas would be one day, but Matilda and Hero had as much aversion to the natural world as their mother. They stayed in the warm in front of the television while Thomas said he would help Rabia in the kitchen. The fridge, as she had hoped, was well stocked with bread and butter and cheese, with salad in cellophane bags and fruit in plastic packs. Mr. Still had disappeared. In the distance, but somewhere in the house, she could hear a hammering and a sound like something heavy being dragged across the floor.

Darkness would come early. It would soon be the shortest day of the year, sunrise at eight in the morning and night arriving at four. Mr. Still pointed all this out as they sat down to lunch. Therefore they must be sure to get out in the fresh air while it was still broad daylight.

"Why is it *broad*, Daddy?" said Hero. "Why not *wide* or *long*?"

He didn't know. "I've got a surprise for you." He smiled, evidently doing his best to be a kind, loving father. "We didn't have a Bonfire Night party and you didn't go to one. You missed out and that's a shame, so I thought we'd have one down here, this afternoon. We'll have a bonfire of our own and I've brought a lot of fireworks. Now what do you think of that?"

"I hate fireworks." Matilda removed a chunk of game pie from her mouth and laid it on the side of her plate. "There's this girl at my school burnt her hand on a firework and it was so bad they amputated her little finger."

"Oh, yuck," said Hero. "I can't eat any more, that's put me off my lunch. That's disgusting."

"She's American and Americans call your little finger a pinkie. Even if it's not pink. She asked the doctor if she could have the burnt pinkie to keep but they wouldn't let her."

Rabia wanted to reprimand the girls but she didn't like to when their father was there. He ought to do it and suddenly he did, shouting, "That's enough. I don't want to hear another word out of you till you've cleared your plates. Do you hear me?"

Hero got up and left the room. Matilda began to laugh, and that set Thomas off. He had thrown most of his food onto the floor, fortunately some sort of laminated wood. "Please excuse me, Mr. Still," Rabia said, "if I take him into the kitchen and give him his lunch there."

She managed to feed him, clean his face and hands, and get him and his sisters, the two of them protesting sullenly, out onto the lawn and through the gate into the field. There, fitful sunshine and the temperature's rising just above freezing had melted what snow remained. Mr. Still, determined to be cheerful, had laid a fire Rabia could see at once wouldn't burn. He had used damp sticks from the woodland, piled with solid planks, and nearby stood a can of something she was almost sure was petrol.

"Forgive me, Mr. Still, but I don't think that will catch fire. May I try to—rearrange things a little? Could we have some newspaper, do you think? And, I'm sorry, but if you put petrol on it, you may set the trees on fire." And yourself, she thought, but didn't say it aloud.

Instead of getting angry as she had expected and feared, he went away and fetched stacks of newspaper and a plastic bottle of paraffin. Getting her hands dirty—it couldn't be helped—Rabia squatted down and remade the fire. What was he burning apart from the twigs and logs? She now knew what the hammering and dragging sounds had been. There was quite a lot of wood and sheet plastic that had been chopped by someone who had scarcely ever chopped anything before. Mr. Still had hacked about and split and cracked open a thing that at first she took to be a boat and then identified as one of those luggage boxes people carried on the tops of cars. Well, he knew his own business best, she would have liked to believe but couldn't. The fire was ready to light. She stepped back, well away from it, taking Thomas in her arms and keeping the girls with her. Mr. Still poured on the paraffin and put a match to it.

Rabia shuddered when she thought what might have been if he had been left to use petrol. The bonfire began to burn steadily, the flames mounting until they reached up to lick the varnished underside of that case thing. Mr. Still set off the first of his fireworks, a green-and-silver rocket which burst in fountains of emerald showers.

"I'm bored," said Matilda.

"I REMEMBER WHEN my father broke his wrist," said the Princess on Sunday morning. "It took three months before he could use his right arm."

"That was different." June contemplated the illustrious autographs. "It didn't matter so much. You told me he was left-handed."

"He could use both, he was ambiguous. I'm only telling you because it means you won't get the use of your arm back till March, and it's a terrible thing if that poor dog has to depend on the kindness of visitors all that time."

June said all right, she would take Gussie out, but if she fell over and broke her other wrist, don't say she didn't warn her. She took it slowly, Gussie tugging on the lead. Mr. Still, at the wheel of his car for once, had to stop suddenly to avoid knocking her down outside Dr. Jefferson's. His brakes squealed and he sounded the horn for good measure. He was opening the window to say something to her, but June forestalled him. Her tone was sour.

"Better leave the driving to Beacon next time."

She watched the car park outside number seven and those badly behaved daughters of his get out. Then—surprise, surprise—came Rabia. No sign of Lucy of course. Rabia was carrying Thomas. She adored that child. It would be hard on her when number seven was sold, Mr. Still bought that place that was for sale next to his sister's, and Lucy took the kids to her parents' country house. Rumour had it that Lucy's own nanny lived there still and Rabia wouldn't be needed. June went on round the block, slipping once, her heart in her mouth, but no harm done this time.

21

SINCE SHE HAD BEEN Jimmy's girlfriend, Thea had smoked a lot more. Damian and Roland had noticed and remarked on the smell on her clothes.

"I hope you won't indulge in your habit," said Roland, "while you're preparing the food for our party."

"It's stress," Thea said to her sister while she was doing her hair. "Being engaged doesn't suit me."

"You mean being engaged to Jimmy doesn't suit you," said Chloe, painting one lock after another of Thea's red hair with viscous black tint.

"There's nothing I can do about that. Is this stuff supposed to itch? I need to scratch my head but I don't want that stuff on my fingers. You don't think I'm allergic, do you?"

"Everybody's head itches when the tint goes on." Chloe gave Thea a comb to scratch with. "Why don't you break it off? With Jimmy, I mean."

"It would hurt him terribly."

"You worry too much about hurting people."

"I don't really. I worry about what they'll think of me."

Chloe laughed. "You going to put those candles in their front window this year?"

"I bought them this afternoon," said Thea. "I don't suppose I'll ever see the nineteen pounds they cost me."

It was traditional at Christmas now, almost a sacred trust. Lord Studley's father, who had lived at number eleven before him, had begun it, the result of spending a holiday in Norway where it was the custom in a village he had stayed in. He came home, brimming with excitement at starting something similar in Hexam Place. So, that December, a few days before Christmas, five smallish, squat candles appeared in his drawing-room window. He had persuaded his neighbours at number nine to do the same and had the following year bullied most of the other householders to set candles in their front windows, only old Mrs. Neville-Smith, mother of the present occupier of the lower half of number five, the Collinses then at number two, and the Princess refusing to conform.

June was the only servant to observe this custom from the beginning. That is, to watch others observing it. When she admitted Lord Studley to the house and showed him in to try his powers of persuasion on the Princess, June was already prepared to buy the candles for number six and set them in the drawing-room window. For some reason her employer was adamant. No, she wouldn't have it. Gussie liked sitting on the windowsill and would knock them over. The house would catch fire. June watched the neighbours, one by one, doing what Lord Studley asked. The following year she bought a dozen candles (there was no restriction on number) in glass jars guaranteed fireproof and was the first in the street to begin the illuminations. Lord Studley came round himself to congratulate her on the show. As for the Princess, she never noticed, and when she did, sometime around the turn of the century, she had taken into her head that it was her idea and that she had even started the tradition herself.

Lord Studley was dead; his son had inherited the title and was one of the small number of hereditary peers who still had seats in the House of Lords. He and his wife, Oceane, enthusiastically maintained the tradition of the candles. The only households which did not, June had observed, were the Stills at number seven and the Asian couple in the lower half of number four, a surprise really as June would have expected Hindus, which she supposed they were, to go in for lights in a big way. Last year Lord Studley had written severe letters to number four and number seven, admonishing them for not keeping up with the tradition and urging them to remember their candles this time. Now, as everyone in Hexam Place knew, Preston Still had moved out, a divorce was impending, and it seemed that the family was held together by Rabia, the nanny. It was she who, having got indifferent permission from Lucy ("Oh, do as you like, I don't care"), took Thomas buying candles and candleholders and brought number seven into line with the other houses in the street. The Asian couple took no notice of Lord Studley's letter and struck a note of defiance by filling their drawing-room windowsill with seven pots of red and white poinsettias from the Belgrave Nursery.

Because Simon Jefferson took no interest in candles or even Christmas itself but went away to stay with his sister in Andorra, number three was left in the safekeeping of Jimmy. With his usual generosity, Dr. Jefferson told his driver to enjoy himself, have friends in, have a party. Jimmy put more candles in the drawing-room window than anyone else in the street and would have set the curtains on fire if Thea hadn't snatched the offending candleholder away in the nick of time. She had expected Jimmy to find fault with her new hair colour, but it seemed that he loved everything about her even if the admired feature underwent a dramatic change.

"It's like you were born with it that shade," he said. "It looks more natural than the red did."

"My mother says I hadn't any hair when I was born."

Thea was already regretting changing the colour. Montserrat had given her a big hat from Accessorize for an early Christmas present. Under its brim there would have been no ginger showing to provoke unruly teenagers.

"What do you think of twenty-seven January for our wedding date?"

"Oh, Jimmy, I can't. That's the day of Damian and Roland's civil partnership and I'm doing the food."

No harsh words had as yet passed between them. Jimmy had been unfailingly amenable and loving and easygoing. Now he exploded. "I don't believe it! I'm not hearing this! We can't get married because you've got to make sandwiches for a couple of shirt-lifters' thrash—a mockery of marriage if you ask me."

"I don't ask you. Never never use expressions like that again. It's disgusting, I didn't know you were a rank homophobe, I can't believe it."

The traditional way for lovers to mend their quarrels is by making love. Jimmy instigated the lovemaking by carrying Thea upstairs to Dr. Jefferson's four-poster, somewhat against her will. She protested but weakly and soon gave in. Nothing more was said about a wedding on January 27. Given the scarf, an early Christmas present, Jimmy reacted as if he had been presented with a treasure he had longed for all his life. Thea was genuinely pleased with his offering of a black faux-fur jacket, very like Montserrat's, which Thea had always admired.

Downstairs on the drawing-room windowsill the flames burned steadily as they did, more extravagantly than elsewhere, at Lord Studley's. The Kleins had gone to New York for Christmas, so there were no candles in the house on the corner. Thea herself had bought, installed, and lit six pink ones at number six because June's bad arm made any such activity on her part impossible. Living on an upper storey herself and without a ground-floor window, Thea had also set up candles in Damian and Roland's window and got a good deal of criticism for their colour and shape but no thanks. At number four, Arsad Sohrab and Bibi Lambda had for the first time just about given way to Lord Studley's bullying, removed the poinsettias, and placed two meagre candles on saucers at the back of the blinds, behind which they glimmered faintly.

JIMMY, in the kitchen at number three, was planning the Christmas dinner he intended to cook for himself and Thea. A duck had been ordered from the butcher in the Pimlico Road. He would collect it on Christmas Eve. The green peas came frozen, while the Maris Piper potatoes sat in a bowl, waiting to be peeled and dropped into cold water. He was grating orange peel for the sauce when the doorbell rang. It was Dex, come for the bag of tools he said he had left behind the last time he had been here. The evening before there had been a phone call from Mrs. Neville-Smith, snowbound in Wales, asking Dex to scrape off what ice and snow remained on the steps of number five as well as the front garden and path, ready for their return. She would pay him the day after. Another call came almost immediately after. It was Peach, the beautiful voice severe now, cross and purposeful. "Remember you have to destroy the evil spirit. The psychopomp. You have to do it soon. Now, as soon as you can."

Jimmy was a stranger to him, his face a featureless mask as nearly everyone's was, his voice harsh and unrecognisable. "I could do the front here too," Dex said, "once I've got my tools."

"I don't know. Dr. Jefferson's away. I can't speak for him."

The mask grew darker and uglier. "OK. Maybe you can phone him." Dex had infinite faith in mobile phones. His was the home of his God and so might other people's be. "Like before the snow goes."

The gardens of Hexam Place had no sheds, only a cupboard in the area. Jimmy sent Dex down the area steps to the basement door, went down there himself from the inside, and found the toolbag inside the cupboard. Dex checked that everything was there, nodding at each object he pulled out, secateurs, shears, a long trowel with a pointed tip like a dagger, a small fork, a pruning knife, and a variety of other implements. The spade he used when he tended Dr. Jefferson's garden he left behind in the cupboard along with a broom, a rake and a hoe, the fork and the shears, ready for future use here and perhaps for other gardens in Hexam Place. The toolbag was now much lighter.

"I don't know if I can let you leave that stuff here," said Jimmy. "You shouldn't have left it in the first place."

"Dr. Jefferson won't mind."

"We'll see about that. If he says take it away, I'll be on the blower and you'll have to come back and fetch the lot, Christmas or no Christmas."

Dex set off up the street, the little lights twinkling on either side of him, white candles and red candles and in one window a dog sitting next to some pink candles. He didn't like dogs but he liked the lights. He walked all the way back and down again.

PRESTON STILL had been to see his son and his daughters. Not to give them their Christmas presents, children must have their presents on Christmas Day itself, that's the rule, but to hand them into the safekeeping of Rabia. The gifts themselves were shop-wrapped. Rabia could see that, for she rightly guessed that Preston was incapable of making a parcel with festive paper and tying it up with glittery string. His awkwardness in the matter of the bonfire would never be forgotten. She put the presents on the top shelf of the cupboard in her own bedroom, out of the children's reach, beside the three stockings she had prepared. She had never done this before for any children, but she read in a magazine how to do it, the kinds of small toys and sweets you put inside, and found it simple enough. She was particularly looking forward to seeing Thomas's face when he woke up on Christmas morning and found this sparkling cornucopia of little gifts at the end of his bed.

Lucy had taken the girls ice-skating. Thomas was having a nap. Rabia eyed Preston keenly as he stood over the boy, watching his sleeping child. His face didn't change. She often looked for signs of tenderness and love in the expressions of these parents but seldom saw even a hint of what she hoped for.

"I'll be back to fetch them on Christmas Day," he said. "I'm taking them to my sister's in Chelsea. Lucy too maybe, but who knows?"

Rabia came out with him and over the gallery watched him go down one flight of stairs and then another, half-expecting him to head for the basement and Montserrat. But he marched without a backward glance towards the front door and slammed it after him, as had become his habit these past weeks.

THE PREVIOUS CHRISTMAS DAY Thea had spent with Miss Grieves. As was the case with most of her good deeds, she hadn't wanted to do this but had succumbed to what she thought of as her duty. That was before the advent of Jimmy. When she told him she intended to cook dinner for Miss Grieves and herself and eat it with her, he had been nearly as angry as over the wedding-date debacle.

"I can't just abandon her."

"Get someone else to do it. You'll be wanting to take her on our honeymoon next."

The only possible person was Montserrat. On December 23, the busiest shopping day of the year, at ten in the morning Thea went down the basement steps at number seven and rang Montserrat's bell. There was no reply, but because a faint light was showing in the window, Thea tapped on the glass and called softly, "It's me."

A groan was the answer. "What is it?"

"Please let me in. I want to ask you something."

After another groan, quite a long time after, the door was opened. Montserrat was in tracksuit pants and a sweatshirt that belonged to Ciaran. "You'd better come in, but I've got the mother of all hangovers."

"Damian says that it's only since all these Asians came to live here that we've started talking about the mother of things. Because they do. We used to talk about the father. And that's quite funny because they're supposed to be misogynists."

Sitting down on Montserrat's tousled bed, Thea thought how much she would like it if Jimmy said things like that. If he observed people and their speech and habits and made perceptive comments. But he didn't and never would. Montserrat had sunk down in a heap on the far end of the bed.

"Shall I make us some coffee?"

"If you want it. I don't."

Thea told her about Miss Grieves and the Christmas dinner. She would supply the ingredients and a Christmas pudding and mince pies already made.

"Sorry but that's out. I expect I'll be spending it with Preston. He's taking his kids to his sister's and then he'll be taking me to the Wellesley for lunch."

Thea didn't believe her but could hardly say so. For one thing Thea doubted if that exclusive and fashionable restaurant would be open on Christmas Day. "I'll have to try and find someone else."

"Leave her to her own devices, why don't you? It's not as if she's disabled. I see her chasing the fox up those stairs most days. It'll have to stop anyway when you're married."

Thea had also been going to ask Montserrat if she would come last-minute shopping with her to Oxford Street, but now she changed her mind. The resentment she felt wouldn't make for pleasant companionship. Montserrat too preferred to be alone until she met Ciaran to go clubbing that evening. The lie she had told about dinner with Preston troubled her, not because it *was* a lie but because it might all too easily be found out. As for shopping, she might venture into the chaos and melee of Oxford Street later in the day.

"In case I don't feel up to it, would you go into HMV and get me a DVD for Rabia? I'll have to give her something. D'you think she'd like *Doctor Zhivago*?"

"I don't know," said Thea, "but I'll get it."

WALKING DOWN Hexam Place for the third time that day, drinking in his fill of the lights, Dex saw the evil spirit come up the area steps at number seven. He hung about, letting her get well ahead of him, then he began to follow her. Past the flickering lights in number nine, past the bold and blazing lights of number eleven, and on towards Sloane Square.

He wanted to steer clear of that underground. But if she got into a train, he would follow her, not do as he had done last time, when he had failed. She avoided the station. She was going to get on a bus. Dex left her to seek a little warmth under the bus shelter while he stood outside. He did as he sometimes did when he wanted guidance, touched a series of numbers on his phone, eight digits starting with a seven, in the hope of hearing his God's voice, but there was nothing, only words from a woman telling him the number had not been recognised. It might be the evil spirit speaking, but he wasn't sure of that.

The bus came and he got on. The evil spirit went upstairs while he went for the seats at the very back. From there he would have a good view. The psychopomp, Peach had called it, the guide who led evil spirits to hell.

22

W HEN A POPULAR SALE is on in Oxford Street or a new,
much hyped store is opening or December 23 comes
round, the crowds are not like the crowds in other cities. They are
nearer the huge gatherings of people assembled for some religious
ceremony or political upheaval. The difference is that they are
mostly but not exclusively women, and they are constantly on the
move. The movement is slow and sporadic, broken by hesitations
outside shop windows or pauses at traffic lights, where impatience
to get across is intense and risks are taken with life and limb.
Regularly, people fall as they try to cross on a green light and are
injured, occasionally one will be killed, collapsing under a bus, but
mostly the crowd moves on, a sluggish river of women and the rare
man, come to help carry the bags. It is never possible to strike out a
plan for oneself or take one's time or even change one's mind as to
direction of route or selection of store. It is wiser to stay away. One
joins in where one can, moving along at a pace set hours before,
following those ahead and being followed by those behind.

It was so for Dex, who managed to come up close behind the
dense mass of black hair and the black coat as the evil spirit left
the bus and to follow her as she slipped into the train of shoppers,
heading up towards the circus. She didn't look round, no one did,

you looked ahead, ever onward, hoping for a gap in which to spot a certain doorway you could plunge for, elbowing and thrusting, scarcely breathing. The evil spirit seemed to have no particular shop in mind, no recognisable door to make for. He fingered the trowel in his pocket, the long trowel with the pointed head, and the sharp pruning knife. Which to choose? Which to use? Perhaps the trowel was not sharp enough, while the knife was sharp enough for anything.

Somewhere ahead, maybe in the circus itself, a band was playing, someone was singing, all of them surrounded by red and yellow streamers and great green and white banners under the silver Christmas lights. Of the people around him and ahead of him, many were on their mobiles, talking and listening, laughing, enjoying themselves. Dex tapped a number into his and this time it rang. The voice that answered was a man's, a soft voice, not Dex's God's, but like it. It was unusual for this to happen but wonderful when it did. The voice that wasn't quite Peach said, "It's a wrong number, but Merry Christmas just the same."

Dex said, "Thank you. Merry Christmas," and, as he did so, realised that he had never uttered those two words before to anyone or had them uttered to him.

The music was loud now, the voice shouting and sobbing. Dex could see only the backs of heads, mainly the black, curly head in front of him. He pulled the toolbag up so that he was holding it right up in front of his chest. It kept him from being too close to the evil spirit, from touching it. In his other hand he clutched the knife. No one was looking at him, everyone could only look ahead, shuffling along, moving to the rhythm of the crowd's footfalls. Dex lifted the knife in his fist and thrust it hard through the black coat, through and through and through. The sound the evil spirit made was drowned by the drums and the saxophone and a CD all playing at the same time. Dex stood still, let the crowd move past him, clustering now around the falling girl. There was little blood to be seen, the furry coat must have sucked it up. The evil spirit was now a heap of black fur lying on the ground like a dead bear. Now a constant broken, choking screaming began from the crowd, and the music suddenly stopped. The singing stopped and the band on the dais fell silent. The sound was replaced by everyone talking, shouting, repeating over and over, "What's happened? What's going on? What is it?" and then a man's voice like a bell tolling: "Someone's been killed."

CLOSING OXFORD STREET on this, notoriously the busiest shopping day of the year, was at first unbelievable to retailers and the public. This was *their* day of days, their last-minute day. But they had no choice. Entrances to the stores were closed, and though rowdier women from the crowd banged on the doors demanding to be let in, most fell in with the police demands to proceed into side streets, to tube stations, and to bus stops on diversionary routes. The clearing of the shopping centre took a long time.

It was impossible for the police to establish who had been moving along in the vicinity of the dead woman when the stabbing took place. Dex felt the trowel in his pocket, glad he hadn't used it. He liked his little trowel and had never seen another quite like it. To have used it to destroy an evil spirit might have spoiled it for him, making him not want to weed and plant with it again. The knife he had wiped on the raincoat of a man he was thrust against in the exodus, then he had slipped it into an open handbag. Whose handbag he didn't know, just a big red bag belonging to a woman who had left it wide-open as she struggled along. A wrong way to behave, Dex thought, because it encouraged crime, put temptation in the way of bad people who wanted to get money they hadn't earned.

His success pleased him. The world had been cleaned of another evil creature and he would be rewarded for it. The back streets of Mayfair were strangely silent and empty. Dex didn't think why this might be. He heard police-car sirens and the deeper howl of ambulances and supposed there must somewhere have been a serious accident. In Park Lane he got on a crowded bus and it carried him away towards Victoria.

THE REGIONAL NEWS at noon was almost entirely devoted to the fatal stabbing of a woman in Oxford Street. The Princess watched it with Gussie on her lap and called June when it was too late to see or hear much beyond the police's saying it was murder. The woman had not yet been identified. The huge crowds whose preference on this special day was Oxford Street had been dispersed with difficulty. June watched, fascinated to see women young and old herded onto buses and driven into tube stations. She supposed the murder had been done by one of those gang members, the only difference being that it took place in a Christmas crowd in the West End rather than in Brixton or Peckham.

She gave the Princess her lunch on a tray, a chicken breast with oven-cooked French fries and defrosted peas, and took herself off to the dining room with a sandwich to prepare the agenda for tonight's meeting of the St. Zita Society, the last of the old year. Typing with her left hand took a long time. As chair, she intended to be firm with those who wanted to resume discussion of the canine-excrement question. That must come to an end this evening and not be raised again. The St. Zita Society had done its best and had failed, as must sometimes happen. She would establish with Thea what arrangements she was making for Miss Grieves's Christmas dinner and, rather more subtly, for serving a suitable meal to herself and the Princess. June had to keep going back over what she had written, correcting the mistakes made by her stumbling left hand.

She added "the gardening question" to her agenda and "disposal of Christmas trees" and then she was done. The little pink lights had to be checked. One of them had burnt down faster than the others. This puzzled June but was hardly important. She replaced it and the one next to it with new candles. The Princess was asleep, the lunch tray still balanced precariously on her lap. June lifted it off, noticed that the brandy bottle had joined the flagon of sparkling water the Princess hadn't touched, and helped herself to a generous tot.

The lights behind the blinds at the home of Arsad Sohrab and Bibi Lambda had gone out. Henry, sent by Lord Studley to check on all the candles, rang their bell and reminded them of the importance of keeping up the tradition. Arsad said, "What importance? You tell me." But Henry couldn't. He lacked his employer's logical mind and adversarial skills. "I don't know. Just do it," he said, and passed across the street to where Jimmy had failed to replace the candles at number three.

"His lordship relies on you," Henry said severely. "You've made a good job of it up to now."

Jimmy, who was wearing an apron with a grinning cat on it over his jeans, invited him in and gave him a glass of the port, which had already been broken into. "Have you seen Thea?"

"Not since this morning. She was on her way to do some last-minute shopping."

"It's not like her not to answer her phone."

Henry had his own share of what he called "woman trouble." He raised his eyebrows at the grinning cat, said, "You can't keep her tied to your apron strings for ever, you know," and laughed at his own joke.

The Neville-Smiths had returned and placed two candles in handsome brass holders on their windowsill. As Henry was passing, Montserrat with Ciaran came up the area steps, and the two of them persuaded him to join them for a pre-Christmas drink in the Dugong. Maybe he should stick to tonic water as he had already had the port with Jimmy. He was due at Huguette's around two. Any more drink was out of the question. He had to drive Lord Studley to a Coalition Christmas party at Spencer House at six.

Now all his meetings with Huguette took place at her flat in Chelsea. It was safer than number eleven Hexam Place, and as he broke a rule and drove to Carlyle Square in the Beemer, he could see no reason why this arrangement should not continue for ever—well, for several pleasant years. The improbable had happened. She had got a job with a PR company much favoured by the Conservative Party. No doubt Daddy had helped, thought Henry.

Her flat was small but luxurious, consisting of a pretty bedroom, a minimalist living room, a lavish bathroom, and a kitchen smaller than the larder in her father's house. Henry had to say no to a share in the bottle of Chablis Huguette opened, and they went straight to bed. Thanks probably to his abstemiousness, he enjoyed himself even more than usual and Huguette was rapturous about his performance. If it could always be like this, he wouldn't resist when she talked about telling her father of their relationship and future marriage. Time flew by as it always did when she was in a sweet and clinging mood, and it came as a nasty shock to catch sight of his watch on the bedside cabinet and see that it was 5:21.

"My God, I've got to go! Your dad'll kill me."

Henry was never so carried away as to forget his job and his duty, and instead of dropping his clothes on the floor he had draped them carefully over a chair. He was stepping into his underpants when he heard the faint creak of the lift and a high-heeled footstep in the passage outside. How they both knew who this must be, neither could have said, but they did. Huguette flung open one of the wardrobe doors and pushed him inside, thrusting his clothes after him. The doorbell didn't ring. Henry heard the letterbox flap lifted and a familiar voice call, "Hi, darling. It's Mummy."

It would almost have been better if the caller had been Lord Studley himself. Inside the wardrobe it was stuffy and the scent from Huguette's clothes almost overpowering. Skirts and trousers and jeans and long scarves and stoles hung down, teasing his face. Henry was afraid to move much in case Oceane heard the noise he made. He was also aware that Huguette had given him his clothes but left his shoes under the chair. The memory came to him of a film he had once seen about the duke of somewhere or other visiting his girlfriend and having to get into a cupboard just like him because her other lover had arrived and her other lover was the king. Charles the Second, he thought it was, and maybe it was the other way round and the king had to get into the cupboard when the duke arrived. It wasn't a good film.

He listened, hoping that Oceane hadn't seen his shoes or the Beemer—it was parked some distance up the street—and that she'd say she couldn't stay long. It seemed she had brought the shoes and handbag which were Huguette's Christmas present because Mummy and Daddy were off to France on the following day. But as for not staying long, she had accepted a cup of tea and then a gin and tonic and was admiring her present, now apparently on Huguette's feet, and telling her that the bag came from Chanel. Huguette had also failed to hand Henry his watch, but he could guess that it must by now be a quarter to six. He was hastily fumbling his way into his clothes.

Oceane had a clear and penetrating voice. He heard her ask for a second gin and tonic and remark that Huguette's father would shortly be going to a party. "Naturally I was asked and naturally I said no."

"If I go and get dressed, do you think we could go to the Icebar?"

Oceane laughed. "As if it wasn't cold enough outside!"

With exceptional perceptiveness Henry thought how having qualms about this igloo-like drinking place where everything was composed of ice showed her age. No young person would ever have made that remark. "And then we'll have dinner at the Ivy. They'll always give me a table."

"I'll call Henry and he can take us. Daddy can go to his party in a taxi." Huguette came into the bedroom, whispered to him, "When I'm dressed, I'll take Mummy into the kitchen. You can get out of here, give it two minutes, and then ring the doorbell. OK?"

She had saved, if not his life, the best part of it. He heard her placating her father, telling him she'd order him a cab. Her resourcefulness was a surprise to him, and he decided that next time she proposed to him he would give in. The arrangement and the several pleasant years would apply just the same when he was a married man.

THE *EVENING STANDARD* had the story and so did the BBC's regional news at six thirty. Montserrat hardly ever watched television, but she fetched the paper from the corner shop and walked home looking at the picture, which filled the front page, of what looked like a million people in Oxford Street, nearly as many police, and something lying alone on the pavement. It was too dark to read anything smaller than the headline: FATAL STABBING OF SHOPPER.

The dead woman had not yet been identified, or if she had, the police were not telling. It wouldn't be anyone Montserrat knew, she was sure of that. Indoors she read an interesting story about someone being killed by her pet cat, an animal of exceptional size and ferocity, and another concerning a model who had broken her leg through wearing shoes with seven-inch heels, and then she got dressed in a frock and filmy stole for her surprise visit to Preston Still, adding as an afterthought the red quilted jacket that was a Christmas present from Ciaran.

June and the Princess got no dinner that evening. June was obliged to open a can of spaghetti Bolognese and forage for ice cream in the freezer. She was late for the meeting of the St. Zita Society, but that hardly mattered as the only other member to turn up was Dex, who sat as usual by himself, drinking Guinness and listening to the various voices, pleasant and unpleasant, that his pressing of digits on his mobile conjured up.

Alone at number three, Jimmy had a fridgeful of food and no one to eat it. He had sent three texts to Thea, left her four voice-mail messages and three e-mails. None had been answered. She had left him, he was sure of it, had been half-expecting it ever since she made it clear Damian and Roland's civil partnership was more important to her than their own wedding date. Yet when his mobile finally rang, all this misery and all these doubts were overthrown and he knew it was her, calling to tell him that she loved him and had been absolutely unable to get to a phone all day.

It wasn't Thea. It was her sister, Chloe.

"Are you sitting down? This is going to be a shock." Her voice had a catch in it, like a sob. "You want to prepare yourself."

"What is it?" Yet somehow he knew.

"That girl that was stabbed in Oxford Street. That was Thea. The police got hold of me to identify her. My number was on her mobile and yours is too. I was her next of kin."

23

Y OU," SAID PRESTON STILL, opening the door to Montserrat.
"Who did you think it was?" she replied.

He was looking at her as a man might look at a ghost before
he realised it couldn't be true, that whatever this was it must be
a manifestation from his imaginings. She was suddenly terribly
frightened. She thought of the car and herself spread-eagled across
its grid, of the shove into the middle of her back that nearly resulted
in her falling onto the tube line. Now the idea of entering his flat
brought on a shivering he stared at.

"What's wrong with you?"

If she accused him outright, she was too scared of what he might
do, but something kept her there, unable to retreat or take a step
forward. When she spoke, she stammered. "It's Thea who's dead."
She was afraid to say it was Thea he had killed.

He didn't seem to know whom she meant. "Who's Thea?"

"My friend." It seemed to her now that her voice was someone
else's or coming from a long way off. "Girl with red hair, only it's
not anymore. It's dark, like mine." The moment she uttered those
words, even before they were fully out, she knew. She went on
making the parallels. "And she's got a black jacket like mine and
she's my height and she was going where I meant to go." It was

too much for her, and she broke off into a hysterical laughing and crying, clutching on to Preston because there was nothing else to hold on to, screaming and crying into his face.

As a door on the other side of the hallway opened, he pulled her inside, hissing at her to stop, to stop, keep her voice down, be quiet. She fell onto the floor. She would have kicked out at him if he hadn't quickly stepped away. He picked up his mobile phone from the table, and she recognised the digits he gave as his reference number at the cab company he used. "As soon as possible," he said. Then he said, as she struggled to her feet, edging away from him, "When that woman was stabbed this morning, I was in my office in Old Broad Street at a board meeting with half a dozen other people. When you tell the police, I think you should tell them that too."

She said nothing. He took her down in the lift, and the cab was waiting outside. The driver must have thought it odd that she didn't speak and Preston Still didn't speak but opened the door for her, closed it, and walked away up the steps without looking back. It was cold inside the taxi and Montserrat asked if she could have some heat, please. The driver appeared to be one of those who scarcely speak. The heat came on and he maintained his silence, finally saying as they drew up in Hexam Place, "Going away for Christmas?"

Montserrat shook her head and, realizing he couldn't see her, said, "No."

She got out, making no reply to his parting words, whatever they were, she hadn't heard them. Before she even got into the house, while she was still going down the area steps, she called Ciaran. Something strange had happened to her. She had lost her friend, her friend had been killed by mistake for her, she had been enormously frightened, but now when she heard Ciaran's voice and spoke to him, she was filled with an emotion quite new to her. She didn't want him just for sex or for a man to be with.

"Oh, Ciaran," she said, "please come to me. Please come now. I do love you so."

CHRISTMAS EVE and Thea was dead and Jimmy couldn't quite believe it. He hadn't seen a paper. All he knew was what Chloe had told him, and Chloe wasn't reliable. Once she had told him Thea had been to the cinema with her when Thea had really been serving drinks at the party Damian and Roland had had to celebrate their being together for ten years. That was an outright lie, and so might this be because Chloe wanted Thea to break their engagement. Jimmy wasn't sure whether he believed this or that Thea's death was the reality. Chloe couldn't have made that up about the police, could she? Or a stabbing in Oxford Street? She could, though. It wasn't so very way out. He ought to go up to Mr. Choudhuri's shop and buy a paper, but instead of going, he began walking up and down and round the house, looking out the front windows.

The night before, after he put the phone down, he had gone into Dr. Jefferson's bathroom and found a foil pack of what he thought were sleeping tablets. The name was new to him, he had never heard it before, but he took two of the pills so that he would sleep and not be able to think about what Chloe had told him. It was the first thing that came into his mind when he woke up. That is, when he struggled through apparent layers of fog and fluff and something thick like soup and lay there telling himself nonsense like Thea's being dead. It took about an hour of dozing and coming round for him to recall the phone conversation and what exactly Chloe had said. Now he stood at the window, looking down at Beacon, who had just walked along and got into the Audi, and then at June, her plastered arm in a sling, walking that little dog. Both of them wore quilted jackets, June's red, the dog's dark blue.

The candles on the windowsill had burnt down and gone out. He must have gone to bed and into that drugged sleep without putting them out. The house might have caught fire. Dr. Jefferson had a good stock of candles and it was only a matter of setting them into the holders and putting a match to them, but Jimmy hadn't the heart. Thinking about cooking Christmas dinner tomorrow was equally dispiriting—no, worse, impossible. He looked at the duck. He had collected the orange sauce in a china bowl, the potatoes waiting to be peeled. He put the duck into a carrier bag and carried it out into the front garden. Beacon was bringing the Audi round to park it outside number seven. Jimmy walked down to the bottom of the street in his short-sleeved shirt, not noticing the cold. He tapped on the Audi's off-side front window.

Beacon got out, said, "That was a terrible thing about Thea. I'm very sorry."

So it was true. In a way Jimmy had always known it. "Would you like to have this duck? I've no use for it now."

"That's very good of you. We've got a goose, but Dorothee will be pleased to have this bird as well." Beacon cleared his throat, assumed what Montserrat called his vicar's face. "She is with God now. Where she's gone, there's no more pain. Sorrow and sighing shall flee away. You have to remember that."

"Yes, thanks. I will. Enjoy the duck."

CONTEMPLATING THE PLASTER that sheathed her right arm, June said, "I've been thinking that if I'd done it back in September, this thing would be off by now and I'd be able to cook our Christmas dinner."

The Princess was trying to unzip Gussie's quilted coat and had already received a small nip. "You couldn't have done it in September because there wasn't any ice to slip on." The Princess made growling noises at Gussie, very like his own. "You're a naughty dog to bite poor mama."

"We shall just have to have one of those ready meals from Waitrose or somewhere, madam." June was about to go out again, easing what the Princess called June's "stone arm" into her red quilted coat sleeve, when Rocksana arrived with a young Chinese man, his face, as the Princess put it, with more metal studs in it than the back of her leather sofa. His name was Joe Chou, he was a guitarist and Rocksana's new boyfriend.

"I hope you don't mind," Rocksana said, accepting a gin and tonic for herself and one for Joe Chou. "I mean, you don't think me unsensitive, Rad being your sort of nephew, but you can't argue with love, can you?"

"We weren't close," said June, taking off her coat.

"And now someone's murdered your friend Thea. It's got to be the same person, hasn't it? Only it makes you wonder how many more people down here are going to snuff it. Now tell me what you're doing for Christmas?"

"Bugger all," said the Princess.

"That's what I wanted to hear because you're going to have it with us. Me and Joe have got a carful of nosh outside, and we're going to come and cook it for you, turkey and all the trimmings. Pop outside and bring it in, Joe, there's a lamb." Rocksana lit a cigarette and held out her gin glass for more. "The fact is I've had to give up my place in Montagu Square that was Rad's, I can't afford it. And Joe's only got one room, so you're doing us a favour letting us have Christmas here. I forgot to mention Joe's a chef when he's not being a guitarist, so you'll get a brilliant meal."

He came back and was rewarded with more gin. June eyed the overflowing carrier bags and the boxes from a well-known patisserie. "More to come," said Joe, tossing down his drink at two gulps. "I've already got a parking ticket."

"Never mind, angel. When you've brought all the flowers in we'll be on our way."

Banksias and gazanias and multicoloured other varieties. Khalid Iqbal would have known their names and so, probably, would Dex Flitch. June wondered if they had enough vases to accommodate them, so put the food away first.

The duck having been taken home to Dorothee, at three in the afternoon Beacon picked up Mr. Still from the office he would not be returning to until December 28 and drove him, not to Medway Manor Court, but to Hexam Place. His wife, Rabia told him, had just left in a hire car for the Cotswolds and her parents'. Before that she had sat down in the nursery with Rabia and poured out her heart to this unwilling but acquiescent audience. The girls were watching a DVD and Thomas was asleep.

"My marriage is over," Lucy said. "Preston has put this house on the market, only no one's supposed to know yet. It will absolutely destroy me to have to leave it. I can't live alone with those kids. We shall talk about it over Christmas, of course, but it looks likely that I shall take them to live in my parents' house. It's huge and there's a big flat in it—well, a whole wing really. That's where we'll live."

Rabia said nothing. She tried to smile encouragingly but couldn't. Her lips were as stiff as if she had had an anaesthetic at the dentist's.

"My old nanny's there. She's nearly eighty but she adores children and she'll be a real help to me. I know I couldn't take you away from London, so that solves that little problem really. Preston will be talking to you about it. You don't have a contract, do you?"

Rabia didn't know. She couldn't remember signing anything, and contracts were papers that had to be signed. She was glad that while Lucy was speaking, when she was saying all these things, Thomas was out of sight and asleep.

Lucy's car had come before much more was said. Rabia carried her cases downstairs for her, and Lucy said she was a treasure, not a word Rabia much liked applied to herself.

"I'm going to hate having to let you go."

By the time Mr. Still arrived the children were all ready and their cases were packed. Mr. Still said nothing about contracts or her having to leave, barely spoke to Matilda and Hero and not at all to Thomas. For once he didn't ask if the spot on Hero's cheek was chicken pox or why Thomas was so pale. When they were all gone,

Rabia was alone in the house. Or she thought she was until, while she was standing on the gallery, leaning over the rail, she heard a burst of laughter from Montserrat's flat. She was still standing there, thinking how she must go back, tidy the nursery, and change the sheets on all the beds, when Montserrat appeared on the stairs below, more closely entwined with a young man than perhaps Rabia had ever seen her before. They looked up, laughing, and called "Happy Christmas" to her.

Rabia thought it would somehow be wrong for her to say the same thing back, so she said, "Thank you."

That evening she went to the mosque with her father but sat of course with the women, wearing her long black skirt and a new black coat, her head covered by a hijab with a gold design on it. Her thoughts had been straying in a way they should not have done, to Thomas at his auntie's in Chelsea, a big house no doubt with everything in it that money could buy. Would she be kind to him and loving? Would she give him the food he liked and praise him when he ate it? Rabia knew she must not keep thinking of him, she must put him out of her mind, prepare herself to forget him, look to the future and new relationships, new commitments.

It was cold, frost already clouding windscreens, lying on hedges and brickwork. She and Abram Siddiqui walked along in silence for a while until she broke that silence by telling him there was no point in her returning to the empty house in Hexam Place that night and could she stay with him?

"Of course, my daughter," he said. "You know I would like you to stay with me always."

But she waited until they were there, walking along this street in Acton where many of the houses belonged to people like themselves of Pakistani heritage, but a few had Christmas trees in their windows and holly wreaths on their door knockers, before broaching her intended subject.

"There is something important I want to say to you, Father."

He let them in, took her coat from her. "Will you make tea for us, Rabia?"

The neat little house was warm. Abram often said, with forgivable pride, that he hoped he could now afford never again while indoors to shiver in the bitter English winter. As if the temperature in the high twenties centigrade were not enough on its own, he added ten degrees to it by switching on the gas heater, whose flames licking artificial coal looked like a real fire. Rabia brought in the tea. She handed him his cup, sat down in a low chair, her black skirts spread to cover her feet in their small black pumps.

"Father, if you are agreeable and the idea pleases you, I would like you to see Mr. and Mrs. Iqbal and tell them I'll be willing to marry their son Mr. Khalid Iqbal. Will you do that?"

"My Rabia," he said.

IF A MURDER VICTIM is a woman, the first suspect the police look at is her husband or fiancé or partner or lover or boyfriend. Newspaper readers and news watchers know this. They wait avidly for an arrest and feel disappointment if this particular man is pronounced cleared, a witness now, not a possible killer. Jimmy knew this but he had never thought much about it. He had never imagined himself in such a man's position or considered how it must feel for someone who was innocent, and already had his grief to contend with, to be suspected of the very crime which had plunged him into misery. And until the two policemen rang Dr. Jefferson's doorbell on Christmas Eve in the evening, such an eventuality never crossed his mind. Everyone knew he had been in love with Thea, had been engaged to her, was soon to marry her, including this Detective Sergeant Freud and Detective Constable Rickards, whose red hair reminded him of Thea's as it used to be.

They asked him where he had been on the morning of December 23 and he told them he had been here, in this house. No, he hadn't been out. He had been preparing for Christmas with his fiancée. They wanted to know if anyone could confirm that, and he had to say that he had been alone, he had seen various residents of Hexam Place from the windows, but he didn't think they had seen him.

"What about Rad Sothern?" said Freud. "Did you know him?"

"I don't know people like that." Jimmy couldn't understand why they brought him up now. "That was months ago."

"Just seven weeks, in fact," said Rickards.

Most mystifying to them, it seemed, was how and why Jimmy was there in Mr. Simon Jefferson's house at all. All right, Jimmy was his driver and kept an eye on the house while his employer was away, but *lived* there, had his girlfriend there with him, was cooking Christmas dinner for both of them.

"Do pretty well for yourself, don't you?" Freud was eyeing the bottle of gin on the sideboard, the half-empty bottle of Scotch, the as-yet-unopened bottles of wine. "Drowning your sorrow at Dr. Jefferson's expense, were you?"

That made Jimmy feel like crying, but he managed to hold back the tears like a child missing an indulgent parent. He told Freud and Rickards that while in the house on Friday morning he had seen from the window June in her red coat, walking the dog in its blue coat, Henry at the wheel of the Beemer, Bibi Lambda on her bicycle, and Rabia pushing the little Still boy in his buggy. They said they would want to talk to him again.

"Everything stops for Christmas, doesn't it?" Jimmy was trying to be ingratiating.

"Not in our business," said Freud coldly.

24

T HE PREVIOUS YEAR Dex had spent Christmas Day in a
church hall near Chelsea Creek. The people who came
there to have their dinner were looked after by a group of young
girl volunteers who waited on them and served their food. He had
been told by the social worker who looked in on him from time
to time that it would be the same this year, and it was. Not all the
people were homeless; some were like him, living in one room
on their own, with no wife or children. The men outnumbered
the women by three to one. First of all they had a cup of tea, then
they watched TV, and at 12:30 p.m. Christmas dinner was served
at a long table covered in red paper; there was turkey and stuffing
and sausages, roast potatoes and cabbage, followed by Christmas
pudding and custard. One of the women said the stuffing came
out of a packet and the custard out of a tin. Dex didn't care. It was
the best meal he'd had all year. A big glass of Guinness would have
made it perfect, but there wasn't any, of course there wasn't. He
didn't really mind.

After dinner he slept a bit in an armchair with wooden arms and
a cushion with Mickey Mouse on it because everyone else slept.
They woke up for the queen and then Dex went home. His room
was stuffy and smelling of unwashed clothes and mothballs. He

switched on the television and sat down in front of it to see a woman talking on a five-minutes-long news bulletin about finding his knife in her handbag. Now he rather regretted putting it there. He had done good service with it, making the world a better place. Suppose he had to destroy another evil spirit? Stealing was wrong, he knew that well, but just for once he might have to break that rule and take a knife from Dr. Jefferson's kitchen if Peach needed him again.

IN SPITE OF Thea's death and the sporadic visits of the police to Hexam Place, the little candles in drawing-room windows continued to burn. Even Damian and Roland, allowing theirs to go out before they left for Roland's mother's on the Friday evening—out of respect for Thea, charitable people said—relit them on their return on Christmas night. Apologising in a perfunctory sort of way, DS Freud and DC Rickards turned up on their doorstep ten minutes later, observed by Montserrat, to make what they called routine inquiries. Montserrat and Ciaran had had their Christmas dinner with Ciaran's sister and a bunch of friends, eaten little and drunk a great deal, and, returning, decided that the run of number seven should be theirs. The family had gone away and so had Rabia. They slept for a while on the drawing-room sofas and, recovering after a restorative concoction prepared by Montserrat of wine, water, and soluble aspirins, stationed themselves at the big window to watch the world go by, or such of it as moved about Hexam Place.

Light from streetlamps rather than candles glittered on Rickards's red hair and Freud's well-polished shoes as they mounted the steps to Damian and Roland's front door.

"That'll piss those two off," said Montserrat. "They've only just got back from their mum's. Or one of their mum's."

"I reckon it's just a formality and they'll arrest that driver guy."

"It won't have been Jimmy. I saw Jimmy in Jefferson's place at the time it was happening."

"You did?" said Ciaran. "Wow. You'll have to tell them."

"Yeah, I know. I just thought I'd wait a bit. I've got something to tell you, Ciaran. I don't know what you'll think."

They continued to look out of the window for a while, Ciaran's arm round Montserrat's shoulders. Miss Grieves came lumbering slowly up the area steps of number eight, dragging a black plastic bag behind her.

"The council won't take that," said Montserrat, "not on Boxing Day, they won't. I tell you what, those cops ought to talk to her. She sees everything goes on down here. Hey, look at that."

What Ciaran was to look at was Henry, who had appeared from Lower Sloane Street holding hands with the Honourable Huguette.

"I don't believe it. Are they going into number eleven?"

"I can't see from here. Who are they anyway?"

"If I went in for fairy stories, I could say the princess and the swineherd, but the reality is they're Lord Studley's daughter and Lord Studley's driver. How about that?"

Ciaran said, "You said you'd got something to tell me. Like what?"

"Let's have another drink first. There's whisky in that cupboard thing."

While they were raiding the drinks cabinet, the fox emerged from the Princess's front garden and set about tearing open Miss Grieves's rubbish bag. It helped itself to a turkey drumstick. She watched it from the area and, unable to do anything about it, stood at the foot of the steps shouting and shaking her fist. The fox left with its booty the way it had come.

WHEREAS *bun in the oven, up the duff,* and *knocked up* were expressions Henry was familiar with, the terminology used by Huguette in the text she had sent him the day before yesterday he had never before heard. *In family wy! b OK now. xxx H.* He had to phone her and ask, to be told she was more than three months pregnant and her father wanted to see him. Henry nearly fainted.

"No, it'll be fine. I wouldn't say he's like over the moon. But what d'you think he said? 'At least he's a fine specimen of manhood,' he said. 'It'll be a handsome infant.' Couldn't you just die laughing?"

"And he's going to let us get married?"

"He's going to *make* us get married. What d'you think he said? 'No daughter of mine is going to be one of those single mothers,' he said. 'Remember, I'm a Conservative.'"

So Henry had gone to see Lord Studley at number eleven, climbing up the elegant flights of stairs to the office on the second floor. The House was not sitting, nor were ministers required in their departments, so the Beemer would remain clean and shining in its garage. Lord Studley behaved much as his own great-grandfather might have behaved to an unsuitable but successful suitor for his daughter's hand, delivering first a scolding, following it with a commentary on the few consolations to be had: Henry was young and healthy, had never been married before, was not a stranger to the family, and Huguette seemed devoted to him. After that, since there would be no driving that day, sherry was offered and accepted and both agreed that the wedding should take place as soon as possible.

There was no sign of Oceane.

THE WHOLE STORY of Rad Sothern and Lucy, Preston Still's early return to number seven, his assault on Rad, and Rad's fall down the stairs to his death at the bottom was related to Ciaran. Then Montserrat told him about the box on the roof rack, the drive to Gallowmill Hall, and the subsequent disposal of the body.

Ciaran was unfazed. If anything, he was admiring. "If you tell them all that, you won't be able to tell them how you saw Jimmy on Thursday morning."

"Why not?"

"Get real, Montsy. Think about it. They're not going to believe you, are they? Maybe they'll believe one but not both. You have to choose what you want them to believe, Jimmy or Rad Sothern."

"Don't you believe me?"

Ciaran was quiet for a minute. "OK, yes, I believe you, but you're my woman. Of course I do."

"What shall I do, then?"

"Obviously you can't let Jimmy go on trial for murder. You saw him in the doctor's house while Thea was being murdered in Oxford Street. You did, didn't you?"

"You said you believed me, Ciaran. Of course I did."

"Then you tell them that and write an anonymous letter to the police about Rad Sothern and your Mr. Still and the box and the tyre et cetera, et cetera. Write to that guy Freud."

"Will he like take any notice?"

"He won't dare just let it go," said Ciaran.

A NUMBER OF WOMEN at the mosque as well as family members took it for granted Rabia had found a second husband through a Moslem marriage agency. She was quick to deny it. Such transactions, though sanctioned in the community, seemed to her improper, even vulgar. These arrangements should be made through parents or, if that was impossible, through uncles and aunties.

Now the deed was done and Khadiya Iqbal was already making wedding plans, Rabia looked forward to her future life as one might to a holiday destination so remote and exotic as to be beyond imaginings. One day it would happen and be infinitely strange, every day filled with unfamiliar things and experiences. She would once again have a permanent companion who was not a child, yet someone quite different from herself. Someone she could love? That she would try to, do her best, but as she thought this way,

Thomas came into her mind and she pictured her post-Christmas reunion with him, the little boy's expression puzzled until he saw her across the room and leapt into her arms.

The Still family was to return home on the Tuesday after Christmas, while Rabia came back on the Monday afternoon. She knew the house had been empty but, possibly, for Montserrat in the basement flat. She tapped on her door but there was no answer. Upstairs, on the first floor, she looked into the drawing room and got rather a shock. At first she thought the mess must be due to burglars, bottles empty and half-empty, glasses and cups and mugs everywhere, the furniture moved around, boxes of DVDs lying open on the floor in front of the television. More likely it was Montserrat and a friend or friends celebrating Christmas. Zinnia would be back next day but so would Mr. Still and the children. Rabia fetched a tray and began picking up the crockery and the glass. Father and now Khalid say I'm good, she thought, but I don't want to be too good, this isn't my job, and if any of them say how good I am, I shall get cross. But they won't, of course they won't. It doesn't matter anymore because I shall soon be gone and that will be the end of it.

Thomas did leap into her arms the way she predicted, and she felt such a surge of joy that was like excitement, making her breathless, that the tears came into her eyes. She had to fight them back and try to smile.

"Say *sweetheart*," said Thomas.

THE POLICE MIGHT have told Jimmy that they weren't going to arrest him, they weren't going to charge him, he was off the hook. But they didn't. They didn't tell him that Montserrat Tresser of number seven Hexam Place had seen him through the window at number three at the relevant time. They told him nothing. They just didn't come back. He waited nervously, missing Thea, sometimes speculating as to who could have killed her, sometimes feeling low.

Simon Jefferson, returning from Andorra on the Wednesday after Christmas, was suitably and gratifyingly sympathetic when Jimmy told him about Thea.

"Take the rest of the time off till after the New Year."

"I won't do that," said Jimmy. "Better that I have something to do, keep my mind off things."

None of the members of the St. Zita Society knew exactly what was happening with the police and Preston Still, but everyone speculated and produced theories. It began on New Year's Eve when early in the morning Freud's little Honda turned up outside number seven. Freud and Rickards, observed by June, who was walking Gussie, went up to the front door, spoke to Zinnia, and came down again almost immediately. June asked them whom they were looking for and, when there was no answer, said that Mrs. Still was in Chipping Campden and Mr. Still now lived in Medway Manor Court.

The car disappeared into Lower Sloane Street. Later that day a radio news bulletin led on a story about a suspect in the Rad Sothern death. The police were releasing no name yet, but a man had been arrested and was being questioned. Henry, over the moon, as he put it, after his engagement party, told Sondra, who had been serving the drinks, that Beacon had told him the man was Mr. Still. Sondra, who had never said anything about it before, said Zinnia had told her this was because Rad Sothern had been having a fling with Lucy. Not that this surprised Sondra as it had always been her opinion that Lucy had been round the block a few times. Beacon was shocked and seriously considered giving in his notice but had taken no steps so far.

The soon-to-be happy couple collected Jimmy from Dr. Jefferson's, where he had settled in, and took him to the Dugong to cheer him up. Jimmy had heard that the police had got a search warrant and been to Gallowmill Hall hunting for a roof-rack box but had failed to find it.

"That'll be my box I sold to Montsy," said Henry. "Well, *sold—gave away* is more like."

"Rad Sothern's body was in that box," said Jimmy. "I think I'll have another rum and Coke since it's New Year's Eve and I'm not driving. Anyway, they never found it. Another thing, they've been talking to an RAC man who changed the wheel on Mr. Still's car that same night. You'd think a big, so-called intelligent guy like him could change a wheel, wouldn't you?"

"I don't believe a word of it," said Ciaran, who had just come in. Montserrat put her arm through his. "And nor do I."

"They'll keep questioning Mr. Still all night, Dr. Jefferson says. He's really upset about it, I can tell you, being a mate. He says they can keep him there for thirty-six hours. I keep thinking if only Thea was here—it'd be quite a drama for her, wouldn't it?"

"Maybe he killed her too," said Huguette, but not till she and Henry were outside and on their way to yet another celebration, this time in Soho.

25

WHILE NOT WISHING to sound callous, Damian and Roland said to each other in Zinnia's hearing that, shocking as it was, Thea's murder would make little difference to their way of life. It might even be to their advantage as they would now be able to let the two top floors at a higher rent. Zinnia listened to Roland's phone call to the agent, and if she couldn't quite guess this woman's responses, she could hear the disappointment in Roland's voice. No doubt he'd been way off the mark in expecting a thousand pounds a week for that flat, and that was before the agent had even seen it. As for Thea's contribution to their domestic arrangements, it seemed they had underrated what she did. Zinnia could have told them, but didn't, that Thea had been secretary, housekeeper, gardener, and occasionally caterer all rolled into one, getting no thanks for it and no money. They needn't think that she, Zinnia, was going to make up the shortfall, though she might if they paid her.

No mention had yet been made of anything of the sort. Both Damian and Roland grumbled all the time about running out of soap, rubbish bags, and lightbulbs, the houseplants dying for want of water, having to serve their own drinks and do their own shopping. Who would now do the catering for their civil partnership party?

Zinnia told June she nearly died laughing when she heard Damian on the phone to his mother, tentatively enquiring if she and his aunt, who sometimes cooked for Belgravia dinner parties, would produce luncheon for 119 people at number eight Hexam Place on February 3. This was even funnier than the call to the estate agent, and Zinnia told June all about it, not leaving out his mother's "Bloody hell, Damian!" which you could have heard all over the flat if not in Hexam Place itself.

"I knew what would happen," Zinnia said to June, "and I was right. They've had to send cards to all those people they invited, apologising and telling them the wedding's off. Of course it's not. It's just going to be very quiet and the two of them having lunch at the Ivy with their mums and Lucy Still and Lord and Lady Studley."

"And that nongay pal of theirs Martin Gifford," said June, "so there won't be too many women."

THE POPULATION RETURNED more or less to normalcy on the first Tuesday in January. It was Jimmy's birthday, a sad occasion. If Thea hadn't met such an awful fate, they would have gone out to dinner and celebrated and talked of wedding plans. Or so Jimmy told himself, tears in his eyes as he opened the rear door of the Lexus for Dr. Jefferson. This went straight to the paediatrician's heart when he discovered that it was his driver's birthday, and telling Jimmy to wait "just a second" while he went back into the house, he reappeared with an envelope in which Jimmy later discovered was a cheque for two hundred pounds.

This was Dex's first day back at work. He arrived at nine thirty, carrying his big cloth bag containing the pointed trowel, the hand fork, the secateurs, and the shears, just as Jimmy got back from Great Ormond Street Hospital. Jimmy barely spoke to Dex but went quickly indoors, telling himself it was too cold, the wind too sharp, to stay out there longer than he had to.

Dex was used to the cold. When he was a child, his mother used to shut him in the outside toilet, sometimes for hours at a time, only in the winter, though. There was no point in doing it in the summer. She got one of his stepfathers to put a bolt on the outside specially for this purpose. So the cold was nothing when he had a warm coat and those stretchy gloves you could buy for a pound in the market. The ground was free of frost, though might not be for many mornings if the pictures on the TV were true, little white pellets fluttering about on the gray and the green. Frost and then snow had prevented a lot of the cutting back he would have done in early December. He began trimming the lilac and the philadelphus, remembering to be careful with the latter; no blossom would come on this year on those branches which had been pruned. The cut wood he placed in a large plastic bag. Better if he could have used the green carriers whose contents could be recycled, but because of the cuts Westminster Council had ceased providing them. Each branch and twig he cut up into small pieces for the sake of neatness.

He was starting on the dogwood when his mobile began to ring. This didn't happen often, and when it did, Dex always hoped it might be Peach. Once or twice since Christmas it had been, but not to speak to him, only printed messages Dex thought were telling him good things about the phone, things that would save him money. This call wasn't from Peach but from Mrs. Neville-Smith. Would he call next door and collect his money for sweeping up her path and the pavement outside and while there trim the hedge? Dex always said yes. While he liked Dr. Jefferson very much, he didn't like Mrs. Neville-Smith at all. This wasn't so much because she wasn't nice to him but because of her name. His second or third stepfather, the one who'd put the bolt on the toilet door, was called Smith, Brad Smith. He was the first evil spirit Dex ever encountered. Dex didn't know then that it was his mission in life to destroy evil spirits, so Brad Smith was still in the world, doing wicked things. Dex said yes to Mrs. Neville-Smith because of the money.

He worked till the clock face on his phone said 11:30, then he knocked on the back door to tell Jimmy he was finished and to ask for his money. Sometimes he wondered how Jimmy, who was only a driver and a workingman like himself, managed to live in Dr. Jefferson's house—eat there and watch TV and sleep in a bed there—but he would never ask. Occasionally, in the past, Jimmy had made him a cup of tea or, a wonderful moment, a mug of chocolate when Jimmy was having one himself. There was nothing like that this morning.

Jimmy handed over the money. "Dr. Jefferson'll give you a bell when he wants you again."

"He said Thursday."

"Sure of that, are you? I'll check with him. Don't count on it till you hear from me."

This was perhaps calculated to make Dex wonder where the next pound was coming from. He took his tools with him next door to Mrs. Neville-Smith's.

Jimmy sat down in front of the television and put his feet up on the coffee table. There were things to do—go home to his own flat, check that all was well, give it a bit of a clean, clean and polish the Lexus, see to the paperwork Dr. Jefferson left to him, renew the tax disc, check that the Residents' Parking wasn't about to expire. But not on his birthday and not when he was sick at heart. He was bereaved, practically a widower, and he needed to look after himself at least till the end of the week and maybe till Monday. Dr. Jefferson must be fetched from Great Ormond Street, of course, but apart from that, today would be a day of rest. Remote in hand, he switched the channel to the Tuesday lunchtime quiz programme and leant back against the cushions.

WITHOUT EXACTLY REGRETTING the anonymous letter—the first letter she had written to anyone for five years—Montserrat felt nervous about it. It was possible to know practically everything these days. She was vaguely aware that it hadn't always been like that, but it was now. Where someone or something came from, where anyone lived, who had touched something, worn something, who had written something, sent something, got in a train or on a bus—the list was endless. Did that mean the police knew who had sent that letter? Wouldn't they have come and seized her if they did?

"Stop worrying," said Ciaran. "What can they do to you? We've got ninety thousand people in prison and the jails are bursting at the seams. Get real, Montsy."

She didn't want to see Preston Still or phone him. The police might be tapping his phone, and as soon as they heard her voice, they would know she was the author of the anonymous letter. He might still be at the police station or they might have let him go back to Medway Manor Court. But surely, if they took the proper notice of her letter that they should, he would *never* go back there.

Lucy had arrived home in a hire car. Zinnia had told Montserrat that Beacon had refused to drive Lucy on account of her immoral life, but Montserrat wondered if Preston wouldn't let him. There was nothing in the papers about Preston. Montserrat was afraid to look, but Ciaran told her. Surely they had questioned him? Surely they had got a warrant to search Gallowmill Hall and the luggage room? She hadn't mentioned the changing of the wheel on her car because naming her car would have led them directly to her. Nor had she written a word about the RAC man. But the roof-rack box would be enough, wouldn't it? Rad Sothern's hairs inside it, his DNA, all those traces which these days were so helpful in bringing criminals like Preston to justice. They would get a warrant to search. They would have done that by now, but what was the outcome? If only she wasn't so frightened of asking.

NUMBER SIX Hexam Place was the property of the Princess, not June. In most of their altercations, the Princess made this point. "You want to remember," she would say, "that this house belongs to me" or "I am the mistress of this house." There was no danger of June's forgetting it for, every so often, after the Princess was asleep, she would open the top drawer in the drawing-room bureau and read the Princess's will or the copy of it, the original being in Mr. Brookmeadow's office in Northumberland Avenue. The will, witnessed by Damian Philemon and Zinnia St. Charles, left "everything of which I die possessed" to June Eileen Caldwell and was signed by Susan Geraldine Angelotti, known as Hapsburg, and dated "this fourteenth day of October 1999."

June had seen it many times but never been *permitted* to see it. Damian and Zinnia (an unlikely pairing) must have been "roped in," as she put it to herself, while June was taking Gussie's predecessor on one of those long walks needed by a Labrador, up to and round the park. Zinnia had told June of its existence or, rather, that it was the latest testamentary replacement. Now, one evening in the first week of January, the Princess having gone to bed early, June was examining the will again. It was the last of several wills made over the years, each one securing this inheritance to herself. In all the years she and the Princess had been together, notwithstanding a couple of lovers for each of them, an occasional woman friend, and an Italian family connection attempting to sponge, there had been no serious contenders to be beneficiaries. Things looked different now.

Some few hours earlier June, returning from a walk with Gussie, had come upon Rocksana easing the Princess into her wheelchair preparatory to taking her for a trip to Harrods. June had said nothing, but later on, after the Princess had retired to her room, going in with a cup of cocoa and a small Irish whisky on a tray, she had found Rocksana sitting on the bed holding the Princess's hand. This sight had led to the checking up on the will. Rocksana had talked about going home—wherever home might now be—after Christmas, then about going home after the New Year, but here it was past Twelfth Night (according to Roland) and she was still here.

June's indignation had nothing to do with liking or disliking Rocksana. If anything, June was indifferent to her. But the young woman, model, actress, whatever she might be, was nothing to the Princess. She was, if not a relative, a family connection of June's, or almost. Being engaged these days practically meant being married. If poor Rad had lived, they would probably have been married by now, and June would have been Rocksana's great-aunt-in-law. Next day Zinnia told June that when she went up to the second floor to "give it a quick flip round with a duster," she had found Rocksana there with a tape measure.

"Frankly," said June, "I'm surprised she knows what a tape measure is."

"It's amazing what you know when it's loot that's in question."

"That's true."

June was writing up the minutes of the last St. Zita meeting and preparing the agenda for the next one. Part of the time should be devoted to a memorial for Thea. Jimmy would be invited to speak, but perhaps he wouldn't feel up to it. Beacon might be a wiser choice so long as he didn't bring in too much religion. She was interrupted by Rocksana's asking if June would mind her taking Gussie out for his walk. The Princess had suggested it (or so the girl said, thought June), and Rocksana would be happy to lighten June's load.

June was on the alert two days later when the Princess asked her if she would give the little dog a rather longer walk than usual and reminded her that the vet had said he shouldn't put on any more weight. Mr. Brookmeadow was coming to tea. No, nothing important, only something that had to be done before a notary public, and Mrs. Neville-Smith would also be there. Did the Princess want anything special for tea? Rocksana was seeing to all that, fetching a cake from Patisserie Valerie. June was convinced a new will was to be made and in Rocksana's favour. She cheered up a bit next morning when, although Rocksana told June she was moving into the two top floors, the Princess demanded a short lease renewable after six months.

The St. Zita Society meeting was well attended. Beacon, who wasn't working that day, came over to the Dugong specially, complimented Jimmy on the excellence of the duck, and made a stirring speech about Thea's fine qualities. Apparently she had confided in him that she intended to be married in church and had asked him to give her away. Jimmy wept a bit and bought Beacon a Drambuie. Beacon rarely drank alcohol, and this was taken as a good omen. Dex again sat on his own at a table in the corner listening to his mobile and looking at messages which appeared on it. Jimmy, who was turning the meeting into a wake, bought Dex a Guinness but said afterwards that Dex's smile when he thanked Jimmy "made your blood run cold."

Dex had gone by then. The proceedings had mystified him. They seemed to be about some woman who had died, but who it was, where the death had taken place, and why these people cared, he didn't know. They were all people, not evil spirits, that was clear. The Guinness had been nice, and he had forced a smile of thanks for it, but smiling was unusual with him, he had few occasions for it. Sometimes, when a plant he had grown came into flower and was a good colour or a pretty shape, then he would smile, but that could only be a summer event and never happened at this bitter time of the year. January and February were the times when he best remembered being shut up in that cold place and the door bolted on him.

On the way home he picked up a tin of sardines and a bag of chips for his supper. His room was cold, and though he couldn't afford it, he put on the electric fan. The old lady on the floor below got something called the winter fuel allowance, two hundred pounds. Dex couldn't understand why he didn't get it, but when he asked, he was told he wasn't old enough, and he couldn't understand that either. Why was it better to be old than young? He put on the television. The woman who had found his knife in her bag was talking again, and then a policeman talked about tests being done on Dex's knife. With her black hair and fluffy coat the woman reminded him of the evil spirit he had destroyed, but he had got rid of her so he was no longer either afraid or angry.

His mobile phone made a little sound just as he was getting ready for bed, two little musical notes and then another. He had a look at his screen and to his mounting excitement saw that a message from Peach had come.

As a little thank-you, he read, *for being a Peach customer, we'd like to give you 10 free calls.*

He was pleased, not so much for the cost-saving as for the care for him this showed. In his world not many people had cared for him: Dr. Mettage perhaps, Dr. Jefferson had been good to him. But he felt that Peach really cared. After all, he hadn't asked for these messages, this kindness, it had just come, preceded by the little tune. Peach loved him.

JOE CHOU HELPED Rocksana move in and stayed the night but didn't apparently intend to live here with her.

"The Princess wouldn't have it anyway," said June. Her employer had never taken a stand on any moral issue, but it did no harm to tell the new tenant the rules, formulated by herself. "Not unless the rent goes up fifty percent," she added.

"Joe's just got himself a flat over the restaurant. He wouldn't want to give that up."

June got up at two o'clock in the morning to check on the will. The Princess had been in bed for five hours, Rocksana for perhaps one. Creeping up the top flight every quarter hour in the hope that the crack of light under Rocksana's bedroom door had gone out,

June had made three such journeys, dragging her rockbound right arm behind her until she met total darkness. At nearly three she entered the drawing room and looked for the will. Either the old one or a new one was what she expected, but what she found was no will at all. Impossible to tell whether a fresh one had been made. Possibly it had and Mr. Brookmeadow had taken it away with him to have a copy made; possibly a copy would come back. But perhaps the old will had not been superseded, June was still the legatee, and Mr. Brookmeadow had suggested there was no point in her keeping it at number six Hexam Place when it would be more secure with its fellow in the safe in Northumberland Avenue. There was no knowing.

If there was a new will, Mrs. Neville-Smith had been one of the witnesses, but who was the other? Not Zinnia. She had gone long ago and would be up at number four cleaning for Sohrab and Lambda by the time Mr. Brookmeadow arrived. There was of course a third possibility. A new will could have been made with June no longer the sole heir but with Rocksana and even possibly Zinnia herself as additional beneficiaries. Humbled by stress and anxiety, June thought she wouldn't much object to that, she was not entirely averse to sharing, she could bear it. In a rather more resigned frame of mind, she went back to bed.

In spite of his being a paediatrician, 99 percent of whose patients were under the age of ten, most of the residents of Hexam Place called for Dr. Jefferson when in need of medical attention. He lived in the same street, he was a doctor, and everyone agreed he was nice. Before the separating from his wife, Preston Still had regularly rung the doctor's doorbell (or sent someone else to do it) when one of his children had a temperature or a rash; Damian Philemon phoned when he or Roland had a sore throat; and Bibi Lambda asked for a repeat prescription for her contraceptive pill. Even Simon Jefferson, the mildest of men, remarked to Jimmy that this was a bit much.

He never said no and wouldn't have considered saying no when June presented herself at his front door and told him she had found the Princess unconscious on the bathroom floor. Dr. Jefferson accompanied her back to number six, where Rocksana told him, to everyone's surprise, that she had attempted the FAST test for stroke, examining the Princess's face for distortion, attempting to get her to raise her arm and to speak, none of which had results.

"Best call an ambulance. It looks like a stroke, in which case time is of the essence."

26

THE PRINCESS NEVER regained consciousness. June could see little point in visiting her when she wouldn't know if anyone was there or not, but Rocksana thought otherwise.

"They, like, know you're there," she said to Zinnia, "even if they can't hear or speak."

Rocksana went every day and sat by the Princess's bed. June was made uneasy. She hunted through the medicine chest in the Princess's bathroom and seemed to recall a bottle of sleeping pills that had been there for at least twenty years but was there no longer. A search of Rocksana's flat revealed neither the pills nor the bottle, but June put this down to Rocksana's cunning. Three days after she had been admitted to the hospital, the Princess had a second stroke and died. Rocksana wept bitterly. June put on the Princess's mink coat and a hat made of lesser-quality fur because the weather was still cold and walked up to number three.

Doing this took a good deal of nerve. Only knowing that a fortune might be at stake kept June to her resolve. Dr. Jefferson was a doctor, he lived in the same street, he was famously kind and easygoing. He would listen. But she was afraid. Her mouth went dry as she rang the front doorbell. The butter-coloured Lexus was parked at the kerb, so there was no escape now. He was there.

Jimmy was there too and answered the door. He didn't exactly ask her what she wanted but as good as.

"Oh, hi, June. What brings you here?"

"That's for Dr. Jefferson's ears only," said June in a stiff but hoarse tone.

"Sounds like you've got a bad cold. Maybe you shouldn't be out."

June made no reply. It was the first time she had ever been inside the house. Through the half-open drawing-room door she could see the place was elegantly furnished, so without waiting for Jimmy to show her the way, she went in there and sat down on the kind of chair she thought of as French, with curly, gilded arms and legs and red silk upholstery. The sitting down was not entirely a gesture of defiance aimed at Jimmy but also because she feared her legs were about to give way from nerves.

Dr. Jefferson kept her waiting only two minutes. He wore a sympathetic look, a gentle half-smile, said, "I was sorry to hear about the Princess. I'm afraid you'll feel it deeply."

"Yes, well—yes, of course I do. We'd been together sixty years."

"Dear oh dear, that's a long time. Now what can I do for you?"

June came out with it bluntly. If she hadn't, she wouldn't have done it at all. "I want to know if we can have a postmortem."

"A postmortem? And why would you want that?"

Always one to fall back on drama in difficult situations, June said, "I suspect foul play."

"I am not hearing this," said Dr. Jefferson in a cold voice.

Outside the half-open door Jimmy heard her on the subject of the pill bottle, the Princess's good health right up to the minute she was found lying on the floor, Rocksana's arrival at number six, and her "worming her way into the Princess's affections."

"I think she persuaded the Princess to change her will. Why else would Mr. Brookmeadow have come to tea? And it would have been changed in Miss Castelli's favour. You'll see."

June had more to say, but her voice had faltered and she put her left hand up to her mouth, for Dr. Jefferson's face had changed. He had gradually come to look quite different, to look in fact like another person. Now he was no longer the kindly, genial man who was the favourite of mothers at Great Ormond Street Hospital and whom their children seemed to prefer over their own fathers, but the just judge, stern and uncompromising. Two deeply etched parallel lines appeared between his eyebrows, and his thin lips were thrust forward. Jimmy, within earshot but unable to see through door and wall, gleefully awaited the explosion. None came.

Dr. Jefferson spoke quietly. "It's best to give you the benefit of the doubt, June. You have lost your employer and closest friend, you are plainly not well yourself. As a doctor, I suggest you go home to bed, have a good rest, and let's hear no more of this nonsense."

With that, half of it inaudible, Jimmy had to be content. He appeared at the appropriate time to show June out, saying as he watched her make her way unsteadily down the path, "Didn't I say you shouldn't be out with that cold you've got?"

Back in the kitchen Dex was patiently waiting for Jimmy to return to give him his money. Jimmy had absentmindedly put the envelope in his pocket. He retrieved it and handed it over, rather relieved that when Dex thanked him he didn't also manage one of his spine-chilling smiles. Careful to lock the back door before leaving to drive Dr. Jefferson to Great Ormond Street, Jimmy was back again after about a quarter of an hour. It was too early for lunch but Jimmy felt in need of a snack. The knife block had six slots, the bread knife occupying the one at the top on the left. The slot on the right, which a smaller, sharp fruit knife usually occupied, was empty. Strange, thought Jimmy, but not particularly sinister. It must be all these appearances of that woman on TV, the one who found the knife that killed Thea in her bag, getting to him. That couldn't be the missing one, could it? No, because he was sure that slot had been filled yesterday.

He began cutting bread, spreading the slice with butter and laying on it a thick wedge of cheddar. Eating drove the knife question from his mind and he concentrated on missing Thea.

PUTTING OFF HER resignation from day to day, Rabia decided she must postpone the writing of that letter no longer. Mr. Still had interviewed her and engaged her, but Mr. Still was gone, a divorce was imminent, and it seemed that Lucy alone was her employer now. Of this Rabia wasn't quite sure, but surely her notice should be given to Lucy. Mr. Still lived somewhere else and she didn't know how to find out where. Lucy would know, but Lucy would want to know why Rabia asked. Montserrat might know; Rabia was reluctant to ask her. So she put it off from day to day.

She knew the other reason for this postponement. While she told no one in the Still family that she would be leaving, she was still Thomas's nanny, as close to Thomas as ever. Secretly, privately, she could go on telling herself what she knew was true, that she was Thomas's best beloved, of all the people in his world he loved her best. Once she was gone, once she had announced that she was going, this would cease to be true. It would have to cease, for Thomas's own sake. He must not be made unhappy by her departure. If possible, he must be disturbed as little as could be by her leaving him. Rather to her surprise, when she put this into words—to herself only, silently to herself—she began to cry. Rabia had believed that her tears when Nasreen died were the last she would ever shed. And so it had been until now.

She was crying for a child who wasn't dead, who wouldn't die until he was an old old man, and who wasn't her own. She must lose him, there was no escaping that. She must lose him, marry Khalid, and maybe have children of her own. Drying her tears, she took out from the dressing-table drawer in her bedroom the pad of writing paper she had bought specially for this purpose and the envelope with the first-class stamp already stuck on it and settled down to write her resignation to Lucy. It took her a long time. The three children slept. Rabia wrote one draft after another before she was satisfied.

The letter in its envelope but destined to lie on her dressing table for several days before she would give it to Lucy, she went into Thomas's room and sat for a long time by his bed, watching him while he slept.

JUNE TOO WAS CRYING. It was only natural, she told herself between sobs, that she should weep for the Princess, her long-term employer but also her dearest friend. They had been inseparable, each other's confidante, knowing each other's business inside out. Gussie also cried or howled, searching the house for his dead mistress, although during his lifetime the Princess had scarcely been into any room but the one where she slept and the one where she watched television. He searched and paced and howled and wasn't much comforted by June's hugging him and saying, "It's just as bad for me, you know."

But it wasn't. June confessed to herself after a day of this that she was crying not for her loss but because Dr. Jefferson had rebuked her. If the reproof had come from someone well-known for rudeness and shortness of temper, she would have thought little of it, but from a man famous for his mildness and easygoing kindness to all and sundry, that was scarcely to be borne. So she cried. Her only comfort came from the sympathy meted out to her by the neighbours who, calling to express their sympathy, recognised genuine grief in her swollen eyes and tearstained cheeks.

27

Y OU HAD THE FUNERAL and then the people who had been to it all gathered in the drawing room, and Mr. Brookmeadow read the will. This belief of June's was grounded in her sporadic reading of sensational literature. The first of February was the day of the funeral, and she was planning ahead. The dining room should be allotted to the solicitor, who would sit at the head of the table, while those considered particularly interested took the seats along the sides. Rocksana Castelli, June thought, Zinnia St. Charles. Did witnesses have to be there? June might invite Damian, but would he come? Most unlikely. His own civil partnership now was to take place two days later, and though this hardly precluded attendance at the funeral of a neighbour, she thought that, if challenged, he would plead pressure of personal business.

Dr. Jefferson's unprecedented outburst at her suggestion of homicide on the part of Rocksana, on the part of anyone, had shocked her to the core. Had shocked her so much that she felt it in her bones so that when she kept her appointment to have the plaster removed from her arm, she asked the doctor if the pain she felt all over her was the onset of arthritis.

"At your age," he said not very pleasantly, "everyone has some arthritis."

It was nice getting her arm back, but not enough to make her forget Dr. Jefferson's behaviour. His explosion had frightened her, the way few demonstrations of anger could have. Her erstwhile belief she now saw as mistaken, a natural consequence of suffering bereavement. That was why she invited Rocksana to be present at the will-reading. If Rad's girlfriend now inherited the Princess's house and fortune, June had decided she would not contest it.

Burns's contention that the best-laid plans of mice and men often go wrong is usually taken to mean that the plans are good and their destruction bad, but in June's case the reverse was true. On the morning of the funeral she received a letter. It told her that under the will of HSH the Princess Susan Angelotti, known as Hapsburg, apart from minor bequests to Mrs. Zinnia St. Charles and Miss Matilda Still, her goddaughter, the residue of her estate, being the house known as number six Hexam Place SW1 and the sum of 4,652,000 pounds, mainly in stock and bonds, was to pass to her, June Eileen Caldwell. There were some subdued congratulations and expressions of his pleasure in the sad circumstances, and he was hers sincerely, John Brookmeadow.

June read it again. She wasn't dreaming or hallucinating. The will had been taken out of that drawer only to be remade with the inclusion of Zinnia's name and that of the little minx Matilda Still, and someone else had witnessed it. For the first time in many years, certainly for the first time since the Princess's death, June felt affection amounting to love for the Princess that brought tears to her eyes. She was glad that, admittedly to impress the neighbours and not to look mean, she had ordered a huge bouquet of white lilies, white freesia, narcissi, and gypsophila. The florist brought it as she was reading Mr. Brookmeadow's letter for the third time, and it joined the mountain of flowers piled up in the hall. June, who was still in her dressing gown, went up to her bedroom and dressed herself in the deepest black she had, selecting the Princess's mink coat to wear over it. After all, it was hers now, along with everything else.

MATILDA RECEIVED few letters. Rabia had become the personal postman at number seven since Mr. Still's departure, and she brought Mr. Brookmeadow's letter upstairs. Matilda was eating Cocoa Pops in the nursery with Hero.

"You can read it."

"'Please, Rabia, will you read this letter?'" Rabia corrected Matilda. "If you want me to read it, that's what you say."

"Oh, OK. Please, Rabia, will you read this letter?"

A lawyer was writing, telling Matilda that the Princess had left her five thousand pounds. If Rabia had ever heard the words *to him that hath shall be given,* she would now have thought them apt and true. But they came from the wrong holy book and she did her best to avoid resentful or envious thoughts.

"I didn't know she was my godmother" was all Matilda said for five minutes. Then: "I shall add it to my running-away money. I've probably got enough now to start my packing."

Rabia said nothing. She didn't believe in the running-away scheme, and the chances that Matilda would be allowed to get her hands on so large a sum were remote in the extreme. Holding Thomas by the hand, Rabia took the girls downstairs to wait for the school bus. It was rather less cold, another pale gray day. The bus came at the same time as Mr. Still's car. Hero called out, "Daddy, Daddy!" and Rabia marvelled, not for the first time, as the little girl ran to him, that children love bad fathers as much as good ones, their need for a parent is so great.

Mr. Still went up the steps to the front door, rather unwillingly holding Thomas's hand, and once Rabia had seen the girls onto the bus, she followed them. Opening the front door, she asked him if he had got the letter she had eventually posted. His shrug and shake of the head told her that he hadn't. It was lost, she supposed. She would have to write it again, resign again. Should she tell him about the Princess's legacy? Perhaps.

"The Princess has left Matilda some money."

"Really? I didn't know she knew Matilda."

"She was her godmother," said Rabia, although she knew little about what this meant. Up in the nursery, she showed Mr. Still the solicitor's letter.

"Good heavens," he said, once more shaking his head. "I can't attend to that now. I've some important documents to pick up." He cast a perfunctory glance at his little son. "Is that a bruise on his forehead?"

Rabia didn't say it was where his sister Hero had hit him with a tooth mug. No need to make more trouble when she could deal with what already existed. Anyway, she would soon be gone. With Thomas on her knee she watched Mr. Still from the window while he ran to the Audi, his arms full of papers. On the other side of the street, that gardener man called Dex who sometimes came to the garden centre was also watching him.

"We'll go for a nice walk," she said to Thomas. "We'll go and see *my* daddy and say hallo to Mr. Iqbal. Shall we do that?"

Thomas yelled, "Yes, yes, do it now!" and Rabia, smiling at him, put her finger to her lips.

THE CIVIL PARTNERSHIP ceremony passed off quietly, and the small lunch party was a success. At least according to June it was. She watched Damian and Roland leave in an ordinary black cab and come back in the afternoon in Lord Studley's Beemer, driven by Henry. It was a historic occasion in more ways than one, being the last time Henry would, for the foreseeable future, ever drive someone else's car. Huguette was giving him a Prius for a wedding present two days later. Opening the car door for his future mother-in-law, Henry took great pleasure in addressing her as "my lady," also for the last time. In future, he had decided, it would be "Mama," as copying Huguette and calling her "Mummy" was a bit OTT.

Other changes were coming. Adding her legacy to the savings she already had, Zinnia had discovered she now had just enough to satisfy a lifelong ambition, to go home to Antigua and open a bar on a fashionable beach. She had a flight booked on Saturday, much to the chagrin of half the residents of Hexam Place, who would now be without a cleaner. Jimmy told Dr. Jefferson "no worries" (his new phrase) because he would do the cleaning at number three. He might also become a replacement for Zinnia at number six, number eight, and number seven. He could do it now he had moved in at number three and was, so to speak, on the spot. This was said in the hearing of Dr. Jefferson, who made no attempt to deny it but only smiled resignedly. Jimmy had forgotten all about the missing knife.

MONTSERRAT AGREED with Ciaran that she had become obsessed with Preston Still. Not obsessed in a sex kind of way, she assured him, she didn't even like him anymore, but desperate to know what had happened between him and the police. Had they told him about her letter? Had he guessed it was from her and had he told them so? What were they going to do to him, if anything? She seldom saw him. Occasionally the Audi drew up outside number seven and he was seen to run up the steps to the front door. He never spoke to her, never seemed to notice her, though he looked in her direction and the whites of his eyes showed and his face flushed.

Ciaran wanted her to come and live with him. His flatmate had left and he didn't miss the rent money.

"Or we could go off somewhere it's not gray and damp."

"Spain," said Montserrat, Barcelona in mind. "I'll think about it."

Thinking about it involved plucking up the nerve to talk to Preston. That would mean going to Medway Manor Court, and suppose he refused to let her in? It was the kind of thing that needed to be done on the spur of the moment. See him, go up to him, speak. But she never did see him. If he came to number seven—she knew from Rabia that he did—it was early in the morning before she was up. How many mornings would she have to be up by seven thirty in order to speak to him?

She never saw Lucy either. Three women had replaced Zinnia. They were called Merrie Maids, and they came every morning, so that took care of Lucy's breakfasts. Montserrat spent a lot of time with Rabia. Her curiosity was aroused when the children's nanny asked her, if Montserrat was going out that morning, would she post that letter to Lucy? Montserrat thought Rabia might as well give it to her employer, but she couldn't very well say so or ask what the letter was about, but though she looked enquiringly at her, Rabia only smiled. Her au pair's money, for which Montserrat now did nothing, continued to come into her bank account.

But on the evening of the day she was going to post the letter, with the letter actually in her hand, she was climbing the area steps on her way to meet Ciaran when she met Preston Still stepping out of his car. This was as she had predicted, the spur of the moment, and they were face-to-face.

"Hallo," she said. "Long time no see."

In a chilly voice he said, "How have you been?"

"Absolutely fine. What are the police going to do to you? If you don't tell me, I'll go and ask them."

If they hadn't been out in the street and with that weird gardener guy watching their every move, she thought, he would have hit her.

"Nothing," he said. "*Of course.* How many times do I have to point out to you that it was an accident?"

"Let me guess. They went to Gallowmill Hall and searched and didn't find that roof-rack box because you'd taken it away, dumped it somewhere. Or burnt it or chopped it up."

"I was able to explain everything satisfactorily. And now, if you'll excuse me, I am in rather a hurry." He turned away and bounded up the steps to the front door. Montserrat walked down to the Dugong and sat on one of the seats outside. Preston Still was inside number seven for no more than five minutes before returning down the steps and getting back into the car.

It was too cold to stay there any longer, cold and pointless. Montserrat went into the pub and bought herself a glass of red wine for a change. This might be the last time she would ever come in here. It was time for her to go, shake the dust of this place off her feet, to use a phrase much liked by her father. Lucy would have to find another au pair.

SPRING SHOWS its first signs in the middle of February. It was still too early for those tulips and hyacinths Khalid Iqbal had planted for Thea and at number seven, but the snowdrops had come and gone and purple and yellow crocuses were coming out. Those front gardens where a flowering tree or shrub grew in their centre beds had an almond in bud if not yet in flower and a yellow mahonia with sprays of blossom among its prickly leaves. Dex noted all these pretty things with pleasure, a relief from that ugly thing he often observed, the evil spirit. He was preparing to dispose of it when he could. The difficulty was that it was never alone for more than a minute or two and it never walked anywhere.

Dex was in no doubt at all that it was an evil spirit, though he had come to that conclusion on his own. Peach was silent. He left messages, kind and caring, but he never spoke. Destroying the evil spirit might take a long time, Dex understood that. He would watch and wait.

GUSSIE HAD HOWLED for the Princess for three days, refusing to go out for walks, though June had tried to take him. Then, quite suddenly, his mourning had ceased, he had begun to eat again, and he had bitten June when she tried to put his coat on. With Thea dead and gone, Henry a married man living in a pretty little house in Chelsea rented for him and Huguette by his father-in-law, Zinnia describing in e mails from Antigua the restaurant she had started, and herself no longer a servant, June disbanded the St. Zita Society. It had been good while it lasted, approximately seven months, though she had noticed that while she had always been enthusiastic, the others had mostly not pulled their weight. Now she must be free to concentrate on her project, the redecorating of the whole of number six from top to bottom and putting in a new central heating system. Why not, when she had a house of her own at last? Neighbours suggested she should sell it and buy herself a nice little flat with a second bedroom for when a friend came to stay. June shuddered. She had no friend. The nearest to come into that category was Rocksana Castelli, and June understood she must be got rid of promptly. It would mean breaking the lease, but June had never lacked courage.

She made her way upstairs, her bones aching again, rehearsing the words she would use to Rocksana, but at the top of the top flight, when she was seriously out of breath, Rad's former girlfriend emerged from her bedroom. "Oh, June, the very person I most want to see. I hope you won't hate me, but I'm leaving. I know I've got this lease, but will you be an angel and let me go? You see, I've met this wonderful man and he wants me to . . ."

June didn't hear the rest. She was marvelling at her luck. Courage wasn't necessary, maybe never would be again. This afternoon she would devote to finding a builder. But first to attend to Miss Grieves. Learning that it is much easier to be charitable and kind when one is rich, June was finding that ministering to the aged tenant of number eight's basement was not only satisfying but quite enjoyable. She had even succeeded in eliciting from Miss Grieves what no other resident of Hexam Place had ever managed to do, finding out her Christian name and calling her by it without arousing the old woman's rage.

"Good morning, Gertrude." No wonder she had kept it dark! "I'm popping down to Waitrose in a minute so I want to know what you'd fancy for your dinner." The place was filthy and smelt disgusting. "Now I think it would be a good idea for me to ask Merrie Maids to pop down here one day this week and give this flat a good tidy-up. What do you think?" She really must stop speaking of herself and everyone else popping everywhere. "Shall we say Wednesday morning?"

Miss Grieves didn't argue but said she'd like curry for her dinner.

"Good idea. Maybe I'll have the same. And I'll get you one of those bins with a lockable lid to keep the fox off. I'll pop—I mean, come down—with it this afternoon."

A SIGN OF the times, Jimmy said it was, when Lord Studley's new driver turned out to be a woman. Rosamund was her name. Probably she had a surname too, but no one knew what it was. Such appendages seemed unnecessary these days, for staff if not for employers. Curtains for her if she was caught calling Lord Studley *Cliff*. Greatly daring, Jimmy had experimented, when returning from a long session in the Dugong, with addressing Dr. Jefferson as "Si" and had received no reprimand. But the paediatrician had been half-asleep in front of the television at the time and might not have heard.

Jimmy had watched with interest June's ascent to millionaire and house-owner. And what a house! Not a little semidetached on an arterial road in Acton, conveniently beside a bus stop, which was the best she might have aspired to by her own efforts, but a palace in one of the finest residential districts in the United Kingdom, if not the world. Unfortunately, Si Jefferson (as Jimmy now thought of him) was no more than ten years his senior, if that. But he was progressing in his campaign, had graduated from that poky little room in the basement to one of the principal bedrooms on the first floor and convinced Si of his top-class cooking skills. They not only now shared their evening meal but took it together, and Jimmy hung in there afterwards, watching TV in the drawing room. He had almost forgotten Thea, recalling her vaguely when he saw a woman with red hair.

No one attempted to stop her moving out. On a Saturday, the day the first tulips came into bloom in the window boxes Thea had prepared to delight Damian and Roland, Montserrat stuffed her clothes and makeup—she possessed little else—into the boot of the VW and shook the dust, as Beacon and her father put it, of Hexam Place off her feet for ever. Rabia came downstairs to say good-bye to her, but apart from putting a hundred pounds in an envelope under her door, Lucy took no notice of her departure. Montserrat had resigned by leaving a message on Lucy's voice mail.

"I hope you'll be very happy," Rabia said as if Montserrat were getting married.

"Shouldn't I be saying that to you?"

"Maybe." Rabia laughed. "We will take it as said."

Montserrat had got no farther than the junction with Lower Sloane Street when she remembered she had left her Jo Malone scent and body cream behind in a bathroom drawer. Ciaran had given it to her in the new Red Roses perfume for St. Valentine's Day and would certainly notice if she wasn't using it. She had just parked the car outside number seven once more and was on the top step of the area stairs when a familiar voice laughing made her turn her head. Preston and Lucy were coming down the steps from the front door, Preston gripping her hand as if determined not to let her get away. Lucy's face was set, her mouth tight. She looked thinner than ever.

Montserrat heard him say, "Jogging every morning for me, darling. If that's how you keep your weight down, I must do the same."

And Lucy said, "That'll be the day."

So they were back together. Montserrat wasn't altogether surprised. She would never have put up with him for those four years she had planned. Lucy was welcome, though she seemed to be finding it a penance.

28

IT WAS UNUSUAL for Dex to question the ways of evil spirits. Their rules were not like those of other people. They ate and drank all right—he was remembering Brad Smith—and went to bed at night and sometimes went out to work, but what else they did was a mystery. So seeing the evil spirit who had come to live at number seven Hexam Place appear regularly, if not quite every day, jogging determinedly up the street and back again after about half an hour, was a puzzle but not one that need be sorted.

The evil spirit behaved much like a human being. A banker, he must be, thought Dex, who had seen bankers on television. Once, while running, he took a mobile phone out of his pocket and talked on it, talked to Orange or Apple, Dex supposed. Beacon drove him when he came down the steps after his run and his change of clothes, and Beacon said his name was Mr. Still. Dex knew better. His name was Beelzebub or Moloch.

THERE HAD BEEN no response to Rabia's letter giving notice. Lucy was well-known for not answering letters, for even ignoring their existence. But husband and wife were back together. Beacon had carried Mr. Still's suitcases up to Lucy's bedroom, and from the floor above Rabia had seen Mr. Still come out of that bedroom in the morning. The adultery must be in the past and Lucy's conduct forgiven. But what of Rabia and her future? Perhaps her letter had arrived and been read and shown to Mr. Still but no one had remembered to tell her. Her departure date was probably to be the end of March, when she would move back with her father until the wedding.

The wedding. Within the year she would perhaps have a baby. I cannot go through that again, she said aloud in the nursery while Thomas slept. It may not be because Nazir and I had that bad gene, it may be because I alone had it and any child of mine would be sick and die. I can't go through that again. But what choice do I have? They must have found a new nanny by now to take her place, and one day soon that new woman would walk in here and introduce herself. Rabia thought, I must know, I mustn't let that happen to Thomas without warning, I must get up my courage and go to Lucy and find out.

Rabia no longer took Thomas to that other kind of nursery for his outings. Khalid was there, kind, handsome, considerate Khalid, with whom she must spend the rest of her life. And her father who talked all the time now about the wedding and the Iqbal family. Rabia found herself avoiding him. Instead of going to the nursery she took Thomas in his luxurious pushchair up into Hyde Park or across to Green Park and sometimes to St. James's Park to see the pelicans. One morning when she got back to number seven she found that Mr. Still's mother had come to stay. Accustomed to mothers and aunties and older people in general being treated with the utmost respect, she was horrified next day to hear Lucy screaming at old Mrs. Still. Thomas reacted as he always did when a loud, vociferous quarrel took place between the adults in the house; his eyes wide, his lower lip trembling, after a while of silence, the whimpering would begin and the tears would flow down his cheeks.

The sight of him in distress when another quarrel began, this time between husband and wife, triggered Rabia's courage. Mr. Still had begun coming home early now he was back at number seven, and the two of them were angrier than ever with each other now Mr. Still's mother was in the house. Rabia went down to the drawing room to see Lucy, only to be told by old Mrs. Still that her daughter-in-law was in no fit state to see anyone. But Mr. Still's mother had plenty to say to Rabia.

She understood Thomas's nanny was getting married. This was just as well as she was no longer needed here. "My son is thinking of engaging a Norland nanny for Thomas, if you know what that is. My daughter is very keen on the idea and they discussed it over Christmas. *She*"—a long, gnarled finger was pointed in the direction of the drawing room—"objects, of course, but that is neither here nor there while he is back living in this house, as I hope he will be at least until those children are grown-up. It will be best for the girls to go away to boarding school. Something will have to be done to improve their manners."

"When am I to go?"

"You'll have to ask my son. Lucy, as I understand she lets you call her, can have no say in the matter. It can only be a matter of weeks."

Rabia had to know more than that. She was screwing up her courage to confront Lucy, in her bedroom if necessary, when she came up to the nursery herself, a thin, worn woman, looking all of her thirty-seven years and ten more added on.

"I don't want you to go, darling. Preston was quite pleased when he saw your notice because it means he can get the nanny his horrible sister recommended. He thinks she'd be firmer with Thomas." Lucy gave a heavy sigh. "If he wasn't around, you could stay for ever. I don't want you ever to go. Why did he come back?"

Rabia was unable to answer that. She went into the girls' room, where Thomas was with them watching the television. "Be nice to Mummy," she said to him. "Sit on Mummy's lap."

And Thomas did. Lucy was so surprised and apparently pleased that she hugged him and kissed his plump, pink cheek. Rabia made Lucy and herself a cup of tea and gave Thomas a chocolate biscuit. She could hear Mrs. Still senior calling for Lucy in her loud, raucous, old voice and said as politely as she could, "You will have to go. Your mother-in-law wants you."

Lucy went, having first kissed Thomas, and said once again how happy they could all be if Preston and his mother went away and left her alone with Rabia and the children.

THE FIRST OF these wished-for departures was witnessed by June, introducing Gussie to his dog walker, who had arrived in a black van with a picture of a Great Dane on it. A taxi had drawn up outside number seven, and an old woman in a fur coat came down the steps and started making a scene. June dearly loved a scene and listened enthralled while the old woman berated the taxidriver for not being Beacon in the Audi. Then Rabia appeared carrying two suitcases, there being, June supposed, no one else to do it. The dog walker went off with Gussie and the taxi with the old woman. June thought how lovely it was to have money and not to have to walk Gussie ever again.

She went into the back garden, where it was Dex's second day at work, and looked on approvingly as he dug over the flowerbed he had painstakingly rid of dandelions, ash-tree seedlings, and groundsel. He seemed, she thought, to be enjoying himself, and she knew from her own life experience that you do better work if you like what you do. Ten pounds an hour, which Jimmy, who seemed to have appointed himself Dex's agent, had told her she must pay. It seemed exorbitant but she could afford it.

Dex had already followed the evil spirit that morning. He was unsure whether Moloch, as he now called him, would take the same route every day or even if he would jog every day. All that was certain was that when he came back, he would go to work at being a banker, a job which, Dex had many times been told by the television and almost everyone he spoke to, was the wickedest and most cruel occupation anyone could have. He must be far worse than Brad Smith had ever been.

Moloch had run down Lower Sloane Street, along Pimlico Road, along Ebury Street, up Eaton Terrace, and home. Not far. Dex wondered why Moloch did it, but there was no knowing. The ways of evil spirits were strange. What he would like best would be for Moloch to go into the grounds of the Royal Hospital. He would follow him there.

Tomorrow Dex would be working for Mrs. Neville-Smith. It was a pity about her name, but he had decided the *Neville* part took away the evil of *Smith*. The bulbs he had planted in Dr. Jefferson's garden were not only pushing through the earth now but breaking into bloom, the daffodils first, bright yellow and pale yellow and some with golden petals and white bells. It pleased Dex that those he had set deep in the earth were doing better than the ones planted in tubs by that man from the Belgrave Nursery.

In Hexam Place the staff were changing. Jimmy, while still Dr. Jefferson's driver, had become a resident of number three and been heard to refer to himself as the doctor's "housemate." Montserrat had gone, was said to be living with Ciaran O'Hara in a flat in Alderney Street, and a new au pair had been taken on at number seven by Preston Still. Pauline, the most sociable of the Merrie Maids, told June this woman was a Dane called Inger and so fair in colouring that she personally believed her to be an albino.

"Has she got pink eyes?" June asked.

Pauline was shocked. "I expect it's your age, but it's not politically correct saying that."

June went indoors. She made a mental note to stop employing

the Merrie Maids and take on the wife of one of the builders. When you've got a lot of money, she was discovering, you could please yourself about things like that. Anyway, there was no point in having a cleaner at number six. The house was full of builders, tearing walls down and floors up. They were all Polish, their English poor but their manners perfect, and they called her "madam," the way she used to address the Princess. June hadn't been so happy for years. She even enjoyed the hammering and drilling and, when Roland complained about the noise, told him that you could hear building going on wherever you lived in London.

It wasn't long before June encountered Inger, whose English was a great deal better than that of the Poles. And her eyes were midnight blue. June took her into the Dugong for a drink, and Inger said she would like a schnapps, but they hadn't got any. They drank gin instead. Inger confided that she loved the basement flat at number seven, Lucy and the children were angels, but she didn't care at all for Mr. Still, who snapped at her whenever they met. She'd do anything for Lucy, she said, but she wasn't going to put herself out for him.

"I don't blame you," said June.

"No, but he does. He came back from his run this morning and acted like it was my fault there was no hot water for his shower. What do I know about the hot water? I called a plumber, and when the man said he couldn't come till tomorrow, Mr. Still got very nasty."

"Oh, ignore him," said June.

"That nanny is very nice. We don't have many Moslems in Denmark, but she is so nice."

Rabia thought Inger was nice too. Quiet and well mannered and she obviously adored Thomas. Having kept earlier hours for several weeks, Mr. Still had now reverted to leaving number seven at eight in the morning and often not returning until ten at night. At least, Rabia thought, there could be no more adultery with that

Rad Sothern. If it was wrong to be glad someone was dead, well, she was sorry, but she couldn't help her feelings.

Mr. Still continued to go out jogging, but from being every morning it had gone down to every other morning and by April was only Saturdays and Sundays. Perhaps he had lost heart because, as far as Rabia could see, he hadn't lost any weight.

"You would have to run from here to—oh, I don't know the names—every day to lose weight," said Inger, who as a Scandinavian was considered in the Dugong to be a fitness expert.

"Here to John o' Groats," said Jimmy.

Inger said she didn't know where that was. Mr. Still would be out late that evening—it was Friday—and she had a job to do for Lucy. When first asked, she had thought doing such a thing might be wrong, but when she considered that she liked Lucy and disliked Mr. Still, she said an unqualified yes. The man she had to let into number seven and take upstairs to Lucy's bedroom was having a drink with Damian and Roland at number eight. Inger watched him come across the road and down the area steps. Good-looking, she thought, a great improvement on Mr. Still.

"Martin Gifford," he said when she let him in.

Dr. Jefferson's kitchen was big, and the gas hob was at the garden end next to the Aga. Dex had been seated about thirty feet away at the table on the paediatrician's instructions, while Jimmy, also on Dr. Jefferson's instructions or at his request, made Dex a cup of hot chocolate. The milk would boil over if Jimmy took his eyes off it for a second, so Dex took advantage of his turned back to help himself to a sharp fruit knife, which he slipped into his toolbag.

"He's doing this out of the kindness of his heart." Jimmy set down the mug of chocolate with a bang. A dribble slopped onto the table. "Now you be careful with that," he said as if Dex had spilt it.

"Thank you," said Dex politely.

"A saint in human form is Dr. Jefferson."

While Moloch was a demon in human form, thought Dex. He had no gardening to do that day. He had only come to collect his money, and the hot chocolate was a surprise. Better go now as Moloch was due to emerge from number seven at any minute, and today was the day set for his destruction. Mr. Neville-Smith was in his front garden, putting out a recycling bag, which Dex knew no one would collect until at least next Tuesday. He hung back a bit, avoiding being seen, but he was near enough to hear Moloch call out a cheerful "Good morning, Ivor."

It was the voice of Peach, upper-class, soft and low, but Dex knew better than to be deceived by that. Evil spirits can assume the voices of whom they please, just as they can take human shape. Mr. Neville-Smith said, "How are you, Preston?" and went back into his house without waiting for a reply. Moloch began to jog along, and Dex followed him, younger and thinner than he and well able to keep up.

RABIA HAD HEARD the voice of Lucy's new lover, and it had dismayed her. The children, she thought, the effect this might have on the children. If Mr. Still had stayed away, if there had been a divorce, if for some reason he had never come back, there would at least have been no question of adultery. Lucy might even have remarried and to someone she loved and could be faithful to. But now Rabia herself was going, and what little she might have done to protect the children was at an end.

For she knew that in the absence of Mr. Still, Lucy would keep her and she would be able to tell Khalid she couldn't marry him. She had to stay with Thomas and the girls. If only it could be. But it was bad enough being glad Rad Sothern was dead without wishing Mr. Still might be. Rabia prayed silently not to have sinful thoughts, and while she sat with her head bent and her eyes closed, Thomas climbed onto her lap, put his arms round her neck, and said, "Say *sweetheart*."

PEOPLE WHO ARE jogging never look round. Dex had observed this truth and that Moloch ran on, staring steadfastly ahead of him. He had no idea and never had that he was followed, followed by someone who knew it would be right to rid the world of him. And Moloch was going to do what Dex had hoped during all these weeks of pursuit that he would do. He was turning in to the gardens of the Royal Hospital, gratifying Dex further by taking a path between bushes and under trees, now starting to come into leaf. There was a sweet, fresh smell of spring and a pale sun was coming out.

Dex felt for the knife in his pocket, and as he did so, Moloch stopped. He bent down to retie his shoelace, which had come undone. Silently, relentlessly, Dex closed on him, a firm grasp on the knife he had stolen from Dr. Jefferson's kitchen.

About the Author

Ruth Rendell has won numerous awards, including three Edgars, the highest accolade from Mystery Writers of America, as well as four Gold Daggers and a Diamond Dagger for outstanding contribution to the genre from England's prestigious Crime Writers' Association. A member of the House of Lords, she lives in London.

Turn the page for a special excerpt from
Ruth Rendell's new novel,

NO MAN'S NIGHTINGALE

Coming from Scribner in November 2013

"Ruth Rendell is a marvel. . . . There is no doubt that Rendell is one of Britain's finest writers, in the crime genre or in any genre."
—*Sunday Express* (UK)

"No one surpasses Ruth Rendell when it comes to stories of obsession, instability, and malignant coincidence."
—Stephen King

"Ms. Rendell continues to write in impeccable form, dripping both mirth and malice."
—Janet Maslin, *The New York Times*

1

M AXINE WAS PROUD of having three jobs. These days more and more people had none. She had no sympathy for them but congratulated herself on her own initiative. Two mornings a week she cleaned for Mrs. Wexford, two mornings for Mrs. Crocker, afternoons for two other Kingsmarkham women, did gardening and cleaned cars for Mr. Wexford and Dr. Crocker and babysat every evening where she was wanted for those young enough to need a baby-sitter. Cleaning she did for the women and gardening and car-washing for the men because she had never believed in any of that feminism or equality stuff. It was a well-known fact that men didn't notice whether a house was clean or not, and normal women weren't interested in cars or lawns. Maxine charged maximum rates for baby-sitting except for her son and his partner, who got her services for free. As for the others, those who had kids must expect to pay for them. She'd had four and she knew.

She was a good worker, reliable, punctual, and reasonably honest, and the only condition she made was payment in cash. Wexford, who after all had until recently been a policeman, demurred at that but eventually gave in the way the tax inspector up the road did. After all, at least a dozen other households would have paid almost anything to secure Maxine's services. She had one drawback. She talked. She talked not just while she was having a break for a cup of tea or while she was getting out or putting away the tools, but all the time she was working and to whoever happened to be in the room or upstairs or in the kitchen. The work got done and efficiently while the words poured out on a steady monotone.

That day she began on a story of how her son Jason, now manager of the Kingsmarkham Questo supermarket, had dealt with a man complaining about one of Jason's checkout girls. The woman had apparently called him "elderly." But Jason had handled it brilliantly, pacifying the man and sending him home in a supervisor's car. "Now my Jason used to be a right tearaway," Maxine went on, and not for the first time. "Not in one of them gangs, I'm not saying that, and he never got no ASBOS, but a bit of shoplifting, it was like it came natural to him, and out all night and underage drinking—well, binge-drinking like they call it. As for the smack and what do they call them, description drugs—mind Mr. Wexford can't hear me, hope he's out of hearshot—all that he went in for, and now, since him and Nicky had a kid, he's a changed character. The perfect dad, I still can't believe it." She applied impregnated wadding to the silver with renewed vigour, then a duster, then the wadding once more. "She's over a year old now, his Isabella is, but when she was a neo-nettle, it was never Nicky got up to her in the night, she never had to. No, it was my Jason had her out of her cot before the first peep was out of her. Walked her up and down, cooing at her like I've never heard a bloke go on so. Mind you, that Nicky never showed no gratitude. I call it unnatural a mum with a new baby sleeping the night through, and I've told her so."

Even Maxine sometimes had to pause to draw breath. Dora Wexford seized her opportunity, said she had to go out and Maxine's money was in an envelope on the hall table. The resumed monologue pursued her as she ran out to the conservatory to tell her husband she'd be back in an hour or so.

Wexford was sitting in a cane armchair in autumn sunshine doing what many a man or woman plans to do on retirement but few put into practice, reading *The Decline and Fall of the Roman Empire*. He had embarked on it expecting to find it heavy going, but instead becoming fast enraptured and enjoying every word. Reaching the end of the first volume, he was happy to anticipate five more and told Dora she'd picked her moment to desert him.

"It's your turn," she whispered.

"I didn't know we had a schedule."

"You know now. Here starts your tour of duty."

As Dora left, Maxine swooped, pushing the vacuum cleaner and continuing to hold on to it while she peered over his shoulder.

"Got a guide to Rome there, I see. Going there on your holidays, are you? Me and my sister took in Rome on our Ten Italian Cities tour. Oh, it was lovely but hot, you wouldn't believe. I said to my Jason, you and Nicky want to go there on your honeymoon when you get around to tying the knot there's no untying, only these days there is of course, no point in getting married if you ask me. I never did and I'm not ashamed of it." She started up the vacuum cleaner but continued to talk. "It's Nicky as wants it, one of them big white weddings like they all want these days, costs thousands, but she's a big spender, good job my Jason's in work like so many's not." The voice became a buzz under the vacuum's roar. She raised it. "I don't reckon my Jason'd go away on a honeymoon or anything else come to that without Isabella. He can't bear that kid out of his sight for his eight hours' work let alone a week. Talk about worshipping the ground she treads on, only she don't tread yet, crawls more like." A pause to change the tool on the end of the vacuum-cleaner hose. "You'll know about that poor lady vicar getting herself killed and me finding the body. It was all over the papers and on the telly. I reckon you take an interest though you're not doing the work no more. I had a cleaning job there with her up till a couple of weeks back, but there was things we never saw eye to eye on, not to mention her not wanting to pay cash, wanted to do it on line if you please and I couldn't be doing with that. She always left the back door open and I popped in to collect the money she owed me and it gave me a terrible turn. No blood, of course, not with strangling, but still a shock. Don't bear thinking of, does it? Still, I reckon you had to think of things like that, it being your job. You must be relieved getting all that over with . . ."

Standing up, clutching his book, "I'm going to have a bath!" Wexford shouted above the vacuum's roar.

Maxine was startled from her monologue. "It's ten thirty."

"A very good time to have a bath," said Wexford, making for the stairs, reading as he went the last lines of volume one, describing another murder, that of Julius Caesar: . . . *during the greatest part of a year the orb of the sun appeared pale and without splendour. This season of obscurity, which cannot surely be compared with the preternatural obscurity of the Passion, had already been celebrated by most of the poets and historians of that memorable age* . . .

His mobile was ringing. Detective Superintendent Burden, known to the phone-contacts list as Mike.

"I'm off to have a look at St. Peter's Vicarage, taking Lynn with me and I thought you might like to come too."

Wexford had already had a shower that day. A bath at 10:30 a.m. wasn't needful, only seized upon as a refuge from Maxine. "I'd love to." He tried to keep the enthusiasm out of his voice, tried and failed.

Sounding surprised, Burden said, "Don't get excited. It's no big deal."

"It is for me."

He closed the bathroom door. Probably, Maxine wouldn't open it but would perhaps conclude that he was having an exceptionally long bath. The vacuum cleaner still roaring, he escaped out the front door, closing it after him by an almost silent turning of the key in the lock. Taking an interested member of the public—that, after all, was what he was—on a call or calls that were part of a criminal investigation was something Wexford had seldom done while he was himself an investigating officer. And his accompanying Superintendent Ede of the Met on the vault enquiries was a different matter as he, though unpaid, had had a kind of job as Ede's aide.

This visit, this opportune escape from Maxine, was undergone, he knew, because, once senior and junior officers, over the years they had become friends. Burden knew, none better, how much Wexford would wish to be involved in solving the mystery of who had killed the Reverend Sarah Hussain.

ALL WEXFORD KNEW of the death, apart from what Maxine had mentioned that morning, was what he had read in yesterday's *Guardian* and seen on the day-before-yesterday's regional television news. And seen of course when passing the vicarage. He could have seen more online, but he had cringed from its colourful headlines. Sarah Hussain was far from being the only woman ordained priest of the Church of England, but perhaps she was the only one to have been born in the United Kingdom of a white Irishwoman and an Indian immigrant. All this had been in the newspaper along with some limited biographical details, including information about her conversion to Christianity. There had been a photograph too of a gaunt woman with an aquiline nose in an academic cap and gown, olive-skinned but with large, deep-set, black eyes and what hair that showed a glossy jet-black. She had been forty-eight when she died and a single mother.

Her origins, her looks—striking but not handsome—her age, her single parenthood, and, above all, that conversion made him think that her life could not have been easy. He would have liked to know more, and no doubt, he soon would. At the moment he wasn't even sure of where the murder had taken place; only that it was inside the vicarage. It wasn't a house he had ever been in, though Dora had. He was due to meet Mike and DC Lynn Fancourt in St. Peter's Church porch, the one at the side where the vestry was.

The vicarage was some distance away and he had no need to pass the church to reach it. Heading for the gate that led out of

Queen Street, he passed a young man pushing a baby buggy, a not particularly unusual sight these days, but he recognized this one as Maxine's son Jason. As industrious as his mother if not as vociferous, he must be having a day off from his job as a supermarket manager. Curious to see the child whose father worshipped the ground she crawled on, Wexford looked under the buggy hood and saw a pretty, pink-cheeked blonde, her long-lashed eyes closed in sleep. Wexford hastily withdrew his head from Jason's glare. No doubt the man was wary of any male person eyeing his little girl. Quite right too, he thought, himself the parent of girls who were now middle-aged women.

He was a little early and by design. In his position it was better from him to be waiting for them than they for him. But Burden was seldom late, and the two of them appeared almost immediately from the high street. All the years he had known him, Wexford had never ceased to marvel at Burden's sartorial elegance. Where did he learn to dress like that? As far as he knew, Mike went shopping no more than any other man of Wexford's acquaintance. And it couldn't be the influence of his wives, neither of whom, Jean, long dead, or Jenny, the present one, had had much interest in clothes, preferring in their own cases no more than attention to "neatness and fashion," as Jane Austen has it. But here was Burden today, his abundant but short hair now iron grey, his beige jacket (surely cashmere) over white shirt with beige-and-blue figured tie, his beautifully creased trousers of denim though discernibly—how? How could one tell?—not jeans.

"Good to see you," Burden said, though he had seen him and eaten lunch with him, three days before.

Lynn, that he hadn't seen for as much as a year, said in a respectful tone, "Good morning, sir."

They walked along the path among gravestones and rose bushes towards Vicarage Lane. It was October and the leaves had only just begun to fall. Green, spiky conkers lay on the grass under the chestnut trees.

"I don't know how much you know about this poor woman's murder, Reg," Burden said.

"Only what I read in the paper and saw on TV."

"You don't go to church, do you?"

"I hesitate to say my wife does, though it's true, and you know it already. She knew Sarah Hussain but through church, not socially. Where was she killed?"

"In the vicarage. In her living room. You tell him, Lynn. You were one of the two officers who were the first to see the body."